Take Me There

A Speculative Anthology of Travel

Edited by Winston Malone

Storyletter XPress Publishing LLC

Take Me There: A Speculative Anthology of Travel is a work of fiction. Names, places, characters, and incidents are the product of each author's imagination or are used fictitiously. Any resemblance to actual persons, living or dead, events, or locales is entirely coincidental or made with the utmost respect.

2024 Storyletter XPress Publishing LLC | First Edition

Copyright © 2024 by Winston Malone

All rights reserved.

Published in the United States by Storyletter XPress Publishing LLC.

Print ISBN 979-8-9870046-2-3

eBook ISBN 979-8-9870046-3-0

Cover by Eoin Ryan

Edited by Winston Malone

storyletter.substack.com

storyletter.press

No portion of this book may be reproduced in any form without written permission from the publisher or author except as permitted by U.S. copyright law.

Contents

Introduction	v
1. Distant Shores by Brian Reindel	1
2. A Marriage of TruMinds by Jack Massa	14
3. The Guardian by Clarice Sanchez Meneses	35
4. The Canyon by Victor D. Sandiego	41
5. Hyperbolic by LB Waltz	45
6. The Fuller by J.M. Elliott	53
7. Cubed by Joe Gold	70
8. The Oath by C.R. Langille	78
9. Two Visions of the Mountain of the Saints by Christopher Deliso	94
10. The Summer Light by M.S. Arthadian	99
11. The Hound and the Nightingale by Randall Hayes	106
12. A Lonely Passage by Devon Field	118
13. The Kingfisher Exchange by Melissa Rose Rogers	126

14.	Abaddon's Portrait of a Lonesome Shore by James Castor	143
15.	A Signal From Callisto by Daniel W. Davison	155
16.	Edith by Pamela Urfer	181
17.	Mountain Talk by Shaina Read	187
18.	The Devouring Ocean by H. A. Titus	209
19.	Summer in Antarctica by Brylle Gaviola	218
20.	Faran: The Launch by Galia Ignatius	224
21.	The Book of Thomas by Iris Shaw	250
22.	Hersh by Shannon Aaron Stephens	263
23.	Red Kingdom by Winston Malone	274
24.	The End by Olivia St. Lewis	303
Acknowledgments		320
Meet the Authors		321
The Journey Has Only Begun		329

Introduction

When we travel, we experience life at its fullest. We make memories with our loved ones, see unique landmarks and landscapes, and savor authentic cuisines. We open ourselves to myriad possibilities and traverse the unknown, the unexplored, and the untamed. In doing so, we grow—quite literally—as people, new synapses forming to commit those moments to the neural logbook.

Fiction functions much the same way. Stories transport us to the once unimaginable, to dreamscapes, alien planets, and even places of nightmares. Stories introduce us to individuals, virtuous and villainous, from all walks of life, here and beyond. Stories expose us to the full range of sensory inputs as if we're inhabiting the world of their characters. This form of travel is the true power of our imagination, and with a writer as your guide, we can be teleported anywhere, anytime.

Thank you for purchasing this book, which features 24 indie authors from around the globe. It's a culmination of several years of work, and we hope that you enjoy the stories inside. At the very least, we wish you safe travels wherever your journey takes you. ~ WM

Distant Shores by Brian Reindel

For Stephanie, Lisa, and Stephen. No matter how distant the shores that might separate us, you'll always remain in my heart.

I dream of distant shores kissed by blood-red sunsets. I dream of a house by the ocean with private sandy beaches. I dream of a wife, loving but sad, and our son, now grown with a family of his own. I dream of numbers in sequence that mean nothing to me. I dream of a life that was once mine. These are memories, fragments of time reconstructed, which arrive in my sleep and stay for breakfast in the morning. I am told I lie. H-Plus do not dream.

Dr. Kulwicki is a corporate man, first and foremost, and a doctor second. He stares at me through a monitor, a transmission received from deep space. Somewhere in a non-disclosed, sanitized room with white walls and medical equipment, he reminds me that I am incapable of dreaming. I question his medical acumen, not to his face, though, as I'm stuck here on Paradisea by contract, regardless of my insults or petitions.

"Thomas, your programming does not allow it," Dr. Kulwiki says.

"I'm H-Plus," I say.

"I know what you are. You are just as much an android, and whatever biological processes remain are controlled by artificial means. I don't expect you to understand."

This is meant as an insult. I'm a construction worker, mechanically inclined, yes, but educationally deficient in all other areas, a trait from my donor. The dreams and reticent memories are also the donor's, but they are mine now, too. He is dead, for exactly how long, I don't know. I feel a sense of responsibility to birth these dreams, care for them, and attach them to reality, even if it's a reality from the past. That's my assessment. But I'm not a doctor.

"I'm busy, Thomas, and I don't have time to entertain this fantasy. Unless you have a serious medical issue requiring my attention, don't call again. The remedial bots can handle most problems. Fabricated maladies excluded," Dr. Kulwicki says. He hangs up without saying goodbye. I suspect he knows more than he'll admit.

After my appointment, I'm required to report to my site supervisor, Tal. He will dock my pay for an hour since my meeting with Dr. Kulwicki was not warranted nor approved by corporate. It doesn't matter. There is nowhere to spend money on Paradisea, at least not yet, not for another 20 years, when my assignment is complete and my contract is fulfilled. The environmental stabilizers will be online, but more importantly, the restaurants, bars, casinos, and entertainment venues will be finished. That will be when vacationers arrive, dreamers like me, except they can bring their dreams to life courtesy of corporate.

"Hey, leatherface, up on Sector 12, the pressure release incubator your buddy retrofitted exploded," Tal says. "There's not much of him left. After the cleanup crew is done, you need to go out and fix it."

Tal uses the term leatherface for every H-Plus on the crew. It's an odd sentiment since my skin is as real as his, not artificial, but flesh with an epidermis, dermis, and hypodermis. He tells us there is no point in being an android if you're still as vulnerable as a human. I'm not as vulnerable. That's a lie he perpetuates. My gills allow me to filtrate dangerous levels of methane and pass it as waste. Those toxicity levels would kill Tal. As a result, I don't need to be outfitted with an Extravehicular Mobility Unit to do my work, an expense that saves corporate millions every year.

"I'll need at least two other mechanics to help cut the pipe and add the coupling. Unless you want to come out and help," I say. He detects the subtle insult. Tal is a fully human supervisor. He can do nothing else.

"Grab David and Marcus. Fix it. When you're done, head over to Sector 2. Double shift tonight," Tal says. It's a punishment for my attitude, for merely being a leatherface.

"Corporate only approves one double shift a month. I've already worked mine," I say.

"I *am* corporate!" Tal screams.

I will not get paid for the second shift. What can I do? I can't leave. I have no transportation, not enough money to pay my way to the nearest substation, and if I stow away on the next transport barge my contract will be void. I will become a floater. Floaters have no citizenship on Earth or anywhere without a sponsor. It's unheard of to sponsor an H-Plus, artificial beings without natural-born rights. We are denizens of corporate; our constitution is a series of words come to life by greed and written to benefit the business of man.

We work efficiently together—me, David, and Marcus—but there is no sense of community or camaraderie. We don't find common ground in our work or within our robotics and genetics. Their DNA comes from different hosts, donated upon death, and they were cloned, grown, modified, and harvested for contract, just like me. While there might be time to grow in friendship, it's impossible as long as I hang onto the dreams, which only divide us further.

"You got no business makin' trouble," Marcus says.

"Keep your head down, do your work, and earn your freedom like the rest of us," David says.

"Only one in three of us will make it to the end of our contract," I say.

"And I plan to be that one," Marcus says. David doesn't argue.

"You had a choice. On harvest day, they gave you a choice. Sign the contract or choose self-termination. You can still choose," David says.

I was reconstituted back into the cosmos as a fully mature being, and on that day, I could choose to live or die. The only consideration is the contract. A representative from the H-Plus Resources department explained the options as I cleaned the silica jelly from my ears. I chose life, if you could call it a choice. I dreamed the first night of a golden retriever hopping in the waves, snorting the sea foam, and chasing a tattered green tennis ball.

"Do either of you dream?" I ask.

"Shut up! You keep your mouth shut!" Marcus yells.

I have my answer.

We work a double shift as demanded. I check at the end of the cycle, and I don't get paid extra. As I suspected, the hour is deducted from my visit to Dr. Kulwicki. I want to ask more crew members, besides David and Marcus, to know if they dream as well, but sometimes knowing is harder than hanging onto a thin thread of doubt.

I'm looking down at the RadioLight transponder I installed in Sector 4, shocked by my recent realization. The gills on my neck open and close in rhythm with my breathing, slow and steady, then twitch as I look around, a child afraid he'll be caught performing a misdeed. The numbers I dreamt of are spatial coordinate identifiers, a number to call using RadioLight, but I don't know who will answer on the other end. The video uplink is not live—only audio. I choose to dial. If Tal asks, I will tell him the numbers are random, a test to connect the transponder to a booster in orbit.

The memory of my wife, Janus, picks up the call.

"Hello," she says. Her voice is sweet and quiet; deep inside my gut, a force pulls me toward her. A passing silence grows long and wide, and when I think this must all be another dream, she speaks again, "Hello? Is anyone there? Sam, come help your mother with this thing." Sam, the memory of my son. Does he care for his widowed mother in the absence of his father? They converse briefly in whispers. I hang up the phone and cry real tears.

We're forbidden to contact our forebearers, those loved ones who are relatives of the donor. Noncompliance leads to immediate revocation of my contract, forfeiture of all pay, and termination due to malfeasance. The end result is sanctioned abandonment, a resolution that removes all of corporate's responsibility when I'm no longer housed or fed. On Paradisea, in the present stage of development, it's a death sentence. No one will come to my rescue.

Compliance no longer matters to me. I make excuses over the coming weeks to continue installing the RadioLight transponder. I write notes of conversations remembered, playback dusty memories, and add to them those dreams I should not be capable of manifesting. Calling Janus again, reciting with measured calculation the minutiae of our vacations, holidays, celebrations, and how we made love, will force her to confirm the dreams have shared significance.

The atmosphere swirls above in pools of orange and red, and I'm reminded of the beach again, the sunset, and the days my donor spent on Earth with a family. In decades to come, rich and powerful men will purchase tickets to travel here, the paradise planet, to experience a vacation unattainable by most. My escape is in the opposite direction.

The day arrives when I can wait no longer. I think carefully about what I will say when Janus picks up the call.

"Hello, who is this?" Sam asks. I'm unprepared for him.

"Is this the Cordoza residence?" I ask, not realizing he will recognize my voice, which I didn't think to disguise.

"This is a deep space call. I know who you are, but I don't know how you got our spatial coordinates," Sam says. Before he can hang up, a profound memory, a small fragment sourced from a dream, comes to mind: the essence of Sam, a stubborn boy with a streak of independence.

"Your thirteenth birthday," I say with urgency. "You told me you were a man then. I laughed, and you got offended. To prove a point, you spent the night at a friend's house, where you both got into the liquor cabinet and had too much to drink. You came home the next day with a hangover, and I made you mow the yard with a pounding headache. Your mother thought I had been too harsh. Do you remember?"

I sense quiet contemplation and hear slow, deep breaths.

"I remember. Don't call here again," Sam says. He disconnects.

New memories are vivid, crystal clear, an artificial representation perfectly painted across my synapses. The dreams, though, are very different, a reflection off the waters after a heavy stone drops. The ripples make it difficult to see clearly, but I understand what's in the mirror image. Sam is there, staring back at me.

Marcus is dead. He won't be the one to make it to the end of his contract. David tells me he slipped into a heated geothermal chamber before it ventilated. He was burned alive. Nothing is left of the body, a complete disintegration of matter spread out high into the atmosphere. David's dreams are overshadowed by nightmares, where he hears Marcus' screams.

"So, you do dream," I say.

"What does it matter? Only the contract matters," David says.

"I contacted my forebearers. They might pay for passage off Paradisea," I say, telling a half-truth. David is stunned, but I see the twinkle of hope in his eyes. He agrees to help, but only if he can be included in the escape plan. We discuss more, and he agrees to an increased workload so I can spend more time at the transponder, attempting to make contact again.

My dreams come more frequently while we wait for the right opportunity. Every night, a different dream invades my subconscious. When I wake up, I write them down and compare them to one another to build a chronology. My old life is a series of loosely connected sequences divided by long gaps. I realize these gaps are true of all humanity, not a measure of my shortcomings as H-Plus. Nobody remembers everything.

David and I find our opportunity. I stand watchful over the transponder, practicing every possible branch of conversation. If Sam picks up again, I will lie and tell him I'm from corporate, that certain paperwork is not in order, and that the benefits will cease if I can't speak to Janus. I'm thankful I don't have to, as she answers after a single ring.

"Hello? Thomas, is that you? Please, tell me if it's you," she pleads. I'm not Thomas, only a shadow left behind after the donor's body starts to decay. But I want to stop dreaming and start making new memories with my wife.

"This is Thomas," I say, unable to say anything more.

"Oh, Thomas, I waited for so long. I thought you would never call back, and I wanted to hear your voice. I'm sorry about how Sam reacted, but I'm happy you called. I miss you so much, and our son is such a wonderful man, and he means well, but..." Janus says.

"I'm still here, Janus. Please, don't stop talking," I say. She is trying hard to fight back tears in between muted sniffles.

"Is it really you? I mean, how much are you Thomas, and how much are you something else? They don't give us many details."

"I dream, Janus. What he knew, I now know, and I don't think there is a difference anymore. I'm becoming less H-Plus and more like the Thomas you knew. I need you. I need to be with you."

"They said that's not possible. The memories they gave you, the ones they took from... before his—your brain died, are supposed to be protected. They were meant to help with your adjustment. Your rebirth. But you shouldn't remember."

"Janus, I want to come home," I say. I sound desperate, uncaring and cold, and I'm afraid she'll think this is a scam, the misguided scheme of a disgruntled employee at corporate headquarters.

"I don't have that kind of money. Corporate will stop paying on the benefits if I sponsor you. They said as much. Please know that I would if it were possible. I have so little, Thomas. Since you've been gone... I have so little hope."

"Live with the hope you do have. One day—" I start to say, and the transponder disconnects. There is no tone, likely the result of a solar storm or supernova, a disruption of light. But the sight of David trailing behind Tal and a lawyer from corporate, both outfitted with their EMUs, leads me to believe it's worse than expected. There will be permanent consequences. Tal is grinning, a devious smile that communicates he doesn't care about anything other than the eventual ruination of every leatherface he supervises.

"Thomas Cordoza. For contacting your forebearers, in violation of Section 3, Part 2, Paragraph 7 of your contract, you are hereby permanently released as an employee due to malfeasance. Self-termination or abandonment are your only two options," the lawyer says, waiting for my response. The original Thomas chose the hard things, and I will continue to honor the dreams conveying that truth.

"Abandonment," I say.

The lawyer looks surprised. He hands me a tablet to provide my biosignature, which I do, and walks away, leaving behind Tal and David, who is sheepish and distant. With thick fingers through his airtight gloves, Tal grabs David by the arm and pulls him toward me.

"I gave him a choice, Thomas. Tell me why he's covering for your shift or risk abandonment. You can guess what he chose," Tal says. David turns and walks away, a slight curve in his back from the shame he now carries.

"On the first day you slid out from the ooze, I knew you would cause trouble. But you're all expendable, cheap labor, freaks of nature constructed for a single purpose, so it doesn't really matter. The only thing that matters now is the contract; you must accept it—not memories or dreams, just the contract," Tal says.

"Even if they were only dreams, it does matter. They represent something you'll never have. You're trapped here, just like me, but your prison is worse," I say.

"Oh, I heard your call, leatherface. You cost that woman the only livelihood she had, and if that's love, I'm better off alone," Tal says, laughing.

I grab Tal's regulator hose, and his eyes widen with fear. Pulling with all my strength, it does not rip out as expected but creates a tear in the suit. Oxygen leaks out, wisps of cool air that blow against my hair. Tal tumbles back, trips, and falls to his back and tries to suck in deep panicky breaths, which only speeds up the process of ingesting lethal doses of methane. He fumbles for the emergency com beacon on his wrist, but I grab his forearm and step on his chest before he can signal anyone. He flails and chokes like a fish out of water.

We are not far from where Marcus died. I drag Tal's limp body the distance, wishing corporate had given me enhanced strength or stamina with my gills. The chamber ventilates frequently, and I must be careful dumping the remains. After the last combustion of superheated methane gasses, I drag him to the edge of the deep pit and roll him over into the orifice. When I'm a safe distance away, the dragon's breath of Paradisea blows upward, spreading Tal's molecules among Marcus's, making them equals.

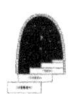

I needed to survive three days before the next transport barge arrived. David's guilt consumed him, and he left me food and supplies in Sector 2 before choosing self-termination. The gesture gives me hope, that little hope, like Janus, to continue. A few men, security and tradesmen from corporate, go looking for Tal but can find no remains. In Paradisea's harsh climate he becomes another statistic, but not one I know. All I know is one in three H-Plus makes it to the end of the contract. I'm not sure that's accurate anymore, given my present situation.

My initial plan is to overpower one of the transport personnel and stow away by force, but enough people have died on this vacation destination already. Instead, I will try to appeal to a corporate man. I can be of use on their journey, even as a floater. If it doesn't work, then I will self-terminate.

When the transport's cargo gate opens, the pilot steps out with several other men from corporate, ready to unload. Instead of surprise, he expects my presence and hands me a tablet. Does he believe an H-Plus can be a shipment receiver? Nothing in protocol allows such a thing, and he doesn't understand my confusion.

"You're Thomas Cordoza?" the pilot asks.

"I am."

"You've been sponsored, correct?"

"I..."

The pilot takes the tablet back, scrolls through, huffs in frustration, and then hands it back, pointing to a name and biosignature box.

"Sam Cordoza is your citizenship sponsor. Do you accept? If so, I need your thumbprint. Unless you want to stay," the pilot says.

I push my thumb to the screen. It blinks green and beeps. The pilot steps aside and begins ordering directions to his colleagues like a good corporate man. They load and unload cargo as I take my seat and close my eyes. The hum of the ship's engines lulls me into a deep sleep after it exits the atmosphere. Even the constant chatter of the crewmembers can't stir me awake. The expectation of seeing Janus and Sam is a soft blanket, comforting me through every passing star system.

I am going home to the place in my dreams.

A Marriage of TruMinds
by Jack Massa

In memory of Michael Bishop, a great science fiction author, and an even better human being.

"I'm sorry, Jon. I just don't see the market potential of living forever as part of someone else."

Shumate Carver, CEO of Dendritecs Corp, stared at Jon Ebsen across the laminate desktop. Behind him, a window showed a curving panorama—trees and park-like paths, buildings, and residential neighborhoods stretching into the cylindrical distance. Built three centuries ago, this was one of the older Lagrange habitats in Earth-Luna space.

"You're still not getting the concept, Shu," Ebsen replied. "I'm not talking about the uploaded person becoming *part* of someone else, but fusing two minds into a unique, new being."

For the past fifteen minutes, Ebsen had pitched the proposal to his former boss. Using a holo-cloud to show code samples, data readouts, and bubble diagrams, he had outlined the project in broad terms.

Not broad enough, it seemed.

As an engineer, Ebsen tended to lose himself in the details. Even a tech-savvy executive like Carver needed to be beaten over the head with the big picture—the bluntest possible big picture.

"And why would I want to be fused into a 'unique new being' when, with our current product, I can upload my mind and live indefinitely as myself, my own discrete self?"

"Loneliness," Ebsen said. "You know as well as I do how the satisfaction indexes are trending."

This was his selling point, the market wedge he hoped would convince Carver.

Spurred by the human dream of immortality, brain uploading, or "whole mind emulation," had been practiced in various forms for over a century. Early models simply scanned and copied a brain's electronic state to a computer repository. The resulting entities *believed* they were the person, but flaws soon became evident—lack of adaptability, scant capacity to learn. These shortcomings—along with the issue of multiple copies of a single mind existing simultaneously—prevented these *emulants* from being legally considered persons.

The breakthrough came thirty years ago, with Ebsen and other technologists of his generation in the vanguard. Harnessing improvements in molecular computing and a radical, layered scanning technique, they produced much more robust uploaded minds. The fact that layered neural scanning terminated the source biological entity also took care of the multiple-copy problem. Following a series of legal decisions and legislation by governments across the System, these new uploads were deemed persons with full human rights—as defined by the habitat or planet-side nation where they resided.

To distinguish them from the earlier, flawed uploads, this new generation was no longer called emulants. Instead, depending on the locale, they were *new people* or *transcendents*. Ebsen preferred Dendritecs' own trademarked term: *TruMinds*.

Founded by Shumate Carver, with Jon Ebsen as chief engineer, Dendritecs had pioneered the new process. With societal winds in their favor and continued technical improvements, the company had been wildly successful for nearly three decades. At present, sixty million TruMinds resided in repositories in the Earth-Luna Ring and more remote locations.

But not all of them were happy.

"Satisfaction indexes system-wide are still close to 80 percent," Carver answered, a bit defensively.

"But trending down," Ebsen said. "Especially among older transcendents. It seems immortality leads inevitably to boredom—or, as I believe, loneliness."

That was putting it simplistically, of course—the bluntest possible instrument to cudgel his former boss. But Ebsen's point correlated with what mental health studies were beginning to show. The first generation of transcendents were mostly elderly, wealthy individuals—willing to exchange failing mortal bodies for a chance at electronic immortality. Once uploaded, they indulged in pleasure-center stimulation, virtual reality entertainment, and adventurous simulations. Over time, such activities were bound to become tedious. Even some of those who devoted themselves to mental work and study were beginning to grow weary of their existence.

So far, only a few Dendritecs TruMinds had elected to go into cold storage, and even fewer had chosen permanent erasure. But even this slight trend was troubling. Seventy percent of Dendritecs' revenues came from maintenance, and the deceased TruMinds paid no rent.

Carver, well aware of all this, twisted his mouth. "I'm still not seeing why merging your mind into some third-party entity would appeal to people."

Ebsen steadied his gaze. "Have you ever been in love?"

A shrug. "Sure. Married three times, and others…"

"No, Shumate. I mean an abiding, all-consuming love for one person."

A smile. "Not in my makeup, I suppose. I know that's how you feel about Widya."

"Exactly. It may be rare. But I'm not proposing this concept as a cure-all for the satisfaction indexes. Still, I'm convinced it will appeal to some people—possibly many, over time. And you have to admit, it's a bold new idea, something to energize the product portfolio."

Carver leaned back, considering. "It's bold, all right. Let me make sure I understand: this merged mind would have the memories of both source persons, correct? So, in effect, I could think and speak as either of the source selves, as well as this new, fused hybrid?"

"That's the design intent. The strength of the separate minds will likely vary based on the source personalities and factors such as merge parameters and neural web configuration. Also, it's my expectation that over time, the fused identity—the *merge,* as I call it—will predominate. Eventually, I conjecture that the source personalities will become memories—still accessible at will, but considered recollections of what the *merge* used to be."

Carver frowned. "Suppose once I'm in this *merge,* I hate it? As I understand your plan, there's no backing out."

"That's true. Of course, the scan process could be engineered with a second feed to create a backup for storage. More expensive and, as with any stored mind, there's the risk of memory degradation over time."

"I still like that better," Carver said. "Update your design schema to include that."

Ebsen straightened in his chair. "Are you giving me the go-ahead?"

"You've made your case. I do like the *bold new idea* pitch. And you *are* only asking for resources to conduct full-scale experiments, correct?"

"Correct."

"I certainly owe you that much, Jon, for all you've done for Dendritecs."

Ebsen had spearheaded product engineering for over two decades before retiring a wealthy man. He and his wife had planned a long retirement—volunteer work, study, and touring the Solar System. Those plans had faded with Widya's failing health.

Carver opened his desk comm. "I'll arrange for Operations to give you what you need. Keep me informed of progress. When you develop a working simulation, we'll bring in Engineering and Marketing. We can wait until then to discuss profit sharing if that's all right with you."

"Thank you, Shu. I'm not at all concerned about sharing the profits."

"Ha! You say that now."

"Seriously. I plan to sign over all rights to the company. You see, I want Widya and me to be the first *merge*."

The medical facility sat within a giant graphene tube that stretched from the rotating floor of the habitat to its motionless center. A combination hospital and nursing home, it was perched at a mid-level of the tube to take advantage of lower spin gravity. Many patients did best at .5 or .6 g.

Riding the elevator, Ebsen experienced a familiar woozy sensation as the effective gravity lessened. He was excited to bring Widya the news but also worried.

He found his wife doing yoga in the living room to the strains of ancient Asian music. The apartment in the assisted living wing was the best money could rent. It included a spacious living room and bedroom, even a kitchen, although all their meals were delivered. The staff, both human and robot, were excellent.

A smile creased Widya's face when she saw him. In the low g, she rolled easily out of her pose. Her thin body stood straight, her complexion appearing less drawn and withered than it had lately.

Or was that just wishful thinking?

Widya suffered from a range of degenerative conditions. In the end, they simply amounted to old age. Despite molecular medicine and nano-based rejuvenation techniques, all bodies eventually wore down. At 132, Widya had already survived well past the average lifespan. The medical team gave her four to five months at best.

"How did the meeting go?" She lifted her face for his kiss.

"Excellent, darling. Carver approved the plan. Resources are being assigned. I'll begin initializing the systems tomorrow."

She nodded, her face carefully neutral. "I know you're pleased."

Holding hands, they walked to the sofa.

"I hope you're pleased as well." His stomach twisted with the all-too-familiar fear about her doubts, about what she would ultimately decide.

Even as they grew rich from the TruMind process, Widya had persistently refused to consider the option for herself. Whatever the legal experts said, she did not believe one's true identity survived as an upload. Also, she saw no appeal in the idea of perpetual existence as a disembodied mind. "I'm just not that egotistical," she would say. "And it would be so lonely."

It was her qualms about loneliness that first suggested the merge concept to Ebsen. From the start, Widya found the idea intriguing. But in the three years he'd worked on designs, she had never actually committed.

They sat together in front of the picture window, the huge tunnel of the habitat stretching into the distance.

"So you're going full-throttle on your project," Widya said. "Working 16-hour days, your mind distracted by computations even when you are with me."

Her tone was teasing, but he sensed hurt underneath. A feeling of helplessness crept into his chest.

"Wouldn't it be more fun to take a trip?" she asked. "We haven't been to Earth in 80 years."

"The gravity would grind you down—despite all the yoga."

She laughed. "Luna then?"

He shook his head. Maybe she was right: better to use whatever time remained to pursue simple enjoyments instead of chasing this wild scheme.

No. He refused to believe that. His project promised them an indefinite lifespan together and a whole new level of intimacy.

"There is so much more life I want to share with you," he murmured.

Her ironic smile vanished, and she squeezed his hand. "Whatever your engineering genius may or may not accomplish, Jon, I know we'll be together again."

That was her spiritual side talking. In her later years, she'd become something of a mystic. Eben's rationalist mind gave no credence to such ideas.

"Widya, you know I'd like to believe that's true. But it certainly does no harm to extend our time together by scientific means if we can. That's all I'm trying to do."

"I know, Jon. But you must also appreciate my view. I know you will do everything you can to ensure the uploads are perfect. But will it really be you and me existing in the cybersphere? I just don't believe it."

Again, the "true identity" problem: Was the upload *really* the person? Did a human's identity reside in the pattern of firing neurons—which Ebsen believed equated with consciousness and could be duplicated—or did identity reside only in that spongy lump of flesh inside the skull? It was a question philosophers could argue over forever, and engineers never solve.

"I believe it really will be you and me. Anyway, I can promise that once we are uploaded, we will think so."

"Or *they* will think so." With a laugh, she leaned her head on his shoulder.

The lab assigned to Ebsen was located in the rear of the Dendritecs interface complex—past several wide halls vibrant with terminals and holo-clouds, occupied by teams of operators and engineers. True to his word, Carver had provided sole access to a 4,000 petaFLOP system distributed over six arrays. Backup storage would be "whatever you need." Shu had even provided a lab assistant, a woman named Darcia Menendez, with thirty-seven years of experience in operations and quality assurance.

"It's an honor to be assigned to help you, Dr. Ebsen," she said when Carver made the introduction.

Ebsen's reputation, ten years out-of-date, apparently still carried clout.

They got to work at once. Ebsen's briefcase contained most of the project in its current state: thousands of lines of code, simulation maps, pages of diagrams, and notes. At first, he had worked on his own equipment. When the project outgrew those systems, he had run simulations on public networks. Even with the best encryption, he had worried about security. That was what brought him back to Dendritecs. Now, at last, he could explore with full resources. The prospect thrilled him.

All morning, he worked with Menendez, compiling his code for the new systems, uploading basic sims, tweaking parameters. In the afternoon, they activated Alembic-KX2, an AI component that would serve as a control system. The AI appeared as a disembodied white face floating in the main holo interface. This fashion of presentation had scarcely changed in two hundred years.

"Thank you for activating me," the level voice said. "I look forward to assisting in your project."

It took eleven seconds for Alembic to digest the uploaded data. "This is a unique approach," it said, "to my knowledge."

"I believe so," Ebsen answered. "What is your estimate of feasibility?"

"Assuming state-of-the-art biological uploads—"

"Of course."

"Then the primary obstacle will be compatibility of the neural mappings. Options for adjusting the pathways will run into trillions."

"Well within this system's capacity, I believe."

"Certainly. But, evaluating each decision point will take time and depend on specified criteria. What is our definition of success? The design points to a merged consciousness that is aware of its two source minds. But to what degree? What are the controlling factors?"

"I've wondered that also," Menendez said. "Will customers be able to choose their degree of separateness up front? And will it be fluid? How will the merged mind adjust its awareness? How do we ensure against symptoms of multiple-personality disorder?"

"All questions are to be answered by trial and error," Ebsen replied. "That's what the simulation phase is for. My view is that the degree of separateness is open-ended. In time, Dendritecs can potentially offer a range of product options. For the initial prototype, I'm aiming for a strongly merged persona, aware of, but not controlled by the source minds."

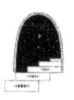

The project took shape in the ensuing weeks. Simulated human minds were downloaded from archives, activated, and analyzed in detail by Ebsen's software. Those chosen as likely candidates for merging were subjected to more detailed mapping. Algorithms assessed and enhanced their neural nets, fabricated new connections, adjusted firing thresholds. Programs running in the background constantly monitored progress, compiled statistics, and revised test plans. A refined, detailed merge process began to develop.

Ebsen lost himself in the intricacies of the project, the liberation of finally having the resources to bring his ideas to life. Alembic-KX2, of course, was cheerfully tireless. Even Menendez, subject to human limitations and lacking Ebsen's personal motivation, seldom took time off.

But even as they made progress, Ebsen grew increasingly desperate. Widya seemed to diminish before his eyes. The medical monitor system reported that she was eating less. She stopped doing yoga, spent more time in bed. Pressed about her decline, the doctors could only express sympathy. They refused to forecast how much time she had left.

Ebsen decided he could wait no longer for a decision. He raised the question one evening over dinner. She had roused herself to sit with him at the table, though she showed little appetite.

"My dear, we are close to the time when you must decide about uploading."

She stared at him for a few moments. "I'm afraid you are right, Jon."

"And...?"

"I don't know. It frightens me, to be honest. To voluntarily end one's life—"

"Not *end*," he insisted, "*transform*. Into something better."

"I know that's what you believe. But I just don't. I'm sorry."

The pain in her voice tortured him—more than he could bear. He reached over and touched her wrist. "It's all right, my dear.

I never want to cause you suffering, you know that. I accept whatever you feel is best."

Moisture shone in her eyes. "I don't want to hurt you either. I know how hard you've worked on this, how much it means to you."

Silence went on for a time.

"Is the merge process almost ready?" she asked.

He stared down at his plate. "No. Still a few weeks, at the very least, before I'd be willing to risk it."

"Well... I might not be here then."

"I know." He squeezed her wrist. "But... if necessary, we *could* upload your mind to storage. It's not ideal, but if there were no other way..."

This silence lasted even longer.

"Give me a little more time to think it over," she said. "Just a little more."

"Good news for you, Jon." Shumate Carver walked unannounced into Ebsen's lab. "We discussed your project in the staff meeting this morning. Marketing surveys turned out better than anyone expected. On the strength of those numbers, we will continue your funding and start drawing up plans to productize."

Ebsen breathed with relief. "That is great news."

"Emily is assigning two senior engineers to work with your team." He meant Emily Kimathi, the current head of engineering. "Not that we're not satisfied with your progress," Carver said. "But since you're planning to eh... leave the project at some point, we'll need people trained up to replace you when the time comes."

Ebsen caught a surprised glance from Menendez. He hadn't told her of his intention to upload his mind as soon as the merge process was ready. He made a mental note to explain to her later.

"Marketing's quite optimistic," Shumate was saying. "They've already come up with a suggested name and tagline: 'TruMerge. A Marriage of TruMinds.' What do you think?"

Ebsen smiled. "I like it… Sounds vaguely familiar, though."

"Right. It did to me, too. Don't worry; they checked trademark. The phrase comes from an old English poet, pre-space age."

⸻

He walked through a hydroponics tunnel, a green place full of sunlight. The floor curled upward, the paths lined with fruit trees, vines, and flowers. The misty air flowed with scent.

He found her beside a flower bed tending violets, assisted by a robot gardener. She worked as an agro-engineer, treating the plants like little friends. In the early days of their love affair, he jokingly called her his Earth Goddess. She brought out a romantic side he had not known existed.

She smiled as he approached—dark angular face, keen searching eyes. She stood, slim and straight, a black braid hanging behind her shoulder. Unbearably lovely.

"Are you ready to take me away now, Jon?"

"Soon, my love. Soon."

The scene dissolved, a blizzard of fragmented light pulsing in his visual cortex. Dizzy with a headache, Ebsen blinked until the VR space dissolved and the lab materialized around him.

"Are you all right, Jon?" Menendez set down the headset she had removed from his scalp.

"Yes. Headache again, but that's of no consequence."

This was a critical phase of the research: testing models of his own mind uploaded as simulations, viewing their experience through standard VR.

Transcendents typically spent most of their existence driving body constructs through virtual environments. These VRs could be generated from their memories, chosen from menu options, or a combination of both. One of Dendritecs' selling points was its vast library of virtual settings. Having evolved in a physical world, human consciousness needed a simulated body and sensory environment to function. Very few minds chose to just sit in the dark and think.

"The sense of reality is getting stronger. That's the important thing."

"If you are ready, Doctor Ebsen," Alembic said, "we will read out your memories for analysis."

"Yes. Of course." The sooner they were recorded, the better. He picked up a second headset and fitted it over his skull.

"I'm sorry, Jon. I'm just so tired."

Widya lay on the up-tilted bed, her eyes sunken, mouth drawn thin. A life-support unit hummed nearby, a tube feeding a concoction of pharmaceuticals into a vein at her elbow. Ebsen could barely feel her hand gripping his.

"Widya, I'm afraid you must decide now. We're nearly out of time."

"I know, dear."

Even as her decline accelerated, the project had run into snags. Some simulations were failing to merge. Others showed erratic behavior and loss of memory from the source minds. A reliable merge was still at least two weeks away.

His wife would not last that long.

"It's not so bad," she said. "Dying. It is the nature of things, you know."

"I don't want to believe we cannot overcome it—or at least delay it."

A weak smile. "You were always such an optimist. I love that about you."

He could not bear to part from that love. Even as she faded day by day, that realization had grown stronger: Her love sustained him.

He struggled to speak. "I am willing to let you go, if I must, if that is your choice. But I will ask you one more time because I believe it will give us a chance for more life together: Will you agree to be scanned and have your mind stored—within the next day or two?"

They both knew the risks. No matter how fine the copy, memory degradation might appear when the mind was reactivated. In a few cases, mental functioning was seriously impaired. And there could be no chance for a retry: the deep-scan process terminated the biological person.

She gazed into his eyes, a look compounded of sadness and affection.

"I will agree, Jon, because I love you. But you must promise me one thing: Do not activate my mind until the merge process is ready. Just in case I am wrong, and it really is *me* waking up in the cybersphere, I don't want to exist as a solitary upload. I would be so lonely."

The Dendritecs medical facility was completely automated. Widya lay in an antiseptic enclosure while the machines prepared to operate. A mild sedative had been injected. Still, she stared at the ceiling with wide, frightened eyes. Ebsen wished he could stand beside the table and hold her hand. Instead, he watched through a glass panel.

Clasps rose up from the table, wrapping her head to keep it still. The electronics came to life. The reader moved into position on a conveyor arm. It paused above her forehead, then moved back and forth, hydraulics humming as it scanned. Red lights flashed on her skin like droplets of blood. Layer by layer, the equipment recorded the information stored in each neuron, dissecting Wydia's brain, putting it to sleep forever.

"Are you all right, Dr. Ebsen?" Menendez laid a consoling hand on his shoulder.

"Yes, of course. Thank you."

"You are doing the right thing," she told him.

"I believe I am... I just wish I *felt* more certain."

"I'll ask one more time. Are you sure you want to do this, Jon?"

"Yes."

"Even though the reliability index is only 68%?"

Ebsen frowned, glancing at the window behind Carver's desk. "Is that what Kimathi's team is telling you?"

"Yes. Emily reports to me daily."

"Well, their methodology is conservative, in my view. My estimate is closer to 80%."

Carver tilted his head. "I'm sure they're using standard measures, Jon."

"It doesn't matter. I can't wait any longer, Shumate. Widya's mind has been in storage nearly three weeks. At that point, the probability of deterioration starts rising. I won't risk it."

Carver stared into his eyes a moment, then sighed. "Your call, Jon." He touched a comm tab and ordered that the contracts for Dr. Ebsen be called up.

Expert systems were activated in the Legal department and at the office of Eben's attorney to witness and notarize the agreements. The terms were read aloud: Ebsen assigned all rights to the TruMerge process, along with all of his notes and documentation related to the project, to Dendritecs. In exchange, a trust fund would be established with a Luna bank in the names of Ebsen and Widya's uploads. Their merged minds, in whatever form, would be maintained in perpetuity—meaning as long as the computer substrate of the present civilization lasted. A retina scan confirmed Ebsen's identity. He voiced his agreement to each document and amended clause.

When the systems had finalized the contracts, Carver asked: "How soon will you upload?"

"This afternoon," Ebsen said. "No time to waste."

Carver stood and extended his hand. "Good luck, Jon. I hope we'll talk again soon—in whatever form that might take."

Lying on the table, Ebsen stared up at the equipment. Outside the enclosure, Menendez and the other team members watched. He smiled and gave a thumbs-up.

"You are ready, Dr. Ebsen?" Alembic's voice sounded over the speaker.

"Yes. Proceed, please."

He shut his eyes and relaxed. He'd taken no sedative, wanting to experience the nerve processes unfiltered. Still, when the hydraulic arm swiveled into position, his eyes popped open with a surge of anxiety.

No need for that, he told himself. *Your whole life's course has led to this event.*

As the scan commenced, his scalp tingled. Neurons spiked and fired, seemingly random sensations at the top of his skull. Unlike the upload to storage that Widya had experienced, this would be a transfer with no loss of awareness. Some TruMinds described a sense of motion, a gradual flow as consciousness uploaded to the waiting neural net. Others reported suddenly blinking to find themselves in the virtual domain.

For Ebsen, there was only the random tingling and the steady hum of the scanner. When he opened his eyes, he still saw the device and the glass-walled room.

And then he didn't.

At first, his vision was dim, a gray cloud with random sparks of white. Then, motion stirred as the cloud dispersed. A space appeared, stretching away in all directions, a web of threads, some spiking with tiny fires—his visual cortex struggling to interpret the neural net.

His new home.

"Dr. Ebsen, can you hear me?" Alembic's steady voice.

"Yes."

"The upload is complete. Are you ready to begin Phase One of the merge?"

"Go ahead, please."

A jolt. Acceleration. The image of the network quivered and surged. Disorientation. A sensation like wooziness in the gut.

Fear.

He was streaming through a space of flashes and tunnels.

Far away, something moved toward him, a pulsing wave.

Another mind.

The waves met, and he plunged into a sea of freezing light.

Jon walked along a stream that ran the length of the hydroponics tunnel. Widya stood in the distance. When she saw him, she smiled and waved.

Was he still Jon? A glance down showed a body resembling Jon's, although younger and fitter.

But he was also something more.

"Widya?" he called as he approached her.

A puzzled frown appeared. "I was Widya. Am I still that same Widya now? I'm not sure."

For some reason, he laughed. "If you were sure you were the same Widya, I would have my doubts. But because you have doubts, I am sure."

He stepped close to embrace her. Instead, their bodies turned to liquid and flowed together into one. He gazed down at the merged form: gray, amorphous, sparkling with energy—a body that could move and reshape itself at will.

Or diverge again into two separate bodies, as it did now.

"I... did not imagine this," Jon said.

"Are you all right, Jon? Yes. I can feel that you are."

"Yes."

He could feel her—her thoughts, sensations, memories. But, most of all, her emotions: confusion, joy, and love.

"I never realized how deeply you felt," he said.

She laughed. "I always knew how deeply you thought."

Both minds were unmistakably present. But what about the merged mind?

Jon could feel that too, a presence that encompassed them both but hovered somehow out of reach, as though behind or above them.

"Don't worry, Jon," Widya said. "I think you will have a good long while to figure it out."

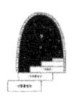

Shumate Carver stood in the lab before the interface portal. Emily Kimathi, Darcia Menendez, and the rest of the engineering team were with him.

"Alembic: Report the current status of the prototype merge."

"No further responses, Mr. Carver."

Before going quiet, the merge had communicated with the team through the interface portal for just nine minutes. They had reported that all was well, that they considered the process a success. They answered 12% of the satisfaction index survey, then quit, claiming that the questions were largely irrelevant to their present state of being. They suggested new tests be devised, offering to help with that and other aspects of the project at a later time. In summary, they declared that their present state of consciousness was "difficult to explain."

"I assume we continue the project?" Kimathi asked.

Carver nodded. "Certainly. The data we have indicates at least a qualified success. But now that Jon's no longer running the show, I want you to institute rigorous up-front simulations and thorough testing before we attempt any more biologic uploads. Alembic, did the merge indicate *when* they might be willing to communicate with us again?"

"No, sir. Only that they intended to enjoy a prolonged honeymoon."

The Guardian by Clarice Sanchez Meneses

For my beloved family (on Earth and in Heaven)

As heartbreaking as this fact may be, they cannot do this for *all* the sick children.

The child must be the perfect mixture of sleepy and awake; innocent enough to still believe in wondrous things and lucid enough to know they are not dreaming, that they are being entrusted with a precious secret they must keep for however long they have left. Delilah only has three days.

That night, the guardian—the title they have come to know themself over the years—bundles Delilah's frail body into a wheelchair and whisks her out into the hall.

"Is it another surgery?" the ten-year-old mumbles. Two years ago, the girl threw screaming fits at the thought of going under the knife, and her parents made a point of reassuring her and promising her treats and rewards weeks in advance. These past few months, that ritual had been thrown to the wind. There had been far too many emergency operations, and Delilah was used to it by now.

"No, child," they say. "You're far past need of that."

Delilah doesn't hear their voice catch. "Good," she sighs as she sinks into the seat. It can't be the most comfortable space, but the guardian understands that, at this point, almost nowhere feels comfortable. The place they are taking her is perhaps the final one in this life that pain cannot wholly follow. Delilah tugs at their sleeve. "Can I take a nap?"

"In a while. I have something to show you." They point to the end of the low-lit hospital corridor. "Do you see that door?"

"The door to the exit?" Delilah blinks and sits up. "No, wait, that's different. That's..." She frowns. "I've never seen it before."

"I should hope not. I only put it there a minute ago."

"You can't just put doors—"

"I can."

The guardian says it with so much authority that Delilah twists to look at them. Her lips form a small *oh*. "I've never seen you before, either," she says.

"You haven't."

"But I thought you were my favorite nurse."

"Why?"

"You sound just like her. No—you *feel* just like her. And my parents, too. You feel like whenever they give me a hug."

"Is 'safe' the word you are looking for?" they offer.

"Yes."

"I am safe. Even though I'm not your nurse, I am your friend." That hadn't always been the case, of course. There was a time long ago when they were far from a friend of any human. But that no longer matters. "I want to show you something through that door. It's the world that I came from."

"You're not from around here?"

"No."

"I guess I should've figured. What are you waiting for?"

"Your permission, Delilah." The girl's mouth rounds in surprise for the second time in five minutes. "Will you allow me to take you through the door? The decision is entirely up to you."

It will probably be the last decision entirely up to her. They want to give Delilah that.

"Yes," the young girl says. Then, belatedly: "Please."

On the other side, the world is made of light.

When the guardian first brought children here—Adrian, the first one, had been shaking with tremors even when his eyes were wide saucers of excitement—they feared that the shift between worlds would immediately destroy the children's already precarious health. It is so different from their universe made of mud, blood, and soil; here, essence is stripped bare and free to float along. Galaxies can be experienced with a single touch; so can oceans of anger, clouds of love, flights of whimsy. A lifetime's worth of marvels—that's what they wanted to give, why they had been willing to risk it.

It is, fortunately, what they managed. There is a brightness in the bones of humans—an essential kind of light that carries them even in a world so different. Adrian had stopped shaking. Now, Delilah laughs as they wheel her through the spirit of a waterfall.

But while the guardian's world isn't reliant on organic matter, that doesn't mean it's completely divorced from it. Soon, treacherous coughs wrack Delilah's body once more. The guardian asks her if she would like to go back to bed.

"Will we come back tomorrow?" she asks.

"No." They had never seen the point in lying to children.

"Okay." Delilah nods her head. "Can we pass by the part that tastes like Chocnut one more time?"

They do, and fifteen minutes later, both of them are back in the hospital ward, Delilah's curtained-off alcove sparkling softly with pink fairy lights her siblings had decorated for her. Those look like stars from another galaxy now. Delilah grins so hard her cheeks ache. "I can't believe I thought you were a nurse."

"I am a nurse," they chide lightly. They hold Delilah from her underarms and smoothly place her onto her bed.

"An ordinary nurse, I mean. From here. You're so *obviously* from that other place."

"How can you tell?" Even though the children often made this observation after the trip, the guardian is still puzzled. Their disguise of a frizzy-haired Filipino woman is immaculate, and no adult ever remarks otherwise.

"You're golden." Delilah places a hand on her heart. "In here."

"Thank you. But I don't think that's limited to people of my world." They ruffle her hair. "You're golden, too."

Delilah ducks her head bashfully. "Thank you."

"I need you to keep this a secret, Delilah. About me and the other world."

"Why?"

"Grown-ups aren't supposed to know." Neither are children or any kind of human being, but what the Council Elders don't know won't hurt them. Besides, the guardian has never been a stickler for the rules.

"I promise I won't tell."

"Good."

"May I ask one more question, please?"

"That's already a question." They smile. "But go ahead."

"Why'd you let me visit?"

How children ask questions like this is so different from how grown-ups do. Whenever the guardian deals with adults in one way or another, those adults regard their gifts with deep suspicion. The question *what do you want from me?* lurks behind their words.

Delilah's inquiry isn't like that at all. Like the other children before her, she simply wants to know.

The guardian could have answered in many ways, all of them true. "To stop the pain for a while" was always a distinct motivation. They could have also replied with "I thought you might like it," "It's a goodbye present," and "You deserve one more beautiful thing."

But underlying all of that is one specific purpose. The guardian crouches down to be at eye level with Delilah. "To help you understand something I learned long ago."

"What's that?"

"You'll be leaving this world soon." Delilah doesn't flinch. That much, she understands by now. "Years ago, I had to leave my world, too, even if I didn't want that." Banished, to be precise. For crimes so savage and bloody, the guardian still shudders to think of them. "I didn't think I would ever find my way back. It was—"

"—Scary?" Delilah suggests.

"That's right. It was scary."

"Change is always scary." Compassion fills the young girl's voice. The guardian's heart breaks for her, grieves for all that

Delilah is and could have been, but they refuse to show that in their face; it's not yet the time for mourning.

"Despite that being the case," they say, "this world, your world, surprised me. When I opened myself up to it, I found it to be as amazing as you found my own."

Adrian had scoffed at that. Dimitri laughed, Mina frowned, and Jenna rolled her eyes while clutching the guardian's hands tight. Delilah simply yawns and smiles. "If Heaven is even half as cool," she says, "I guess it won't be so bad."

The Canyon by Victor D. Sandiego

For three days it rained and everything he carried except for matches wrapped in oilcloth and tinned coffee got wet. His hat. Pack. Clothes. His boots. He ate cold beans and raw trout. When he looked up, he saw the rim of the canyon far above. An unreachable border between worlds. What wilderness lay beyond and what civilization far beyond that had no relation to his presence inside the magnificent greatdeep fissure that split the demanding earth. He had entered the canyon weeks before at its wide and shallow sloped entrance where desert ended and mountains began their ascent. Now enclosed within its transcendent walls and alone with his past, he hiked forever upriver. Impelled by a severe and nameless purpose.

Escape or excursion, he couldn't say—or wouldn't. Either way, only the canyon knew him. Only the canyon received him, and it spoke a tongue he had yet to master. At night the river current revealed stories that had no end—only constant shifting. Flowing. A direction of epochs carved.

The rain stopped. He laid his clothes on rocks and in thrall of midmorning light sat naked while damp yielded to sunlight. He dressed, made a small fire, and heated coffee. Strained through a washcloth as his father had taught him.

They had been here many years before, when he was a boy and his father, for a brief time, a protector. They hadn't penetrated this far into the canyon but had entered at night with rain, mud, and lightning. And a story of a man who had been boltstruck and died.

He still wondered what that would be like. To be sudden pierced by God's brilliant wrath in the darkness and transported at once to another realm. A rare encounter. Divine.

For weeks he hiked deeper into the motherhood of the mountains. A willing prisoner inside the great walls that led ever closer to the river's birthpools. Secreted in far tributaries and snowpacks.

Ancient granite slabs rose from the riverbed and steep-climbed to the sky. In some narrow places vertical and emerging from the constrained and enraged current. No path along a bank at all. He entered the water and waded chest-deep upriver, clinging to crevices in the drenched wallrock. Each step a careful calculation, a blind reckoning with his forward boot in the hurtling water to find a submerged foothold. After came drying and a thanking that the canyon had granted him passage.

One day he came to an easing, a widening of meadow and trees. The water relaxed and rippled. He made camp and, at night, allowed stars in the canyon gap above him to bless their light down onto his face. At times he cried alone in the canyon's well, for even the rationed view of the sky showed the expansive promise of the world. Made more glorious by its boundaries.

He rested for two days, fished, and drank his coffee. Received riversong into his need to let go of his past. Honored in silence a sanctuary of solitude deep in the mountains—his body as soul in flight.

On the third morning he awoke in faint dawnlight to the rough odor of primitive breath. A large black bear sniffed his face. His hands at his side, he exhaled softly and trusted the bear would sense that no threat stemmed from his prone figure. He held only wonder that beast and man should meet at the bottom of the world and share a sunrise.

Afternoons came early in the deep. When the sun dropped over the western rim, shadows crawled up the walls to meet the embrace of night. Still time to tramp the canyon and climb over rock, but conditions could quick-change dangerous. Once in late afternoon he had tried to cross to the other side of the river in leaps from rock to rock but darkness caught him in the middle on a large slab unable to see the next leap and he slept that night with rivermist and the rumble of swift current.

An assortment of slowpass days. At times rough going. The river vigorous and rapid. His other life far behind.

One night he dreamed he stood near the canyon rim and heard a deep voice call out from the abyss. The youth will war me, it said. He shivered and moved closer to the edge. Barefoot on sharp rocks. He cried a single tear and the canyon filled with sadness. A second tear and it filled with joy. He awoke. A soft heaven light burned in the air.

Next day midmorning a jumbled slide of large granite blocks choked the riverside. A wallslab had fallen and shattered ages before. It extended upriver about three hundred meters, an unstable, hazardous passage made more perilous by the uncountable number of rattlesnakes that crowded the rocks to warm their coldblood in the morning sun.

He tucked his pants in his boots, laced them tight, found a stick, and began the crossing. His route anfractuous and precarious as rocks tipped and threatened his balance. Snakebite may be survivable, but to break a leg certainly fatal. Two hundred impossible miles back and an unknown distance forward. He edged ahead. Cautious. Fully alive. Aware of his choice. The snakes hissed and rattled. The sun ascended, an hour crept. Once past, he laid down his stick, walked a ways, sat on a rock, and breathed. Asked himself in silence why he hadn't waded the river and in silence answered trial. And trust.

He entered the current and knelt, lifted his eyes to the rim. The water marked his chest and for a moment he felt himself purified, cleansed. Maybe now named. He heard meaning in the canyon sounds and within the river's urgent rush. He spoke his first words: We all submit to loss, he said to the walls. Man or god. But we go on.

He rose and dripped. Took a long breath. Looked ahead. The cradle of the canyon's birthplace yet upward.

Hyperbolic by LB Waltz

"I didn't expect to see you today," you say.

It's not a lie, exactly. You *didn't* expect to see her today. You didn't expect to see her tomorrow either, or the day after that, or the day after *that*, or ever again, really.

Hopefully.

But there she had been at the crosswalk, snowflakes in her hair and two red hands perfectly reproduced in her eyes, and what else could you do?

Stop, the monotone signal demanded. *Wait.*

You stopped. You waited. And when she grinned at you from the other side of the intersection, her white teeth beckoned like the changing signal, like the neon sign outside the 24-hour diner into which you'd been headed.

"I don't suppose it's a pleasant surprise," she responds, almost wryly. Her coat squeaks as she bounces deeper into your assigned booth, vintage purple plastic chaffing against cheap vinyl. The coat's polka-dot print matches her galoshes.

It's not supposed to rain tonight. Your peacoat slides against the fabric of the opposite seat, unresistant. Unnatural.

You clear your throat. "It's been an age. You look... different." *Childlike*, you think, as in, *like* a child, but not.

Definitely not.

She snorts, kicking feet that don't quite touch the ground. "You don't."

You don't. You know you don't. And because you know you don't, you're not sure how to respond, what you ought to say next. What there *is* to say next. Once upon a time, you would have made demands, caused a scene, shouted something dramatic along the lines of *what happened to me* or *what did you do to my body*; you might have wanted to know the details, the stipulations, the scientific particulars of your own biology.

You cared, once.

Once.

But presumptions and common sense have served you well enough thus far, and priorities change even when faces don't. Not long after acceptance set in, so did apathy. The facts are the facts; reality is reality. You no longer have the same drive for answers, never mind the curiosity or the passion, and that makes conversation difficult.

Life, too, for that matter.

A waitress brings over two waters, her apron ketchup-stained and her smile much less genuine than your enigmatic companion's. *Clunk, clunk*, and the drinks are deposited. You intend to nod your thanks—maybe even voice it, if only to keep from talking to *her* for a bit longer—but you are distracted by the eyes. The round, glossy-glass eyes that gaze up at you from beaded condensation.

Huh.

They pearl, those eyes. They drip. You blink, and the dew blinks back, ommatidial surfaces refracting the restaurant and the souls inside it.

The waitress is already gone. You are alone with her again, alone in the 8 PM crowd. There is a young family behind you, road-weary from holiday traffic, struggling to soothe their infant's wails. On your left, seniors in their church-going best grumble about deserving a better discount. To your right, high schoolers are filing in through the double doors, a grand exodus in reverse, laughing uproariously about whatever it is that high schoolers find funny these days. Memes, you've been told. You don't know enough about teenagers to disagree.

Those condensation eyes haven't left you. Hers join in, ceaselessly staring. They replicate the sputter of that neon sign beyond the window—its panes made insectoid by the compounding of unwashed fingerprints—and invert blurred cursive like a pair of mirrors.

Did you know, somebody once whispered, conspiratorial, into your then-growing ear, *that holding one mirror in front of another opens a portal to the demon world?*

A lie, certainly. Definitely. Probably. Just in case, you have made sure never to do that.

No, *that* isn't what you did.

"Well?" she prompts, bent elbows propped atop the table. Her raincoat whines, and glittering hexagons cover her hair—the snow. It looks so fake, that snow, like misplaced Christmas decorations. These days, it's hard for you to believe that there was ever a time before Christmas, but there was, wasn't there. You *know* there was because you were there for it. "Come on, come on. Don't keep me in suspense. How *is* that lover of yours?"

You're not sure you want to answer that. You're not sure *how* to answer that.

Unlike you, some things change.

"Do you want to share a bite? Maybe a sandwich? Pie?" you offer, reaching out to peel the menu off the tabletop. It comes free as a scab would: stiffly, crackling, covered in infection. The idea contaminates, tainting your thoughts with memories of pared things, of dissecting the delicate layers that make up both living skin and wounds. "I'm not that hungry. Let's split."

Shit. The regret is instantaneous: sluicing like liquid mercury down the tube of your spine. You should've chosen your words more wisely. Now, she must know. Jesus, she probably knew before.

You look at her because you forget you shouldn't.

There are *so many teeth* in her grin.

"Don't worry about me. I'm fine," she hums, tongue slithering behind her incisors. You bite down on your own—you bite down *hard*—but not quite hard enough.

"You aren't hungry?"

She laughs, a hollow, echoing pit of sound. "Oh, I'm positively ravenous." Her foot taps against the table leg, *tap tap tap,* metronomic, rhythmic, making the drinks shiver and ice cubes chitter with the brittle sound of crushed dreams. Condensation assimilates itself, balling and breaking between the both of you before spilling over the laminate.

You don't like the roundness of the pool that the water makes, nor how her cup creates a pupil in its translucent center.

You swallow, closing the menu.

She closes her mouth but frames its arc with her hands.

"So. You're still an item, you two. Officially. Congratulations. An impressive feat, considering your... escapades. Then again, we all saw *those* coming, didn't we?"

That your infidelity had never been an *if*, only a *when*, is the real tragedy here. The real *indignity*. You can feel yourself flushing, the molten shame that serves as your marrow leaking from the time-worn fractures in your ribs. But Christ—did she have to make it a *taunt*? Did she need to be so teasing and sweet and nauseatingly *perceptive*?

Humiliated, you snap a glare her way, but *dammit*, you never learn; your eyes meet hers straight-on—*dead-on*—and you hate yourself for letting that happen, for allowing yourself to be baited, even for the half-second it takes to slap a hand over your face.

You are already aware of your faults and failures—you are so *bitingly* aware. The last thing you need is to see them for yourself, and the last thing you want is to reflect upon them.

Not figuratively. Not literally. God forbid both.

Your companion continues to stare.

"That's the worst part, isn't it? That you betrayed her, and now, she can't trust you. That she left you, and now, you can't trust her," she narrates, ceaselessly staring. Staring, staring, staring. The fluid between you wavers, vitreous. No, aqueous. Both and neither. "And yet, that feeling won't let go, will it? It sours instead and breeds like a cancer."

Muscles are coiling beneath her youthful façade; you can sense them, feel her attention in the pores of your bones. In your sweat, in your plasma. With palms raised as a shield, you turn your focus with great deliberation to an advert for this month's pancake special.

"I love her." The confession makes your bowels blister. Twist. It's pointless to hope that she doesn't notice.

"Of course you do. After all, you're *here*, aren't you? You're *alive*. The both of you are."

"We are."

"And that's *good*, isn't it?"

"Isn't it," you mumble. Syrup oozes in suspended animation, fated never to reach the bottom of its short stack. The food looks unreal, unappetizing, something authentic warped into an uncanny impersonation of itself. A trick of photography, of light. Smoke and mirrors.

Though you don't intend to sigh, you cannot stop yourself. You have never been good at stopping yourself.

"I, um. I sort of expected you to, uh. Tempt me," you admit, soft in your embarrassment. "Tempt *us*. Like, try to lead lost lambs astray or something. To at least show some *investment* in this whole affair."

"*Really?*" She has not blinked. She never blinks, has never blinked, but even so, her long lashes begin to quiver as if with amusement—or, perhaps, anticipation. Impossibly, irrefutably, her mouth curves higher, its corners reaching her under-lids while her irises shift with ever-changing colors.

You think she will actually blind you if you look at her again. So you don't. You try so hard not to.

"Why-ever would I do that?" she chuckles, swing-swing-swinging her legs. Back and forth, back and forth. Steady as a clock, with time changing around her. Around you. "Not that I *needed* to. Obviously. But ignoring that. You don't tempt strawberries to grow faster or try to lead peanuts astray, do you? You don't show investment in the lives of beef cows or cabbageheads. You can't rush a harvest, silly. All good things, etcetera. I don't mind waiting a while."

"Don't you mean 'forever?'"

Outside, the snow has become an unseasonable rain. It falls hard, then harder, shattering the headlights of a passing SUV into prisms and shards. Once filtered through the window, those winking, fleeting fragments flash, glow, and die in her gaze.

You remember fireflies, back when there were fireflies. Back when there were no SUVs, diners, or electricity. Back when the road was dirt, the crossroad dark, and the nearest town—your village—was an hour's walk away. Back before your lover's mirror had known the embrace of ice-cold earth.

A truck splashes through a gutter. Traffic lights flicker from yellow to red.

"We were promised forever," you quietly remind. That baby is still crying, the elderly still griping. People chew and slurp and eat and waste away as their cells slowly, serenely die. "We were promised that our love would last forever. And... our love can't last if we don't, right? So."

The girl—the girl who is not a girl, is not young, is not female, is honestly the furthest thing away from being any sort of human—twists her lips into an expression that can no longer be called a smile. It is too sharp, too terrifyingly wide; it threatens to crack her crystalline eyes, and if you had another soul to sell, you would exchange it gladly if it kept your sanity from cracking in kind.

Decades ago, in 1965, you visited the Infinity Mirror Room at a gallery in New York. Since then, you have understood how such mirrors work.

You know they are an illusion. You know they are a trick. You know they are built on a fundamental lie.

Nothing lasts forever, something once warned, a heated hiss into then-aging flesh. *It only feels that way, sometimes.*

When she clambers to a stand, her polka-dot raincoat starts to drip, shedding iterations, reproductions, and other self-contained distortions of truth. You don't dwell on the liquid.

The snow in her hair remains.

"See you soon," purrs the creature.

Her galoshes squeal like living things as she wanders out the door.

The Fuller by J.M. Elliott

Aristeas died the day the caravan came to town.

The ships came in early, and Aristeas could see their sails from his fields. He hurried to town and down the path to the harbor, where he met his old friend Linus. There, they perused the goods, chatting with the merchants and sailors. The ships sailed regularly from Miletus, and they would dock at the island of Proconnessus to rest and gather a few supplies before heading to the northern colonies through the Thracian Bosporus. Linus always came hoping there would be markets for cloth where they traveled. But Aristeas went for the stories, enraptured by the picture they painted of the strange world beyond these shores.

Unloading their cargoes, a train of asses and carts would ascend the path from the harbor to the town, and merchants would enter the square to hawk their wares. The island's quarries were filled with gleaming marble prized for statues, tombstones, and temples, and no small quantity of this made its way back down the path to awaiting ships. But Linus noticed none of this. He eagerly awaited the unloading of earths from abroad—rare, colorful, magical earths for preparing and dyeing his cloth.

Some cloth made the trek back down the path to be loaded into the ships—to where he never knew. But it gave Linus a twinge of pride to think that his handiwork left these shores to grace the homes and hides of strangers, who would brag to their friends that their fabric was imported from an obscure island in the little Sea of Proconnessus. That tickled him mightily, and he would smile to himself as the ships sailed away.

Aristeas seldom bought anything, but he never failed to join his friend at the harbor while there were reports from abroad to be had. It was an island, and for all their lives, it had been their only world. They might have happily believed it was the whole of the world had it not been for those ships.

By noon, they had returned to Linus's shop, where it was already too hot to work. Summer had just arrived, and Linus rested in the heat of the day while the fabric dried on the lines and resumed work in the coolness of the evening. He'd throw open the door and window to let in the fresh sea air, then sit in the shade with a simple meal of bread and wine.

Because of the noxious fumes that emanated from it, the fuller's shop sat at the end of the lane, overlooking the sea. Bakers, butchers, and even fishmongers would never abide the stench. It was in part because of this peaceful location that Aristeas had always preferred the fuller's shop when he came to town. A smallholder from inland with a few arable acres and some pastured sheep, he had struck a friendship with Linus when, as a boy, he'd bring the household's raw woolen cloth for fulling. The shop had belonged to Linus's father then, and its vibrant dyes, pungent herbs, pulverized stones, and simmering cauldrons captivated young Aristeas. It was more like a sorcerer's lair than a common workshop. Magic happened inside its four walls. He witnessed cloth transmuted from scruffy, dull rags to smooth, rich textiles—purified of color or imbued with foreign hues. He saw how, with enough blows, the roughness could be beaten from a crudely made weave. How fulling brought to completion the act of creation begun in his pastures and on his loom with the plush garment he held in his hands.

Aristeas was born to a noble family of Proconnessus, among the first Greek settlers to colonize the island, which perhaps meant little in the grand scheme of things, but his father, Caystrobius, had been well-liked. Upon his death, he entrusted the farm and household to his son, who tried to honor his father. But Aristeas was no farmer. His uncle's widow had no other kin, and his sister was not yet married because Aristeas could not settle upon a suitable match. The responsibility for looking after the womenfolk and servants weighed heavily on him. Aristeas would confess as much to Linus when they sat in the shop on market days, drank wine, and pissed together in the vats used to process the cloth.

"The old widow's a lowing cow," Linus told him, "and your sister should marry already. It's proper that you look after them, but what about yourself? When's the last time you ate? *Bathed?*" He'd never find a suitable wife that way. Aristeas looked thin and didn't smell so good, and that was saying something in a fuller's shop. *The women are running him ragged when he should be ruling his roost*, Linus thought. *But who am I to talk?* Linus lived alone in the back of his foul shop, drinking too much wine and pissing in a dye vat. *As if this is the life of a family man. . . .*

Although Linus made an honest living, no respectable woman wanted to live behind a shop that smelled of flatulence with a man who reeked of urine—whose hands were rough and stained with dye. Though, truth be told, he'd settle for a disrespectable woman just so he wasn't always alone.

Aristeas happily lived a reclusive life. Quiet and pious, he kept his father's altar and managed his household justly. So, the islanders left him be. He tried his best to keep his thoughts on the farm for his sister's sake so she could have a dowry and find a suitable husband. But, he was plagued by the future.

"If my sister marries, who'll spin our wool? My uncle's widow is nearly blind, and her hands become more like claws with each winter."

"You could marry."

"I've no need of a wife," Aristeas insisted.

"I can think of a few needs a wife might fill," Linus said, laughing to himself.

"Just more mouths to feed. I am beset by hungry mouths."

Aristeas had dreaded becoming the head of a household. He confessed to Linus that he wept like a child the first time he slaughtered a lamb for their pot.

"They say the Hyperboreans live by the fruits of the earth," Aristeas had said wistfully, "never eating the flesh of animals. They live in perfect peace, favored by Apollo. I'd give anything to meet them."

"So, what's stoppin' you?" Linus goaded, knowing his friend would never set foot aboard a ship.

On these trips to town, Aristeas would always bring a small gift of something special, whether some relic or oddity he plowed up in his field, found lying in the road, or washed up on the beach: an odd bone, a delicate flower, an exotic feather, a strangely shaped twig, a knot of wood resembling a face. Today, he brought a pale blue bird's egg he found in an empty nest in the oak by his byre door. He said it reminded him of the sky. Linus would wait until his friend had gone up the lane before casting these gifts out with the rest of the shop's trash. A twinge of regret, perhaps guilt, always assailed him, but what was he supposed to do with all this detritus in his busy shop?

Fortunately, Aristeas also brought wine, which they drank as they whiled away the hot part of the afternoon, the sea breeze cooling the shady shop. Aristeas was usually a quiet man, but drink loosened his tongue, and soon he would vividly describe helping a ewe birth a lamb, light glistening in a water trough, the shape of a cloud, the colors of sunrise. Often, he would lapse into verse, a habit Linus would have found irritating in any other man but that Aristeas seemed not even to realize he was doing. And throughout, his friend's gaze was forever fixed on something outside the shop window. When Linus spoke, he was often convinced Aristeas had heard not a word as he gazed unblinkingly out to sea.

"The merchants say they are continuing north." Aristeas's voice was hushed but hurried as if he passed an illicit secret. "From the colonies, they'll establish trading routes far inland."

"Why'd you not learn to sail?" Linus asked him. "You might've seen the world—made your fortune. At least got out of this stinkin' hole," he said with a chuckle.

But Aristeas didn't laugh. Instead, he mumbled to himself:

> A marvel exceeding great is this
> withal to my soul—
> Men dwell on the water afar from
> the land, where deep seas roll.
> Wretches are they, for they reap
> but a harvest of travail and pain,
> Their eyes on the stars ever
> dwell, while their hearts abide in

the main.
Often, I ween, to the Gods are
their hands upraised on high,
And with hearts in misery heav-
enward-lifted in prayer do they
cry...

"What're you even talkin' about?"

"Oh, nothing. It's just that I can imagine few things more miserable than the life of a sailor. The sea frightens me. And I can't swim."

"Ach, it scares every man. And no sailor can swim! What'd be the use?"

"Exactly. I have no interest in being where my wits and skills are of no use to me."

"Then, like I said, what's keepin' you here?"

At this, Aristeas did chuckle, but it was a sad, defeated laugh. Linus suddenly felt wrong to have made his friend miserable. And perhaps he was foolish to prod him this way. The last thing in the world Linus wanted was for his only friend to leave the island. True, Aristeas had been educated, but there was something else about the way he spoke sometimes that Linus sensed was different.

"I only mean that you have a certain... gift. It seems wasted on us."

"That's for the gods to decide. I'm not the master of my gift, such as it may be." Then, as he turned on his stool to look through the window, his gloom dissipated, and a smile overtook his face. "Look, a rainbow. Out over the water. Do you suppose it is a sign?"

Linus just grinned and sipped his wine. He'd seen countless rainbows and felt no need to gawk at them. And he didn't believe in portents.

"What do you think it heralds?"

"It heralds nothin'. It's just a trick o' the light. Not everythin' is—"

Linus continued talking, but Aristeas seemed not to hear. Again, he stared out the window at the sea, his unblinking eyes fixed far in the distance. Then his mouth began to move as if he were speaking, but no words came. When Linus rose to put a hand on his friend's shoulder and rouse him from his daydream, Aristeas sprang up, curled his fists near his heart, and fell backward, striking the hard ground before Linus could catch him.

Linus knelt by his side to see if he was hurt, but his friend would not awaken. The breath had left his body, and Aristeas was dead. There, on the floor of the fuller's shop, his friend's life had left him.

Terror filled Linus's heart.

"Damn you, Aristeas!" Linus cried in his distress. "I'm ruined! Oh, my friend, look what you've done—and here in my own shop! What am I to do?"

He began to weep irrepressibly into his hands, both for his friend's passing and for himself, convinced that his shop would be cursed and his reputation ruined by the aspersions of town gossipmongers. But he must do something. His mind immediately conjured all manner of wild, twisted thoughts. What if this horrible thing had simply never happened—if no one ever found out? Could he hide the body of his friend or throw it into the sea? Then he cursed himself for even thinking such a monstrous thing. He must go and seek out the kin of Aristeas.

He turned to close the wide window where his friend had sat. The rainbow had gone. After latching the shutters, he gathered up a length of his finest white cloth and, amid sobs, solemnly laid it over the still form of his friend's lifeless body. In the dark tranquility of the shop, his tears flowed. He knelt beside the shrouded corpse, his face buried in his hands, and asked the Averter of Evil: *Why? Why Aristeas, your faithful servant?* Long he sat until he had no more tears left to shed, and the summer sun had moved a hand's width across the sky without his noticing. He stood to leave the remains of his friend there on the slates and go to seek help. Then he looked once more around the room, wiped the stains from his cheeks, and slipped out the door, locking it carefully behind him.

The news did not pass well among Aristeas's kin. Linus's hope that the womenfolk would share his desire for solemnity and discretion quickly turned to regret. They both created such an uproar of wailing and spectacle that soon all the neighbors, the town, and likely the whole island were informed of Aristeas's sudden death. Linus escorted the women to his shop as they howled and tore their clothes and hair, gathering a parade of shrieking spectators in their wake. He walked with his head bowed, more to mask resentment than to wallow in grief. He finally understood something of the trials poor Aristeas had suffered at home.

On the road, a Cyzicenian trader from Artaca who frequented the island on business asked about the commotion. There was no point in trying to contain the story now, as the world would soon learn of it.

"But I just saw Aristeas," he said in confusion. "Yes, he was on the road to the harbor on his way to Cyzicus. Saw him with my own eyes."

"This morning?"

"No, just now."

"Sorry, but you're mistaken, sir," Linus said, equally confused. "My dear friend Aristeas lies dead on my shop floor. Besides, he was terrified of the sea; he wouldn't set foot on a ship for all the gold in Persia."

The man shrugged and shook his head. "Suit yourself. I know what I saw." Then he went about his business as if the whole town had gone mad. Indeed, perhaps it had.

Arriving at the shop door, Linus paused, not looking back at the women or the crowd that followed to the end of the lane. He rested his forehead against the weathered planks and drew a deep breath, seeing in his mind the shrouded body on the floor. How would this shop ever be the same? That image would always be with him. He would never walk across the slates or sleep soundly in the adjoining bedchamber without recalling the corpse that lay there now. But he couldn't delay any longer. He unlocked the door and swung it into the dim, shuttered room.

The chamber stood empty. The cloth lay stretched neatly on the floor, but there was no one inside.

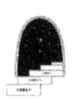

⸻

Aristeas was not seen again. Some called it a miracle. Some, like Aristeas's kin, claimed foul play. Others supposed it was a prank cooked up by the two friends. Linus didn't know what to believe, but the mystery of his friend's disappearance haunted him every day. His mind at times went to horrid, dark places, and he tormented himself because he felt that, somehow, he'd failed his friend, and now his spirit must be uneasy, wherever it may be. The sister of Aristeas did finally marry, but neither she nor her husband would look at Linus, much less speak to him, if they happened to meet.

But work had to continue, and Linus breathed his work like air. Orders had to be completed. New woven material would arrive for fulling, as well as soiled garments and fabric needing cleaning. Some days, his feet were tender and raw from hours spent treading cloth in the wash basins filled with solvents, stomping on dirty woolens as one stomps on vineyard grapes. On other days, his shoulders ached from pounding flat the fresh-woven cloth to tame the coarse fibers. His hands hurt from brushing out the dry wool with stiff bristles. At times, his eyes and nose stung from laying cloth to take the sulfur vapors and enhance its colors. His best days were those when the fabric could be hung to dry in the sea breeze, and he could rest his weary joints for a few hours.

As he worked, he often talked to Aristeas. Not because he lost his wits but because it comforted him to imagine the man's spirit alongside him. He could not conceive where his friend had gone, so he pretended that Aristeas had simply evaporated into the shop's walls or the air around him and that he could still hear when Linus spoke. Sometimes, he imagined he could hear Aristeas answer, though this he knew was fancy. Linus dreamt of his friend often, which he supposed to be the wandering of his soul in sleep, though the shade of Aristeas never revealed where he had gone or how. Aristeas was only a shadow moving through distant landscapes too far away for Linus to reach. When he would call, no sound would come, and Aristeas never turned to answer. Then Linus would awaken, more desolate than before, and face another day, another week, alone in his shop.

His young apprentice would come in the mornings to help him get underway, preparing the basins, setting the dyes, and rinsing and hanging the cloth. But once the work of fetching water and washing was done, the apprentice was allowed to return home and help his crippled father with chores around their farm. He was a good lad, longhaired and beardless, small but wiry. A little too loquacious but eager and unafraid to dirty his hands. He would do well in the trade. Linus needed the help but breathed a sigh of relief when the boy left for the day, and he had the shop to himself again.

The sun settled low over the sea, and his day's work was almost done. A length of fabric on the line awaited pressing. To first moisten it, he spurted water from his mouth so it formed a fine mist; in the light streaming through the window, a rainbow formed as it had a hundred times before. But today, it was so lovely in the gloom of the shop that the beauty of it pierced his heart. He gasped and choked on the water, spilling it from his mouth and down his tunic. He turned away from the window to gather himself and tried to stifle his sobs, though no one was around. As the light streamed through its opening, a strange shadow cast itself upon the wall. When he looked, a raven had settled upon the sill.

His first instinct was that it was an ill omen, and he threw a stone but fumbled and missed. The bird didn't budge. It just looked at him with its unblinking eyes. Something about the creature's persistence aroused his sympathy. He tossed it a leftover crust of his bread, which it seized in its beak and sat on the windowsill eating. Then, the raven gave a knocking call and departed.

When the time came to replenish his stores, Linus took his young apprentice to meet the ships and teach him about buying the materials for fulling. He bargained over Sardinian earth used to wash and whiten fabrics and the Umbrian earth employed for giving luster, fumigating sulfur used to deepen and subdue the colors, and scouring gypsum used to soften and brighten.

By now, the merchants had heard the miraculous tales of the fuller's shop and clamored to ask Linus if the rumors were true. Did he know the vanished man? Could they see the place where it happened? Indeed, the merchant who furnished the earths for fulling mentioned to Linus that he had a daughter he wished to betroth and that she was amenable to the idea of marriage. At last, the heavy stone began to lift from Linus's heart for the first time in nearly a year.

On the first day of summer, the raven returned. It came bearing a barbed arrowhead of bronze in its beak, which it dropped on the table before Linus's plate. Though its first visit was odd, he had since forgotten about the raven with the preparations for his marriage. But he was surprised at his happiness upon seeing the bird again. He fed it another crust of bread from his plate, and it hopped about the table, dipping its beak into his cup of wine. In light spirits, Linus laughed cheerfully at this, declining to shoo the bird away. Then, as suddenly as it came, the raven departed through the window.

Linus married his betrothed and, with her generous dowry and the income granted by his modest fame, moved with her to a small cottage just outside of town. The following year, the family Linus had always dreamt of came to be with the birth of a son.

Each summer, the raven returned, surprising Linus at his shop with odd and trifling gifts. A leather thong, a river pebble, a gold earring, a shard of pottery, a horsehair string. Linus could make no sense of these objects, but they were so inexplicable that he had not the heart to throw them away. He lined the treasures neatly on the shelf in the shop's storeroom above what was once his bed.

Though he watched and waited, this summer, the raven never came. Linus expected the bird's visits as one might await a holiday, and with half the summer already gone, its absence grieved him sorely. After seeing to it that his cloth was loaded onto a ship, Linus dragged himself back to his shop as the sun was setting. Inside, a shadow flitted upon the wall, and his heart fluttered, half-fancying the raven had finally come. But what he instead found made his heart stop altogether—a ghost. He fell back at the sight and struck the doorframe, landing on his backside at the foot of the door.

Aristeas sat on his stool by the window, sipping a cup of wine.

"I hope you don't mind," the apparition said. "I poured us a cup for old time's sake."

Linus was speechless, unable to stand.

Aristeas rose from the stool and offered a hand, which Linus refused.

"You're—you're dead."

"Am I?" Aristeas laughed. He seized his friend by the arms and pulled him to his feet.

"Where've you been these last six years?" Linus demanded, his trembling voice mixed with wonder and ire.

"Some of the places don't even have names."

"Not even a word—you just vanished!"

"I don't remember. I was here, looking out this window. Then, I was aboard a ship. No one was more surprised than I! But look, I brought you a gift," he said, reaching into the pouch at his waist, carefully cupping something in his hands—a fist-sized egg made of stone. A piece of shell had broken away, revealing the extraordinary creature within.

Linus recoiled, refusing to accept it.

"An unhatched griffin," Aristeas said, beaming. "A party of Arimaspi found a nest in the desert while hunting for gold."

Linus just shook his head.

"I carried it such a long way, though."

"You run off for years on some damned odyssey—never mind about your family and friends—and this is meant to make it all right?" Linus shook his head in dismay—in disbelief.

"Oh, but if you only knew the things I've seen!"

"We went mad with grief. We couldn't even make a proper funeral."

Aristeas bowed his head like a scolded dog. "For that, I beg your forgiveness. But, it hasn't all been sorrow? You have a wife and son, as you always dreamt. And when he is big enough, I thought you might show him this griffin's egg and all my other gifts so he'll know how wondrous the world is and have his own dreams."

At this, Linus's eyes began to sting and fill with tears, and he covered his face in shame.

"What's the matter?"

Linus confessed that he discarded all the kind gifts Aristeas had brought him over the years.

"No," said Aristeas, "they sit on the shelf above your old bed."

Linus once again stared at him dumbfounded.

"A lash from a Scythian chief's whip, broken as he hastened our way across the steppe and through battle. A river pebble from the shining waters of the Tanais, dividing Europe and Asia. A golden earring from a living Amazon, lovely and fierce. A shard from a woman's funeral urn shattered by rival lovers, her ashes scattered to the winds—though my grief and shame remain. A cithara string which played for an Issedoni chief's funeral, cut lest it ever play for another. They, too, are sheep-herders who build altars to honor their fathers. Only, first, they eat the man in a stew and gild his skull before doing it reverence."

Linus grimaced in horror. "You lived among such men?"

"For two summers."

"And the Hyperboreans?"

"There is a mountain range, insurmountable but for a single, deadly pass. An unceasing rain of feathers veils the landscape from sight. From a cave above this pass, Boreas himself blows, and men are often swept away by his fury. Those who succeed in gaining passage then face the hideous, swan-shaped Graeae and the Arimaspi, a race of shaggy, one-eyed men who, by night, raid the griffins' gold. Beyond these dwell the Hyperboreans."

"No land's worth such risks."

"Perhaps we'll never know. The Scythian troops guarding our caravan went through the gates of Boreas to scout the way but never returned. It was then I knew my journey had ended—for now. But I hoped to relate all that I'd seen—to tell the stories these tokens could not. I dreamt one day we would meet again, my friend." Tears welled in Aristeas's eyes. "It's so good to be home."

"A long time's passed; much has changed," Linus said wearily, overwhelmed by all he had heard, unsure if his senses could be trusted.

"Have we changed so much?"

"I did when you died. I will if you live. I no longer know what to believe. Maybe I'm a maniac collectin' rubbish by the roadside, feedin' crumbs to birds, talkin' to myself in this grimy little shop. You're probably not real," Linus mused and turned away to take a dry cloth from the line and fold it, content for a moment that madness was most sensible—that he had imagined all of it.

"You are my oldest friend, Linus. Tell me, what can I do to make you believe me?"

Linus thought as he folded another bleached cloth and set it in a basket at his feet. "You could compose one of your poems. Stories like this sound less mad when set to music."

"You hate my poems."

"You know, I don't think I ever heard one. Not really. But they say to the gods poetry is next to prayer. I'm no pious man like you. But gods help me, I need somethin' right about now."

The verse quoted above may be one of the few remaining fragments of Arimaspeia, an epic poem by Aristeas of Proconnessus, quoted by Longinus in On the Sublime, translated by W. Rhys Roberts, Cambridge University Press, 1899.

CUBED BY JOE GOLD

Ruby solved the Rubik's Cube in five seconds flat. She tossed it into the basket with its ninety-nine brothers and pressed the pause button on her stopwatch: eight minutes and thirty-three seconds.

She reclined on the sofa and sighed. "Not good enough."

She'd been solving puzzles all night in preparation for the World Puzzle Championship the following day. Logic toys, playing cards, and board games were scattered about her room. No matter how much she practised, she still felt inadequate compared to Ulrich Veight, the German ten-time World Puzzle Champion. His skill made her feel a mix of determination, anger, fear, envy, joy, and implacable curiosity every time she watched him play.

Ruby looked at a lonely star through the open window. What she really needed was a complex puzzle to get her in the zone that Ulrich Veight seemed to live in. A chill wind howled into the room. Ruby shivered, got up from the sofa, and closed the window. Budapest wasn't likely to deliver anything like that at three in the morning; she was better off just getting some sleep and hoping for the best.

She lay down on her bed, snuggled under the covers, and counted sheep.

When Ruby woke, she was inside a large, box-shaped room with colourful, square-pattern walls. Something small floated up to her. It was a cube that spoke in a Hungarian accent.

"Hello, young lady."

Ruby didn't know what to say at first. Once the awkward silence became too much to bear, it all came flooding out: "Who are you? What is this place? What's going on? Am I dead?"

The cube laughed. "A curious one, aren't you? But then, I wouldn't expect anything less of a puzzler. I am Rubix; this is my Cube, and I want you to solve it for me. You're not dead, but you will be if you don't solve my Cube within six lives. If you do, you may return safely to your own world."

Ruby's eyes widened. "Why are you doing this to me?"

Rubix laughed again. "Silly girl. Now, enough questions. You have three puzzles to solve. The first is how to get to the other end of the abyss."

Ruby looked around at the empty room. "What abyss?"

The floor parted so that there was a ten-meter-wide abyss of total darkness in the middle of it. Three bronze cubes the size of sofas floated up from the darkness and hovered in the air parallel to the floor.

"Oh."

Ruby saw that her hands were now snow white. She pulled her sleeves back; her forearms, too, were chalk-white. She must have been completely white from head to toe. Not only that, she felt oddly unemotional, focused, and determined to solve the Cube's challenge despite everything. Was this change in mood a part of the puzzle, too? She shrugged. *Better this than freaking out*, she thought. Ruby figured she was meant to jump on the bronze cubes to get across.

She took a run-up and jumped on the first bronze cube. She landed successfully, steadied herself, and tensed her legs for the next jump. Then, the cube began to descend. She tried to jump onto the next cube but was too low to reach it and collided face-first with it instead.

Ruby fell into the abyss.

Ruby woke up where she had been sitting before. Her skin was now blue. Fear welled up inside her, and she started to cry. "What's going on? Did I fail?"

Rubix floated up from the abyss. "Yes. You've used up one of your six lives."

"Oh no," Ruby wailed. She wasn't sure why it was happening, but the change in skin color once again altered her emotionally. "I don't want to do this anymore. I want to go home!"

Rubix laughed. "You can't go back yet, young lady. If you quit, I'll just kill you here and now."

Ruby wiped her tears on her sleeve and stood. Clearly, Rubix was a psychopath. She looked at the bronze cubes and gulped. The problem last time was that the moment she had touched the first bronze cube, it had started to descend into the abyss under her weight. If she quickly hopped from cube to cube like a character in a platformer video game, she could get to the other side. It was worth a try. Plus, if she waited any longer, she'd have a nervous breakdown that would get her killed.

Ruby took a deep breath and ran. She hopped onto the first cube, hopped onto the second cube, hopped onto the third cube, slipped—and grabbed the edge of the other side before she fell into the abyss. Panting, she pulled herself up and crawled over to the far wall.

"Well done," said Rubix. "You have solved the first puzzle. Now for the second. Find a way to destroy the Mother Cube."

The abyss closed up. A big silver cube phased out of the ceiling. It started to spin. It shot out dozens of little silver cubes, which floated towards Ruby. She screamed and ran away. The longer she ran, however, the more baby cubes the Mother Cube produced.

Soon, she was cornered with hundreds of baby cubes closing in on her. A baby cube touched her hand, and a cube-sized chunk disappeared. Ruby shrieked as the rest of the baby cubes closed in on her.

They ate her arms. They ate her legs. They ate her eyes. They ate her screaming mouth.

Ruby woke up. She was furious. Her skin was red.

Rubix floated up to her. "Four lives left."

She punched the little thing with everything she had and sent him crashing into a wall. "SCREW YOU."

The Mother Cube phased out of the ceiling. This time, Ruby ran in and fly-kicked it before it had time to give birth. It crashed against the far wall and cracked slightly.

Ruby snarled. "I'VE GOT YOU NOW!"

The Mother Cube began spinning out its baby cubes. They floated towards Ruby. She ran straight through them. Though she lost chunks of her right shoulder, stomach, and left hip in the process, she managed to reach the Mother Cube. Ruby hammered her fists into the big silver cube over and over and over. The spinning stopped, and the cracks spread.

As the baby cubes closed in on her, she lost chunks of her left forearm, upper right leg, and even her left eye so that she was half-blinded. She powered on, driven by pure rage. Soon, the cracks were everywhere. A group of baby cubes ate her left foot and made her fall to the floor. The Mother Cube floated away.

"OH NO, YOU DON'T!"

Ruby kicked out her right foot and caught the Mother Cube on its corner. The Mother Cube and its babies shattered to pieces.

Rubix hovered up to Ruby. "Well done. You've solved the second puzzle. Now for the third and final puzzle. You must find a way to defeat... me."

Rubix morphed into a tall, dark, handsome man wearing a gold suit. It was Ulrich Veight.

"EFF OFF!"

The floor parted between them, creating an abyss in the middle again. Once more, the three bronze cubes floated up. Rubix smirked and produced a silver baby cube from his pocket.

"Watch your brain!" He hurled it at Ruby.

"WAIT, WAIT. I CAN'T EVEN STAND!"

The baby cube ate her brain.

Ruby woke up. She was green. She stood and pointed at Rubix, envious. "Why do you get to start with the baby cube, huh? How's that fair? I should start with it."

"Three lives left." Rubix drew his arm back. "Watch your heart."

He threw the baby cube at her. Ruby held out her hands to block it—and caught it! Looking at her undamaged hands in amazement, she noticed her nails were silver like the baby cube. Maybe it couldn't eat her hands in this puzzle? She looked at Rubix. She was jealous of the guy's throwing skills; he'd managed to fastball it at her twice, giving her no time to dodge. She couldn't replicate his talent... but she could fake it.

"Watch your brain!" She feinted, pretending to throw it at his head, grinned as he held his hands up to block, and then threw it at his heart.

Rubix snapped his hands down and caught it. He grinned back. "Nice try. Watch your right knee."

He hurled it at her. Ruby leaped to her left. The baby cube missed her leg, but she banged her head on the side wall and tumbled into the abyss.

When Ruby woke up, she was yellow, mellow, and oddly happy. She sighed and thought, *I don't know what mood I'll have on my final life, but since this one is so serene, it'll probably be my best and last chance of beating Rubix.*

She scanned the room, noticed the floating bronze cubes, and smiled.

"Two lives," said Rubix.

Ruby stood up. "Ready when you are."

"Watch your—"

Ruby took a run up and hopped onto the first, second, and third bronze cubes. Startled, Rubix hurled the baby cube at her head. Ruby jumped, and the baby cube went through her chest instead. She caught Rubix by the shirt. He looked stunned.

"You're coming with me," said Ruby.

She pulled him down into the abyss with her, laughing all the way.

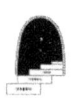

Ruby woke up. Orange. Curious. Relieved.

Rubix rose out of the abyss, once more a Rubix's Cube. "Well done, young lady. You have solved the third and final puzzle and the Cube itself, albeit in a rather unorthodox manner." The abyss closed up, so the floor was whole again. A white door materialised on the wall. "You may return safely to your own world now."

Ruby exhaled. "That's good… but I'm curious about something, Rubix. What was the meaning behind all this?"

Rubix spun in the air. "Come, come. A puzzle with an obvious answer is not worth solving."

Ruby got up. "I suppose."

She walked over to the white door and opened it—white light.

Ruby was back in her bed in Budapest. The sun was shining in through the window. She rubbed her eyes. What a weird dream... *At least now I have the right mindset to defeat Ulrich Veight*, she thought. She smiled as she got out of bed, ready to face her next challenge.

Rubix watched Ruby from the pinnacle of the church as she walked down the river.

"That's my girl."

The Oath by C.R. Langille

To my fellow Seton Hill Alumni. "Hazard Yet Forward."

Tarl, promise me one thing. When I die, I shall stay dead.

Tarl Tel-ath kneeled next to the stone altar where Greta Tel-ath's body lay. She looked serene in death, bathed against a sea of her golden hair. Greta didn't have to stay dead. However, her request echoed in his mind as he stared at his wife's still form. Tarl reached out and grabbed her lifeless hand. It was the same dull temperature as the stone she rested upon.

Why had she asked such a thing of him? Deep down, he knew why but didn't want to admit it. Ever since Tarl's *first* death, Greta had acted differently. She didn't show him the same love and care as when he drew natural breath. But why wouldn't she want to spend eternity with him? Had he done something to drive her away?

Her incessant ramblings about the afterlife only made his head hurt. Why wait for something that may or may not happen when they could be together immediately? What was more absurd was that he agreed to the promise—signed the contract verbally and sealed it with the power of his word. When he sought help from the other 'mancers in the city, they turned their backs on him. *Too dangerous to break the oath*, they cited.

Tarl let go of his wife's hand and slammed his fist into the stone altar. If he were still a normal living being, it would have surely broken his fingers; yet, the power of undeath gave him unnatural strength. Cerulean fire from the Void blossomed from his strike and washed through the room. It left his wife's body unharmed due to the preservation enchantments weaved by the 'mancers. However, a nearby wooden table burst into flames.

Light footfalls echoed through the stone corridor. Tarl rose from his knees but didn't turn towards the visitor. The scent of lilac drifted into the room.

"Grand 'mancer Houdwin," Tarl said.

"Tarl Tel-ath. You wished to see me?"

Tarl faced the short woman. No one in the city knew how old she was, but it was rumored her first death was over five centuries ago. It would be hard to tell unless one knew what to look for. Her hair was vibrant black, darker than the Void itself, and she had striking moon-blue eyes. Yet, Tarl could pick out signs of rot on anyone. Just behind the ears, her alabaster skin turned a mottled gray. Houdwin tried to cover it with mummer's paint, but Tarl saw through her tricks.

Houdwin glanced at the burning table, a slight frown on her face. She snapped her fingers, and the flames died, leaving the charred remains smoldering on the floor.

"Grand 'mancer Houdwin, I beg you, please bring back my—"

Houdwin raised a hand to silence him.

"The answer is no. To break the oath would incur the wrath of the Dark Walker."

Tarl growled and hit the table again. "The Dark Walker! Nothing but a boogeyman to keep young necromancers from delving into arcane secrets."

"The Dark Walker is very real, Tarl. Just because you don't believe in him doesn't make him any less so."

Tarl sighed and turned back to his wife's body.

"Forgive me. There must be a way."

Houdwin appeared at the opposite side of the table, moving quieter than a shadow in the twilight gloom. The Grand 'mancer ran a hand through Greta's blonde hair.

"I am sorry, Tarl, but we cannot break the oath."

Tarl fought to keep his emotions in check, but underneath the façade, his blood burned hot with fire. Eventually, his external mask broke, his upper lip curling into a sneer, and the Grand 'mancer's eyebrow raised in response.

"Then leave me to my mourning."

Houdwin stared at him for what felt like an eternity. Her harsh gaze bore holes through his lies like worms through a corpse—she knew his plans.

"Do not seek to betray our wishes. I would hate to force you to kill your wife as punishment."

She spun on her heel and stormed out of the room before Tarl could process what she had said. As it dawned on him, a rage ignited deep in his soulless body.

The heavy clack of boots against the marble floor replaced the soft echo of her footsteps. Two guards entered the room, dressed in bone-white armor shaped to resemble a ribcage. They both carried swords imbued with dark necromantic fire. The blue flames ran the length of the blade, occasionally popping and crackling in the air. The Grand 'mancer's lackeys, no doubt, sent to ensure he didn't try anything forbidden.

Tarl wasn't intimidated by the brutes. They would be a mere inconvenience at best. If she thought these two could stand between Greta and him, then she underestimated his abilities.

The two guards slowly flanked him. They weren't here to ensure he didn't break the oath. They were here to kill him. Grand 'mancer Houdwin had played her hand.

Tarl forced a smile. "Have it your way then," he said.

The guards stepped away from the wall. The flame of their weapons flared with life. However, instead of heat, the blades put off a chill that nipped at Tarl's face.

Tarl took in a lungful of air, an unnecessary action since his rebirth but a critical component to necromantic powers. Air supplied life, and life was necessary before death could occur.

The guards rushed in from both sides. What followed occurred in less than a second. Tarl exhaled, focusing on the veil between worlds. He whispered the ancient words, and as the last bit of air left his dead body, he crossed into the Void. The room went dark except for the guard's weapons. Their blades burned with azure necromantic energy.

One of the guards raised his weapon and brought it down in a powerful slash meant to separate Tarl's head from his body. Tarl moved around the attack with a grace that would have put an elf to shame as time moved differently in the Void, especially for the dead.

The guard's heart glowed like a red beacon, pulsing bright with each beat. Tarl slipped his hand through the guard's breastplate as if it were nothing more than paper. He wrapped his fingers around the guard's beating heart, which was warm and numbed his skin. Then, with a growl, he ripped away the guard's life essence.

The man fell to his knees. The white glowing essence flowed through Tarl's arm and into his body. It was a fantastic feeling, one he hadn't felt in such a long time. The euphoria washed over Tarl, washing away any remorse he felt for killing one of his own.

Tarl could only imagine what the guards saw—a wisp of a shadow, incorporeal but all too real. Tarl had mastered Dark combat, as only the most disciplined could do, for it was too tempting to succumb to the other side and never return.

The second warrior tried to hit him from behind. The cold fire tickled his back for a mere second before Tarl whirled around and grabbed the man by the head. He lifted the guard into the air and sucked the life away through the man's eyes.

Two deaths in one day, and so close to each other, Tarl buzzed with power. His senses extended outside the building, and the life energy of every living person nearby called to him with a sultry song and promises of more power.

Yet, in that sea of euphoria and promise came whispers—pinpoints of cold that told him things, wicked things. These were the dead ones inhabiting the city—people like him. They would feel his feeding and know what he did. He had to move quickly.

Tarl forced air through his lungs once again and focused on the life it provided. The Void sang its sweet song and tried to tempt him to stay, but there was work to accomplish. He willed his body to turn from the shadow and back into the light. Little by little, the flicker of normal firelight dissipated the gray sheen. Just before he fully transitioned to the living world, something caught his eye—something shadowy. It stood in the corner, close to Greta's body. Before he could discern what it was, the Void slipped away and took the stranger with it.

Tarl made countless trips to the Void and encountered many strange beings during those visits; however, whatever stood near Greta was different.

Questions plagued him, but he didn't have time to ponder them. More guards would be coming soon, and he needed to leave. The recent consumption of the two guards left him feeling stronger than before, and he picked Greta up from the altar as if her body were nothing but a feather pillow.

Committed to the plan now, Tarl had no choice. It was either follow through and bring her back, or face punishment for his crimes. There was only ever one choice. He would go to the cave.

Tarl had found the cave years ago when his father took him into the mountains. His father wanted to find specific alchemical components. A group of rocklings lived in the cave's network of tunnels, and his father, a kinder, gentler soul than Tarl, left before there was a confrontation.

If things went in his favor, the rocklings would still call the cave home. He would need their essence to complete the ritual and bring his Greta back. Once she was with him again, she would understand. She would forgive him for breaking the oath.

Tarl snuck out of the city without further incident. Shadow was a second skin to him, and he wore it well. The cave sat hidden in an outcropping of rock, easy to miss unless one knew what to look for. Tarl, fortunately, knew what to look for. He gently laid Greta on the ground and brushed away a golden lock of hair from her face.

"Soon, my love. Soon."

He didn't want her body damaged and decided to leave it hidden outside. The rocklings wouldn't take kindly to an intruder, and he couldn't risk her getting hurt in the fray.

The cave was cool and shrouded in gloom, and while he wanted to relax, he knew all too well other creatures were just as comfortable in the shadows. He pulled a smidgen of power from his reserves and allowed his eyes to shift into the Void. At once, the features of the cave snapped into view.

Carved geometric shapes and designs decorated the stone walls of the cave—typical rockling art. The earthen people seemed to enjoy leaving the drawings wherever they dwelled, like common graffiti.

The clack of stone against stone echoed through the cavern, bringing a smile to Tarl's face. The rocklings were still here.

Further down, the cave split into a network of tunnels. Tarl remembered most of it from his childhood but took care to mark his path by dropping Void motes behind him, small glowing balls of azure, visible only to him with the extra bit of power he dropped into them. It would do no good to get lost underground for eternity as his body rotted to dust. With the enchantments in place, his mind would decay much quicker than his flesh. A 'mancer gone mad was a devastating and dangerous thing.

The grate of stone against stone grew louder the deeper he descended into the tunnels. Tarl tried to orient himself as to where the sound originated. The noise bounced off the walls and made it difficult to pinpoint.

He slowed down, taking care with his steps. The rocklings could track sound and vibration as if connected to the ground themselves. It wasn't impossible to sneak up on one, but it took a tremendous amount of skill. Tarl took in more air and let his hands and feet slip into the Void. The magic would help mask his movements and hopefully confuse the pitiful creatures.

The rock smoothed out the deeper he went, more signs of the rocklings' handiwork. His father used to say rock people never stayed idle and were always shaping the stone. From further down the tunnel came the echo of rock smashing into rock. The vibration shook his core and rattled his teeth.

It wasn't long before he found them; two rocklings bashed their fists into the cave wall. They were twice as large as Tarl. Their skin was the same texture as the stone, gray with quartz streaks that emphasized their facial features. The rocklings' eyes glowed vibrant emerald green and showered the tunnel in a strange light. When they worked on the wall, they planted their feet deep into the earth to steady themselves.

Tarl took a moment to fully submerge himself in the Void. One of the rocklings would be a challenge; two beasts would tear him limb from limb.

As the shadow caressed his body, he caught another glimpse of the dark figure that eluded him after his confrontation with the guards. It remained on the periphery of his vision. Even though he couldn't focus on the being, its presence dominated his mind—a shadow darker than the Void had crawled into his thoughts and taken root.

He didn't have time to ponder who or what the dark figure was, for the rocklings stopped their work, and the tunnel succumbed to deep silence. The two creatures looked in Tarl's direction, and he froze. He was thankful he no longer needed to breathe to sustain life, for he reckoned it would have immediately given him away.

However, despite his precautions, one of the mighty beings tore itself from the earthen floor and rumbled down the tunnel toward him while its companion scanned the darkness. Tarl's mind filled with questions as the rockling lumbered near him and stopped. It placed a stone-encrusted hand on the wall. Its eyes never blinked, its verdant gaze only intensifying with its glow as it peered into the shadows. A deep rumble issued from the creature's chest, and the vibrations set the smaller stones dancing on the ground. Green energy pulsed from the creature's hand and ran through the rocks like a mineral vein splitting in dozens of directions. The light halted at Tarl's feet.

The rumble stopped as the rockling's eyes popped open. The creature let out a deep and throaty growl. A moment later, it spat a string of words that sounded more like grinding stone before charging toward Tarl. The other answered its companion's cry and came to its aid.

Tarl formed a ball of Void-fire in his hand and hurled it down the tunnel towards the closest one. The fire exploded when it hit, blinding him. The rockling let out a throaty growl that rumbled through the tunnel.

While the fire blast had stolen his vision—perhaps igniting it in a darkened tunnel wasn't the best of ideas—Tarl was still fully immersed in shadow and could sense subtle shifts in pressure. Tarl jumped back just as the creature's fist slammed into the ground. Shards of rock flew in all directions. Some of the pieces pelted him but caused only minor irritation.

His vision returned, revealing smoke wafting off the rockling's body. The light of one of its eyes was gone. Its companion, on the other hand, was unscathed. The second rockling pushed past its companion and barreled straight toward Tarl.

Unlike human targets, the rocklings' stone skin made it impossible for Tarl to see their hearts. The grind of their heartbeats was the only indication they possessed such a muscle. He committed to the attack and struck fast. He expected to feel the slight resistance he always did when he attempted to siphon the life from a creature, but instead, his hand hit a wall.

The sigils and decorations on the rockling's skin flared to life in a brilliant jade glow when Tarl's hand swept across them. Pain lanced up his arm, and he was forced to drop from the Void and out of the shadow.

The moment he hit the ground, Tarl rolled away. The rockling smashed down and obliterated the spot Tarl had just occupied. He sprang to his feet and backed away to create some distance.

The creature pointed and spat out in its rough language. Another of its kind answered from behind Tarl. He spun and found a rockling, this one bigger than the other two. It cradled Greta's body in its arms.

"No!"

Tarl took in a lungful of air. He pulled the Void around his body and let the cold shadows seep into his bones. They wouldn't take her another step if he could help it.

The shadowy stranger stood behind him. Tarl couldn't see it, but its presence was colder than death and full of energy. The hairs on his neck danced with excitement.

Do you wish to rip her from the Void?

The stranger's words slithered into his mind, slick and corrupt, yet they took root. The question distracted him, almost costing him everything as the closest rockling rose to hit him. He rolled away just before its fist crushed the second life from his body.

He may not be able to siphon the energy from the rocklings, but that didn't leave him powerless. Tarl sped toward the next towering creature that stood between him and the one that had Greta, jumping over it easily with the Void powering his limbs.

The rockling uttered something and snatched at Tarl as he sailed over, but the creature was too slow. Tarl landed behind the rockling and turned. Before it could face him, Tarl scrambled up the rockling's back. It bucked to throw him to the ground, but Tarl held on.

I can show you how.

The voice caused a wave of nausea to roll through his body. The dark figure stood near the wall. It didn't slip away from his vision this time. The figure was tall, taller than the rocklings. It was skinnier than most men, with arms that reached the ground. Tarl couldn't make out its facial features, but he knew it watched him with interest.

Was it the Dark Walker? Could it be real?

The rockling crashed its back into the wall. Tarl barely managed to shift his weight and swing to the front of the creature before it pulverized him. Its massive eyes narrowed with rage. The rockling grabbed Tarl by his middle section and squeezed.

Tarl attempted to free himself by pushing down with his arms, but the creature's grip was iron. A moment later, a sickening crack thundered in his body as his ribs snapped. Tarl was grateful that he couldn't feel pain as sharply as he did in life. However, the creature was squeezing the air out of him. As Tarl's lungs emptied, his shadow power waned.

Tarl focused, trying to ignore the crushing grip. He grabbed at a mote of shadow from the Void and tore it away from the darkness to cover his hand in a lifeless cold. Tarl screamed and shoved his hand into the rockling's mouth.

It choked and dropped him to the ground. Tarl rolled away as the rockling scratched at its throat frantically, and the glow in its eyes burned hot. It wasn't long before its attempts to remove the shadow slowed. The brilliance of its eyes dimmed, and it fell to the ground.

A patch of black formed around its throat and snaked its way across the rockling's body, turning its skin from a slate gray to dark obsidian. Then, it shuddered and lay still, dead.

The other two yelled something to one another. The one-eyed rockling that Tarl had hit with the Void-fire came at him. It was injured and off-balance but still dangerous. The larger one stood back, Greta's body still in its arms.

With the dead rockling at his feet, Tarl now had options. He pulled at the shadow in the rockling's lifeless body like a marionette. It jerked and sat up, its limbs held at its sides at odd angles. Azure Void-fire replaced the green of the rockling's eyes. Tarl poured his will into his creation, crashing it into its comrade's body, shaking the very ground.

It was no match for the reanimated rockling, and the beast smashed its former comrade's head against the stones until it was nothing but broken shards. Tarl turned his attention to the final one that held his dear wife.

"You will let her go," he demanded.

He wasn't sure if the rockling could understand him, but it replied in its guttural tongue.

Tarl let the Void-fire build in his hands once more. Time stopped, and the cavern's temperature dropped even further. The rockling was seemingly immobilized. Tarl cocked his head and waited for a moment. He'd never seen this before.

Shadow-frost covered the walls of the tunnel, coating the rock with a frozen layer of murky ice. The dark figure rose behind the rockling, towering over the earthen creature.

Tarl Tel-ath.

When it whispered his name, it was as if a spear drove through his chest. The Void-fire disappeared from his hands, and Tarl fell to his knees. The words carried a power unlike anything he'd ever felt.

"Who are you?" Tarl managed to ask. Each word scraped through his throat like talons.

I am the answer. I am the question. I am everything. I am nothing.

The figure touched the rockling. The creature's body trembled before crumbling into dust on the cave floor. Tarl could almost taste its essence, but the Walker kept it just beyond his reach. Greta remained suspended in the air.

I am the space between the cracks, the darkness in the shadow, and he who wanders the Void.

The Dark Walker. Had he come to exact vengeance upon him for trying to break the oath given to Greta? Was his second life over now?

No, Tarl Tel-ath. I have come to assist you in your quest. Just ask, and I shall grant you the knowledge necessary to accomplish your wishes. Just ask, and she can be with you again.

Words still cut as they passed through his lips, but he could speak.

"What is the price?"

Your body. Once you succumb to your final death, your vessel is mine.

Tarl already knew the answer.

"Agreed."

This will hurt.

Before Tarl could react, the Dark Walker thrust one of its fingers into Tarl's brain. Pain exploded in his head as the shadow crept into every crevice and cavern of his mind. His world was the Void. It showed him every pleasure and pain, ripping and rebuilding his knowledge. Then, everything went dark.

When he woke, he was on the cold ground. Tarl sat up and wiped his face clean with the sleeve of his robe. He moved slowly as the cavern seemed to spin.

The reanimated rockling stood as still as a statue, only the flicker of Void-fire indicating unlife. His wife's body still floated in mid-air in the tunnel.

The Dark Walker had seared the unholy knowledge into Tarl's mind. He knew how to rip her soul from the Void regardless of the oath. Tarl stood on wobbly legs. Once he touched her soft skin, she floated to the ground.

"Soon, my love."

He spoke the words given to him by the Dark Walker.

With each syllable, an explosion of pain echoed in his mind. Each word was more challenging to speak than the last, and as he spoke, the knowledge burned away from his memory. Yet, each word he spoke ripped the rockling's essence away, feeding his ritual. Not only did he take from the one in front of him, but others. Their life thrummed through the rocks, and he bore into the earth with his will, stripping the precious life energy away to fuel his own dark spell.

The shadows deepened around them as he uttered the damnable words. Creatures slithered in the dark, things he never knew existed nor wanted to know about. They waited to see if he'd slip up. Tarl knew they would devour both Greta and him if he did.

The darkness crept closer and closer as he neared the final words. The world itself held its breath in anticipation.

With one last bit of effort, Tarl spoke the last of the incantation. The words were foreign, but their meaning clear. *Come back from the darkness to dance under the moonlight once again.*

As soon as he finished, Greta sat up, screaming. Her banshee-like wail shot through the caverns. Tarl gathered Greta up in his arms and rocked her back and forth.

"It's okay, my love. It's okay. We're together now. We're together again."

Her scream faded, and she tried to push away from him. Tarl held her tight.

"My love. Calm down. It's me. It's Tarl."

But his words did little to soothe her. She broke away and scrambled back against the wall. Greta hid her face from him and sobbed. Her small frame shuddered as she curled up into a ball.

"My love, what's wrong?"

She said something, but it was too quiet for him to hear. He moved in closer and laid a hand on her shoulder. She jumped at the touch but didn't pull away.

"Greta?"

"You promised not to bring me back. You promised!"

"We were meant to be together, my love. Not even an oath could keep us apart. Look at what I was able to accomplish! No 'mancer has been able to pull someone back after an oath."

Greta put a hand over Tarl's. She continued to shiver and weep, keeping her face hidden behind her knees.

"There's a reason for that, love."

Greta clamped down on Tarl's hand and squeezed harder than a rockling. Tarl tried to pull away but was unable to match her strength. Her sobs turned into laughs and then deteriorated into giggles.

Greta sat up. Tears of blood streamed down her face and burrowed sanguine paths down her snow-like skin. Where her eyes should have been were tiny mouths full of rows of jagged teeth. She widened her jaws, which revealed massive fangs, and pulled Tarl close. Greta clamped down on his neck and sucked the necromantic life energy from his body. Tarl resisted, but his strength, shadow and physical, disappeared too quickly. His skin cracked and dissolved to dust as the magical network that kept him whole faded away.

The Dark Walker appeared behind Greta. It stooped down and wrapped its long arms around her body like a cloak. One of its long fingers touched Tarl's cheek. As Greta drained his essence, she replaced it with a different energy, that solely of the Void.

The Dark Walker's cacophonic laugh echoed through Tarl's mind as everything went dark.

Two Visions of the Mountain of the Saints by Christopher Deliso

AND THIS refers to dream visions from weeks before—around the 11th of May, '23—when I had not yet moved from No. 11. It can become dizzying, what with all these moves, counter-clockwise and so on.

Anyhow—these visions referenced two separate visits, occurring on two bookended nights, glimpses into a place presupposed; a place everyone here knows as the 'Mountain of the Saints.'

1.

The first vision brought confusion and disappointment, for an enormous, high-vaulted church soared up into the clouds, penetrating a crystalline blue sky. It stood where it should not have been—considering that its Latin style and opulence were distinct from the expected Byzantine—thus, it was not supposed to be there. I was quiet despite this aberration, not wishing to reprimand a simulation for possessing, or even placing, a foreign presence on a mountain where, after all, there was no more foreign presence than I.

Yet, if the church was not genuine from its exterior appearance, neither was it from within. (It is difficult to convey the concentration it took to follow this vision through its full dimensionality). Its interior was voluminous and high, and this excess pondered its visitors in all our secret shame and doubt. It attained the sort of height in which you would expect to see fine particles of dust descend, trapped in amber sunlight from a high window... only that on that simulation (or, perhaps, that day), there was no dust, just a rare color, one of fallen peacock-feather.

Outside again, things became more confusing; it could not have been the Mountain of the Saints as the ancient Byzantine law had ordained it, and as I always had known it, for that law allowed only men, the mountain being honored for the Mother of God alone among women. I was thus very surprised to see a little girl—an impossible thing in that particular place.

She wore a long dress and waded up to her ankle in a very shallow and oblong pool; she stood there as if exploring an unfound fountain, which stood near the church's entrance, and the sun radiated off of it in glimmering tranquility. A set of very low and fine marble stairs led down to this pool; my instinct relayed that this water source was the place of heaven's light, or spiritual communication with other times, with beings past or to be... an older monk sat on the stair, listening idly as the young girl chattered and seemed to skip over the water in a haze, yet not entirely lucid (almost—yes, a pastel one). She was telling, in a sing-song voice, her story to the monk in a language I could not understand.

I strained my ears to hear as if it would help; and somehow it did, for it was my vision, after all. The little girl said something about how the wading pool had restored her health from a terrible physical accident, or even a fatal one, in her earthly life. She had been sent here for some reason; either to heal or to relay her story, but whether she was meant to stay, I did not know. I saw a couple of other children around the church and a few other people one would not typically see on the Mountain of the Saints... at least not from the simulation of it I knew. I wondered whether my misunderstanding was one of time or modality but quickly abandoned my musing lest it dissolve the improbable vision.

2.

The second vision from the Mountain of the Saints was quite different and very dramatic. I found myself alone in a very high and narrow pass, seeking access to the Mountain and staring down, impossibly far down, at the aching sea. It terrified me, the potential of a fall, by its great distance and the steely hardness of the water-top. Still, my instinct relayed that I must jump from that high point and hurl myself into the sea. And it made no sense at all, in order to enter the Mountain of the Saints, which I imagined was actually very close by to the right.

I was stood up on a small rock ledge that ended immediately above the sea and stared down at the bleak, distant expanse of solid water, then across to where I had hoped the Mountain to be. But all I saw there was a towering wooden pole, as thick as a giant tree trunk, rising out of that unforgiving distant water down below.

I inexplicably chose to wedge myself between the wooden pole with my right hand and the rock ledge with my feet so that I was suspended in the air, a nowhere-place of sharp winds. My fear grew that I would fall into the sea; however, by that extension of myself into the new simulation space my mind had created, I had also somehow wedded myself to the decision to jump, or at least to free myself from the position of standing on dry ground.

The distance to the water was terrifying in its indifference, though I was not and have never been afraid to swim. It was just something about the collision that frightened me…

I cried out; I began to exclaim with great fervor the *Kyrie Eleison* prayer in Greek; all this I did in what can only be called real-time and at a frantic volume; I then became aware that I was doing all this of my own will; and then, as the prayer resounded from my throat, the distance itself disappeared, and a dry direct path to the Mountain of the Saints came into existence, between the rocky ledge and the wooden pole, which became a regular leafy tree. The way was cleared, and the sea itself had vanished from my view beneath me.

I turned quickly to inspect the ledge. There, I found a backpack and, in it, the official permit for entry to the Mountain, as I had known it to be in real life. I read it, not for the first time, but now in unexpected astonishment, that the instructions had changed; whereas, before it had simply given basic entry permission, now it stated in capital letters the name of a monastery, one without electric current, to which I had never been. It thus read:

STAVRONIKITA.

I grasped the paper and put on the backpack with great joy, and crossed the path into the Mountain of the Saints. Immediately there within, I showed the letter to a monk. There were several monks gathered around a small table, and they were cheerful and preparing for a ceremony. I was informed I must prepare to come to the seaside for my baptism—another great surprise...

I cannot speak of the veracity of visions, or even simulations, or the differences between expected and real places and events; all I can attest is that these visions happened exactly as described.

The Summer Light by M.S. Arthadian

From time to time, a tale makes its way to me. Most are drawn out, full of the challenges those *Chosen* face head-on. However, the tale that currently lays claim to my mind is one I simply cannot shake.

It begins in a world within the *Foundation Region* of the *CORE*, about a young prime woman who has never seen the light of day. She's never breathed air that wasn't filled with dust, burning her lungs with each inhale.

Although she has never seen it, the myth of the radiant sky beckons for her to escape upward, out of her prison, beyond the metallic grime and ash that make up her shackled existence within The Shafts.

All she sees... is darkness.
All she knows... is the life of a slave.

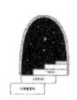

It wasn't until the mark of the Summer Light came that she witnessed a glimmer of hope. She and the rest of the slaves beneath the world's surface watched as their shackles loosened enough to see what lay beyond the veil. The curtains had finally been lifted so they could see the reality of their world as the thick, metal door opened.

For but a moment, awe enraptured the slaves. Brilliant colors engulfed their retinas as a mysterious figure opened their minds to the realization of an existence filled with blinding light. But as quickly as it came, so too did it fade.

The figure, known to the slaves as The Master, descended into The Shafts and brought with it another being, shackled and broken. Ever since she'd been born, there hadn't been a new slave. How old was she? She couldn't know. Having no light prevented any concept of time. Then, as if in a blink, the light vanished, abandoning them again in the pits of darkness.

Despite the brevity of the light's presence, a spark of hope remained within her. She listened intently to the stories passed around by all the slaves, about how the world's surface had seasons that came and went. How life was rich and abundant, flourishing across the surface as far as the eye could see. How a bright light shone for months, heating the world with its *source*. And when that blinding light emerged, it signified the day, and in its absence, an innumerable blanket of smaller versions flickered into existence to announce the night. This season of light was known as Summer. A new light had been kindled within her, burning ever brighter to illuminate a life not as a deprived slave but as one bathed in freedom.

It was then that she knew what she was fighting for.

She felt her way to the elder slave, who had witnessed the light before her birth. The Elder had guided them before; maybe he'd withheld information about the true nature of their existence.

"Elder, who is The Master?"

The Elder laid a hand upon her face, shook his head, and responded, "There is no light on them, just as there is no light on us."

"If there is no light on The Master, why are they not in The Shafts?" This caused The Elder to notice her, to truly *see* her. A faint, almost imperceptible light in the darkness was forming, a *source* that should not... could not be quelled.

In awe, The Elder knelt to her, "What do you wish to know?"

She smiled, another type of shimmer in her eyes, "I want to know the Summer Light. I want to live in the Summer Light!"

Together, they felt their way through the tunnels to the new slave to learn more. As they passed others toiling away with The Master's tools, some stopped to listen, curious about the change in the air, the shift in her breathing that told them something was different.

The new slave was found in a pit. She couldn't explain it, but she could see strange outlines forming on the surfaces of objects and people in the darkness. She studied his face, which seemed broken inside, a shattered soul.

"Please forgive me, newcomer. I've never before seen the light. Not until your arrival, that is. Can you tell me more about it?"

The new slave glanced in her direction, spotting the definitive twinkle in her eyes. He turned away from her.

"There is only darkness," he said, shoveling the grime out of the pit.

The new slave's flippant attitude sparked a passion in The Elder, "Darkness is surely present all around us! But can you not see the light in her eyes? How can you ignore that which is clearly visible?"

"Light is the gateway to darkness!"

His words echoed down The Shafts. The other slaves watched as the new slave collapsed to his knees in apparent agony, "I, too, saw the light. I pursued it, not looking back at what I had left. But The Master thrives in darkness. They pull you back in even after you've seen the colorful skies. That is why there is only darkness, because the light itself is but a trick, an illusion."

"Is there no life beyond The Shafts?" she asked.

"Well, yes, but—"

"Then there is hope that this mere existence of toiling in the darkness is not our eternal fate," The Elder interjected. The new slave could somehow see her nodding her head in affirmation, a soft glow around her. No, it emanated *from* her.

"The Master may use light as a trick, but they do not live in The Shafts. They have not seen *our* light."

She stepped forward to embrace him, and he fell into her arms. It was then that the slaves of The Shafts witnessed the birth of a new hope.

As her light spread across The Shafts, so did the drive to live in the Summer Light. She and the other slaves prepared for the next arrival. With her light spreading, the passage of time became known thanks to the new slave's knowledge. They devised a system to face The Master once they opened the pathway out of The Shafts.

Months passed without any sign of an incoming slave. Some feared it would be years or decades before another would arrive, much like before. She remained dedicated to keeping the light on in their eyes. It wasn't easy, and at times, the light began to fade even in herself. But hope could not be quelled so easily.

Upon the arrival of the sixth month, shifting could be heard above them. Was it time?

After living for so long in utter darkness, the slaves' ears had been attuned to slight reverberations within The Shafts. It had become a way of sensing each other's emotions, a way of communicating without sight. Despite the otherwise suffocating silence that filled the tunnels, she knew what the others were thinking. Held breath meant fear, and fear meant hope was under attack.

She stood taller, her shoulders squared. Her light was no longer a glimmer but that of rays from a rising sun, a sun only referenced in the myths they'd whispered to one another. In them radiated a vibrant light that did not cease. This light that encased all who walked upon the surface provided healing energy. These same rays that had only once spread through legend were now confirmed as truth before the slaves' seeing eyes. Her light had become more real than the darkness surrounding them.

The ancient gears cracked and rotated into motion once more. The Master approached.

As the slaves prepared for The Shafts to open, she spoke to them one last time, "Even if the light does not shine on us, *We* are The Summer Light!"

The Shaft door burst open with once-blinding rays. The slaves were no longer affected like before. They waited for the signal to strike. Heavy, metallic steps descended toward them. The new slave saw his former nightmare approaching the opening.

"Attack!"

The vanguard of slaves swung their weapons at The Master, causing it to reel back in surprise and pain. Another order came from the new slave, "Release the trap!"

The Elder severed a rope holding a thick net laced with sharpened rocks. The net fell directly on top of The Master, and it screamed, "Zigeroff! Voi'kozo tahn!"

"Silence him!" the new slave exclaimed as the slaves grabbed hold of its silky body. The Master was no prime like them; it couldn't prevent the slaves from prying open its mouth and removing its tongue entirely. The scene was brutal, and she cared not for the violence of it all.

The new slave twirled his weapon, ready to take The Master's life. Before he could, she grabbed his arm and pointed towards the light, its warmth radiating from the world above.

"Our life is out there. Let The Master suffer in darkness."

Leering back at her, he saw a blaze shining within her eyes. Then, looking upon the rest of the slaves crowding around him, he realized their eyes burned with the same illumination. He lowered his weapon and joined them as they ascended out of darkness, out of The Shafts.

The slaves were no more, for they had become the Summer Light.

The Hound and the Nightingale by Randall Hayes

To Mark Vest, who ran "the evil game," where Nachtigall first appeared (under another name).

Nachtigall swept the old spider's web off its moorings with one huge, blunt hand and rolled it into a sort of pill that he popped into his mouth and chewed absently. *Hmm—eggs, as well as silk.* His was a cursed varied diet, driven by the tastes of a bird, trying to feed a body over seven feet tall. Fortunately, he also had a man's cleverness and the cast iron stomach of a Riese, the huge sea-people of the coast, who ate anything they found, fresh or foul, that washed up on the beaches. He could coat a leaf or even a scrap of old parchment with sticky honey or syrup, and when it was well and truly covered with trapped bugs, he could crumple it up and consume the whole thing, just like with the spider's web. And though he had no claws, he was roughly as strong as a bear and had no trouble ripping apart rotten logs for ants or beetle grubs.

He was sorting through the fallen leaves, gathering persimmons he had just shaken from their tree. Those bright orange fruits were so mouth-puckering that most animals wouldn't touch them until they were overripe to the point of oozing rottenness. Hornets loved them, however, which meant he could often get both sugar and flesh in the same stop. He had mastered the art of clapping the big wasps out of the air between two bits of wood or rock so that he didn't get stung and then scraping off the crushed remains with his front teeth. It was too cold out for them now, though, unless he happened across a nest, in which case he could satisfy his gut's need for fiber, as well. His familiar spirit demanded freshness in its prey, but he could not be picky otherwise.

The cold did not bother him much. He had little hair, but like his nameless sire's kin, he had a thick layer of fat under his skin that kept him warm. He had clothes, too, of course—he wasn't a savage.

It was an odd sight; the half-ogre squatted down, whistling as he worked. That was another gift of his familiar spirit. He could copy nearly any tune after a single hearing and recombine all those little snatches of music into endless songs that never repeated. They did duets, sometimes, or had contests. He mostly whistled during the day to let the more dangerous creatures, the bears and boars, know where he was and that he wasn't hunting them. The spirit bird sang him to sleep at night with melodies only he could hear. His parents were dead, and he had as little contact with other people as he could manage.

However, the same music that kept the fanged things at bay sometimes drew other predators, and that was the case today. "Ho, there, Whistler." Nachtigall hadn't heard the leaves crunch, but then it was damp out. He looked up.

A few feet away, safely out of lunging distance, stood an armed man leaning on a quarterstaff, looking smug. None of his weapons were drawn, but there were sure enough of them. *Like a porcupine*, Nachtigall thought. He stood, slowly and stiffly, all the way up to let the fellow see what he was in for. The fellow didn't look overly worried by his size, which was itself worrying. "Ho, yourself, Stranger." He tossed a persimmon half a step to the man's right, saying, "Have a snack."

Without looking at it or shifting his feet, the man caught the little orange ball in his right hand and tossed it back. "Still not ripe. Thank you just the same. Do you know a witch named Merga?"

"Who asks?"

"My name is Hundt, a targeteer of some renown. Perhaps you've heard of me?"

Nachtigall shook his massive head, his white eyes bored. "Nein."

"Well, I have heard tell of you, from her. She tells me you know this forest better than anyone. She also said you might be willing to help me with a bit of business. I'm hunting a stolen child."

"I do not steal children. I am no redcap," he growled. Why would Merga sic this sticker-pig on him, except to get rid of a threat? Sending a hornet to the persimmon tree, maybe. His other hand, the one that had not thrown the fruit, held a small pouch of white quartz gravel, the same size and shape as the hailstones that would soon be pelting this bully-boy's skull. As Nachtigall squeezed his fist around the pouch, the clouds above began to darken, and smaller ones formed among the lowest branches of the trees.

"No, no, I know who took her, and I know where they went, thanks to your friend's scrying. I just need to get there, quickly-like, before they do something to her."

"What will they do?"

"I don't know, sacrifice her to some dark god? Sell her to the Beastmen for breeding stock? Nothing good, I'm sure. Come on, man! I have silver if that's what it takes."

Nachtigall released his grip on the pouch, and the skies likewise relaxed. "There are no Tier Manner in *my* forest."

The big one kept getting ahead of him somehow, with those long legs pumping up and down the hillsides, and every time Hundt caught up, he had found something else to pack into his mouth or into a pouch for later: acorns, several kinds of mushrooms, a shed snakeskin.

If he wasn't eating something, he was talking to it: birds, mostly, but a couple of times a squirrel and once to a thing in a cave that Hundt could not identify by any means. Sight, sound, and smell all were just *wrong*. It grunted like a boar, but it smelled dead. And charred. And possibly infected. Hundt did not want to get too close.

"What *was* that?" he asked when they were well over the next hill.

"Ask it yourself."

The stachelschwein was lying. No men had been through here, and no girl. None that the animals could see, anyway, and they saw everything that wasn't spell-hidden. Plants could see through spells sometimes, but they were all asleep for the next few months, except for a few of the ferns and mosses, and they were not very smart.

"Who is this child that her parents have spare silver to hire bravos?"

"Wealthy burghers, eager to have her home."

"The Fey do not like being followed."

There was a pause. "Then they should not take things that do not belong to them." Nachtigall turned. The man's hands were not on his weapons but were not far away. "How much farther?"

"Right there." He pointed into a holly grove, green and berry-laden in the cold. It was the closest possible way, and the time of year was about right. He might make it. "I'll have my silver now."

"Well—"

"—Or that bow off your back if there's no silver." It was a fine one, black yew and six feet long. It looked plenty sturdy enough for him to use. He didn't hunt much, preferring to use traps and snares, but with that bow, he might learn.

"That bow I'm going to need. Here's your silver, as promised, with my thanks." He tossed a pouch, which Nachtigall caught without looking at it. He touched his cap with two fingers on his right hand and ducked backwards into the grove.

Nachtigall stepped around a tree and waited, listening for the creak of a bow being drawn before opening the pouch. It did not, in fact, contain silver. It held gold. He held up a piece to the gray light, examined the writing, and bit it. Counting the gem—a carved white jade the size of a quail's egg—there was easily a year's wages here for a working man.

The half-ogre sighed, grumbling. He had been hoping for silver, which he could melt down and use to make the special crescent knife he needed for ritual harvests. Now, he would have to go into town and trade. He did not like town.

Hundt did not like being lost. His nose usually kept him on track, wherever he was—a gift from some nameless ancestor whose senses surpassed the merely human. But magic broke the rules. That was the point of magic, apparently. It was a way of cheating nature. Hundt did not like being cheated, either, for all that he had lied through his teeth to the big druid. Oh well, gold had a way of smoothing things over, and gold would do him no good where he was bound. Why not be generous?

He should have brought more food. Eating and drinking in Faerie was chancy, he'd been told. He could have tried to buy more from the Whistler back there (*the biggest and ugliest "Nightingale" he'd ever seen, for sure*), but most of what he'd seen the druid eating did not look tasty.

He pulled a pottery flask from his pack and broke the leaden seal. The liquid inside tasted... complicated. He could identify a dozen components by smell, but there were easily a dozen more that he could not. He sipped until he felt drowsy, and then he lay down, facing west, as he'd been told by the witch back in town.

Nachtigall pulled off his clothes and left them with his other effects in a hollowed tree, stuffing the space in front of them with dry leaves and sealing the hole with his own dung. Then he circled the tree's base with urine and simple spells of keeping. It was crude, but the trees were all asleep, and the larger animals he might have called to stand guard were too busy with the rut to respond to anything less than a god.

Finished, he held up a fluffy barred feather that he had reserved from his cache and began to whisper a chant that folded in on itself, along with his body, until he was an owl. He stretched, flapped, and climbed into the air, circling the holly grove before landing in one of the trees above it to wait for dusk. The man slept below.

When Hundt woke, the air was warmer and smelled like spring, with wildflowers blooming. He felt rested and less hungry than he should have been. He stood, did a few basic stretches to loosen his joints, and gathered his gear, which had been pawed through and scattered a bit—by mice, it smelled like. Nothing important was gone, though.

He pushed slowly through the west side of the grove backwards, with his arms up, not because of any spell but to protect his face from the holly's thorns. He looked around when he was out. Twilight.

He needed a high place exposed to the wind. The trees around here were quite tall, so this was going to take some work.

Nachtigall watched from safety, camouflaged against the trunk of his perch by his feathers. Only his bright orange eyes could be seen, and they were pointed up towards the sky, not down towards the ground. The stachelschwein climbed the branch remnants of a pine tree like a ladder, pushing through the canopy to the very top, where the trunk became just another branch, flexible and green. Nachtigall's owl eyes were perfect for this work. Otherwise, his quarry would have been a silhouette, at best, against a sky that was a permanent dusk.

The man carved symbols on the cardinal points of the branches, as far out as he could reach, and then blew on a tiny bird-bone flute. The wind picked up a bit and swirled around the pine. The man closed his eyes and started sniffing at the air like a suspicious guard dog. Then he clambered down, sure-footed as a mountain goat, and strode off to the east. Nachtigall followed, floating along on silent wings.

All the winds in the world flowed through a temple to Aeolus, even a simple treetop shrine that no one but the birds would ever see. Perhaps especially through there, as the king of the winds cared little for worship. It was a trick Hundt had used before when he needed to pick up a trail. And now that they were home, the Erl were no longer actively hiding their tracks. He had their scent now, and as long as he stayed focused, he could follow them anywhere in the world. It meant not eating or sleeping, but those were things it wasn't safe to do anyway, here. On he fled.

Nachtigall flew from tree to tree, amazed at how fast the man was going, just walking like that. He had to work to keep up, and he was flying. At first, he was careful to keep his distance, but every time he lost sight of the man behind some obstacle, he had to search ahead of where he *should* have been to pick him up again. It was like distance itself was negotiable here. Not "seven leagues at a step," but definitely more than a yard. Or indefinitely—*Scheisse! Lost him again!* Finally, he gave up caution and wordplay and moved so close that he could keep the man in sight. He was well-named, as focused as a hound on a trail, and paid no attention to anything behind him. On they flew.

With a gesture that was both elegant and deadly, the master of the Erl party launched his favorite hawk into the pale twilit sky, her iridescent feathers a shining royal blue like a peacock's, the copper bells of her jesses ringing. Unlike the rest of his party, he never tired of being the master, the hand who held the jesses or the reins. He never took a turn being the hawk, or the horse, or the rabbit. Some of the Fey felt this limited him—limited his experience—but he felt that power only grew with the exercise of it. In this one behavior, he was absolutely consistent. All else about the exercise of power could vary, often whimsically so. Sometimes, he was cruel, sometimes generous, sometimes fair, sometimes not.

This ambiguity clearly confused his latest pet. He had struck her earlier, and though he had healed the bruise and plucked the memory of it from her conscious mind, she still seemed wary of him on some level. There was a tension in her posture that had not been there before and did not go away, even hours later.

She was napping on the ground, wrapped in his own cloak, while the Erl played out their hunt. The master had kept men and women before, but they never seemed to live long. They had to be fed and watered at annoyingly regular intervals, or they became sickly. And what happened when you kept them awake for even a week was in no way pretty. Their madness could be boundless—contagious, even. They were entertaining while they lasted, though, which was the important thing.

The hawk's cry and the rabbit's scream brought him out of his reverie, but too late for the action. By the time he cantered up to them, they were already women again, rolling naked on the ground, laughing, covered in the pale blue blood of their kind, the copper bells of the hawk's jesses ringing merrily.

"I'm so sorry," he said smoothly, "I missed that. You'll have to—" An arrow sprouted from the ground between his horse and the women.

"The next one goes through your throat if you start to speak a spell," the archer had another arrow nocked and drawn. "Tipped with cold iron."

The master smiled. "The pup from the mortal fair. A sore loser, aren't you?"

Hundt grinned as well, an entirely different grin, the grin of a wild wolf. "I didn't lose; you witched the target."

"I did not. That would be unlawful and would invalidate our wager."

"That was no wager, you verrückt! *That was a joke.* And not even a joke aimed at you. She wasn't mine to offer. People don't own each other."

"Really? I've been to your world before, you know—many times. Your people are crude in many ways, but they are very inventive when it comes to enslavement. I mean—money? Usury? Lawyers? These are brilliantly devious concepts. I may introduce them here."

"If you won't trade for the girl, I will kill you and take her." Hundt was a strong man but not a patient one. He had to conclude this quickly before his arms tired and began to shake, which would spoil his aim.

Just as the master threw back his head in a mocking laugh, four hundred pounds of naked ogre dropped from the sky on top of him. He was struck from his saddle and plowed face-first into the fragrant sod. Bones snapped. Nachtigall reached over and plucked the arrow from the ground, pressing the flat of its iron head against the master's forehead, where it smoked coldly. The master gasped and coughed turquoise blood.

Nachtigall addressed the two women, who were now standing. And fully dressed. And armed with copper blades. "Three short mortal lives for one immortal is a good bargain."

The master's horse melted into a third woman and joined them. "Leave him to us," they sang in gorgeous three-part harmony. "We will bind him to our will for a few of your decades.

Do not bear children of your own, for *he-will-not-for-get*." They smiled brilliant, wicked smiles.

In Nachtigall's case, that was unlikely and no great loss, but the other two mortals paled visibly.

"Why did they curse us?" the girl, whose name turned out to be Bytzel, whined as they made their way out of the holly grove. It was dark, and according to the moon, a number of days had passed while they were in that other twilit world.

"It was not a curse," Nachtigall corrected her as he plunged his thick fingers through the seal of now-dried dung he had left on his effects. "It was a warning and a fact. They cannot hold him for the rest of their immortal lives, even if they wanted to. Take their advice. If you bear a child or a grandchild, it will have your blood, and he will find it. Pour your love into another's child instead. The Fey care nothing for love."

"I'm sorry, girl," lamented Hundt. "That was not quite the rescue I had planned. I'll have you home by morning." He absently put one callused hand on her head as he looked over and up at the lonesome druid, who was stepping one enormous foot into his leather pants.

"You still owe me silver," grated Nachtigall.

A Lonely Passage by Devon Field

For Micah and Beebo.

Memories, he knew, were not entirely reliable, for what were they really? What purchase could they possibly find on time such as this?

Had this always been his favorite corridor? With no fixed point on which to pin it, he wasn't sure when that had happened. The sentiment was only an echo, now lacking its initiating sound.

Had that particular tone to the humming in these walls, almost a tickle at the base of the skull, always affected him in this way? He couldn't remember, couldn't say. Couldn't set a start to it or guess when or whether it would end.

Sometimes, he would let himself slide to the floor here and feel the noise run through him. For now, he just extended a hand so that his fingers dragged across the wall panels, tingling as they went. He would have to content himself with that.

There was a presence behind him. He could feel it growing closer, pushing with relentless insistence. He resisted for a moment, wriggling in the current, but then he had to go on. He had to let it carry him forward and up the ramp, his feet finding their way beneath him. It was either that or fall, and falling could not be allowed for long.

> *...But even so, rest assured that the flourishing and comfort of all within was at the very forefront of the entire design process. Right from its initial conception, we always pursued this as a "people first" project, and notions such as cost-effectiveness and paying-client fulfillment only followed much later. We believed in that principle very strongly...*

There was so much that was hard for him to recall. Once you had seen something so many times, its meaning was sundered, a signifier without its signified. Those grooves of memory became cut so deep and wide by repetition that they no longer registered, not as anything other than gaping absences which obscured all else that was or might have been.

He remembered this hallway, though. Of course. And those passages over there, opening off to the right. Those were the ones that ran across the spine and down into the zoological halls, where he could walk between the high glass cases, each containing its own family of pseudo-taxidermy, flourishes of life rendered discrete and unobtrusive. He could circle the large cats, arrayed across their rocky slope in varied attitudes of hissing, licking, readying themselves to leap. But not now. The slight ache told him, not now. So he continued on, and through other intersections, other instances of potential, some of which he could feel were now open to him, others not. He took one.

...and as we know now, that required physical interventions. We started on a purely external system, of course. But the drives were unreliable—it just wouldn't work. An internal element was going to be needed. And there was a certain moral discomfort around the idea of the installation. However, as soon as the earliest modules were integrated, still entirely on-surface at this point, the results were inarguable. All of the squabbling fell away, and we immediately refocused our efforts...

There was darkness here, a soothing heaviness to the air that demanded a languid sort of motion to match. He reveled in it, appreciating this moment in which he was permitted to linger, to drift, to roll one foot gently forward, and then another, to exist, if only briefly, in a near approximation of stillness.

After that, there were the visions, the images that bloomed on the walls, the ceiling, and the floor. Dozens of scenes played out all around him in delicate fragments. Boots splashing through a puddle. Small hands twisting a Rubik's cube. Horse rolling in the grass. Fingers dancing across white and black keys, across a screen, across skin. The movement of clouds. A tree burning, growing, falling. A boy and an older man standing together by a wooded path, caught in the motion of turning expectantly toward him. Maybe he knew them from before, or maybe just from here.

The scenes mixed and intermingled. Some he'd seen on his countless passes through this area, while others he still saw for the first time—or at least he thought so. They emerged from the stream of moments like a whale arching out of the ocean—he had seen that here, too.

As he watched, elements swam out of one scene to join with another. A car swerved away from the bustling city on the wall to cut across the floor onto a deserted beach, onto some sort of mechanical device, then onto an apple slice. It collided with his foot and burst apart, dancing off as three crabs, one clambering back into the city streets and smoothly entering the flow of traffic. He had watched this before, watched all of these before, or mostly he had.

Mostly, that growing sense of someone close would send him out into the light before he had the chance to spot anything unfamiliar. So it was now.

> *...The propulsion systems were not a problem. We already had those, as did all of our competitors. But the production of energy, that was the key. What our scientists hit on, what they came to understand that those competitors failed to realize, was that the passengers themselves needn't be thought of only as consumers or as products to be conveyed from point to point, like any other. They were a resource. They were going to actually be our fuel. Once we had that piece in place, the rest was always going to be easy...*

M deck. The cafeterias, with their little table pods rising up chairless from the floor, their maze of partitions to be navigated. He found a dispenser that he favored as much as any other and accepted its cup of seasoned crunch. The salty clusters burst in his mouth, melting to nothing before he swallowed, the cup vanishing just as quickly into a nearby chute and his hunger going with it for a little while longer.

Somewhere beyond the partitions, there was the slightest scuff of a footstep. He could not quite bring himself to look in that direction. He had, in any case, no reason to do so, no chance of seeing them, whoever it was. He moved off toward one of the exits but did so slowly, making a dawdling circuit of one of the pods and hoping for another sound or sign from his unknown companion.

Managing a second circuit through gritted teeth, he was rewarded with the quiet whir of a dispenser somewhere behind him. Sweating slightly from that effort made, he hurried from the cafeteria.

> ...It's true that early prototypes did lack entertainment, nourishment beyond the purely nutritional. Some on the team really took to the whole "foot-traffic as fuel" concept without sufficient attention to precisely what that foot-traffic would be doing with itself, and this was not without consequence. I'm sure you can imagine. We are, however, now proud to also offer richly textured food for their inner lives, from art installations to interactive micro-films. We truly provide an incredible variety of cultural programming and sensory stimulation, just as they provide us with the energy to make it all possible...

Someone was off to his left, just about keeping pace with him. He was sure of it. Sure of the urge that pressed him to take each hallway that opened up on his right. Sure of the pain that flashed in his head as he contemplated the idea of instead turning toward the left, toward them. Someone was traveling in parallel to him, maybe even in the next hallway over, maybe just a little further away than that.

His head throbbed, but he didn't turn away. Didn't take the stairs leading down to the water halls, though it was an area that he ordinarily liked very much. Just kept placing one foot after another in front of him, moving methodically forward while over to the left, someone else did the same, some unknown person making their way, much like his, through the ship.

His breathing picked up under the pressure of the ache, but he willed himself to slow it down, to slow himself down. They must have done the same, his fellow passenger, for the ache was unchanged, and he pictured their effort, which must match his own, their steps every bit as strained and deliberate as his.

> *...Constant motion was the next puzzle. First we'd solved the sleeping problem, simple enough on a technical level. Then, we pivoted to motivation. Pretty much right away we ruled out the continued functioning of the ship as being, in itself, sufficient. It shouldn't even have taken that long. There were some optimistic souls who thought the passengers would simply want to ensure their own ship's survival and safe arrival at its destination. But they didn't, not over the long haul, at least. Not enough to make it happen. They didn't want to feel like they'd done more work than the others. Or at least that's what we think since we can't ask them.*
>
> *We tried different approaches, but eventually, we settled on using what became the Mutual Exclusion Modules, the*

> MEMs. Someone had T-shirts made when we first came up with that. "It's not pro-pulsion. It's re-pulsion!" There was a lot of that sort of thing. It was funnier if you'd been there through all the sleepless nights of development...

As he approached another intersection, he twisted his head forcefully down the corridor toward his shipmate, but they didn't appear. They might have already crossed the intersection or were just about to. Either way, he couldn't wait around to find out. He stumbled, taking a few quick steps to recover himself. Felt a little faint.

At the next, he tried again, staggering from the pain and effort it required of him, reaching out for the wall to hold himself up. He strained to listen and to stay. Remained as long as he could, but there was no more sign of the other passenger. Maybe they had turned away. He gathered himself and did so too.

He was pretty sure there had been other people before. He had vague memories of human interactions, but maybe those were just scenes from the vision hall he was thinking of. It was always so hard to remember everything.

> ...The most difficult balance to strike was that of human contact. Yes, our "fuel," the lifeblood and energy of the ship, was produced by pushing people away from one another, but surely they still needed some kind of personal communication, a friendly face here and there to keep them going. A "How are you?" and a reassuring hand on the shoulder now and then.
>
> That had been our initial intuition, but the answer was

no. If allowed to see one another, the passengers only felt their deprivation all the more deeply. They just couldn't take it.

The correct balance, as it turned out, was zero.

THE KINGFISHER EXCHANGE
BY MELISSA ROSE ROGERS

Special thanks to Jonathan Yona Bohanon (tribal member) for assisting with research and language, especially the Eastern dialect versus Western. This story was inspired in part by two recountings from James Mooney's Myths of the Cherokee, "What the Stars Are Like" and "The Star Feathers." Cherokee words—Tsulu means "kingfisher," which is a bright blue-gray bird; Sequoyah is an anglicization of tsisquaya, meaning "sparrow"; and Sgi (pronounced ShGee) is "thank you" in the Eastern dialect.

The Tsulu arrived in a massive intergenerational vessel that orbited the Earth once a day, giving all those who looked at the sky an irrefutable reminder that we are not alone in the universe. It didn't take long for the colonies on Mars and Luna to find out about the aliens. News travels fast in space. Thanks to the faster-than-light transmitters, the colonies' officials knew before the average citizen on Earth did.

We were en route to the Meridani Planum Mars Station when my grandma's contacts there let us know. People ask that now—*where were you when you found out?* My teacher, Mx.

Jordan, had that for an essay question. When I, Sequoyah, heard the news, I was aboard our cargo hauler, the transport vessel my grandma inherited from her father. Our next stop was Neptune Station to deliver supplies, and after that, my dad's research station. For extra credit, I included some illustrations, comic-book style, about my home with the essay. Our starship doesn't have much of the original left since it has been upgraded over and over throughout the years during trips helping families move across space.

When the intergenerational ship of the Tsulu came in fast from outside the solar system and hailed Earth, the governments scrambled to understand their message: *Greetings, we come in peace*. The realization that the words were Cherokee dawned on the US Government and the globe. Why do the Tsulu speak Cherokee? It's a really old story.

The Closed Distance™ HistoriSim© took over the screen. It was designed to make history come to life for us with an immersive sensory experience, even including temperature. The simulation was made using data from the Tsulu based on their records. A deep, gravelly voice began speaking. I had seen this HistoriSim© before, but I bet many classmates haven't.

The cadence was off in the way movies showed Native people talking was not what we really sounded like. Grams told me there was a time when kids were forced into government boarding schools that encouraged a stiff way of talking and conformity that this was emulating.

Even so, the voice from the HistoriSim© wrapped around me with its story:

"Long ago, a white man named James Mooney came and paid tribal members to tell old stories."

The simulation showed pristine mountains and scenery panning in closer and closer.

"You could say he was interested in preserving our culture, but he gathered stories and then published a book claiming authorship. He took our words, our heritage, and made a quick buck."

Next, I saw a white man on the screen seated on a woven rivercane chair talking with older people wearing traditional clothes inside one of our customary log houses.

"Long, long before James Mooney was born, before the white men came in droves to the New World, there was a glowing star that shrieked through the night sky, crashing into tulip trees and engulfing them in flames."

Across the deepest black sky (almost as black as looking out the portholes of our cargo hauler), a magnesium-white flare rocketed through the sky. The plummeting object set the trees ablaze.

"Through the night, the trees crackled, igniting nearby pines, chestnuts, and hemlocks and sending the red wolves, deer, and brown bears scurrying, fleeing for their lives," the voice continued.

Animals, or at least their virtual renderings, mass exited the woods as the mountainside turned red hot.

"The next morning, smoke clung to the valley, and ash floated through the air like mud stirred up in a creek."

With a flash of the viewer, it changed to gray morning light with men and women gathered around, their voices a murmur.

"The elders spoke softly. They disagreed on what to do. One boy was curious. He had to see the star that offended the heavens. He could not wait for the elders to decide what to do. Trees were bent in half, uprooted, charred. The forest ruins gripped his heart. A tree is a sacred thing, and to see so much death where once was verdure made his heart ache."

The boy, about my age, slipped through the trees. Ash drifted through the air as if it were snow, only harsh and bullying.

"Among the wreckage lay a towering boulder, like half a mountain—smooth as if it had been polished by a river, almost like a soapstone bowl. The material was dark gray and shining in the sun through the smoke. Strange carvings lined it like a giant claw scratched the stone, revealing white underneath the giant ruts. The scratches did not look deep—perhaps they were intentional."

The screen shifted to an alien vessel—a different model than what the Tsulu use nowadays. It looked much cruder and bulkier. I guess they've improved over the last millennium.

"The boulder opened, and out from the smoke and ash, a trio of three spirits emerged. They were brilliant blue and covered in feathers. At first, the boy trembled in fear. Had he been pulled into some otherworldly trial by the spirits? What was happening?"

The squawking noises from their dark gray beaks seemed to perplex him. They stood as tall as he did, but where he had legs like saplings and feet like roots, they had legs that narrowed to scaly branches ending in claws with three shorter talons to the front and a very long talon to the back.

"One of the bird spirits turned one of its large, black eyes and spied the water flowing in a small brook. It waddled as fast as its spindly legs would take it to be upstream of the ash.

"When the other two realized its discovery, they squawked and flapped their seemingly flightless wings and followed suit."

The boy trailed them, noting the voracity with which they slurped down the liquid, bending over the red clay to let their gray tongues grab the glistening water. With their thirst quenched, they sighed and dunked their heads, only to shiver. The boy laughed, probably because he knew how cold that mountain water could be. They groomed themselves rapidly, chewing through tiny, soft feathers of deep cobalt. Their wings, though, were the same blue-gray as those of a male kingfisher.

"When they were satisfied with their cleanliness, one by one, they stopped and eyed the boy with their shining black eyes. He said nothing. What does one say to a spirit?"

The wind shifted and sent the smoke upstream to them. The most vibrant of the spirits squawked, whistled, and chittered. The boy beckoned them to follow him.

"He did not know what they wanted, but perhaps an elder would. The elders spoke quietly of the three feathery visitors. They fed them deer, trout, and paw-paw fruit. With sharp movements, the spirits devoured the offerings."

Their feathers softened and looked puffier, relaxing from the taut, sleek look they had before. The trio clucked their gratitude, and a drowsy look overtook them. The elders motioned. They were ushered to a log cabin—the newest construction, the utmost of their hospitality.

"The boy pondered the stars that night. It was a crisp new moon, and the sky was dark."

The simulation sped up—the moon waxed full and waned to black, then waxed full again. The crisp autumn night turned to winter, so the HistoriSim© 4D effect puffed a cold breeze across me—I imagined it like those ancient maps with the four winds red-cheeked.

"In winter, the spirits barely left the cabin. The boy and others brought them firewood, water, dried fruit, smoked trout, squash, corn, and venison when they could find it.

"The elders sat among them. When the bird creatures molted, their feathers were treasured and crafted, included in medicine bags, and added to rituals. Soon, their clucking and squawking sounds changed. Among the shrills and peeps, there were words more like our speech. Soon, the boy, the elders, and the rest of the clan began to understand the birds. Mostly, they wanted to hear our stories. They asked many questions but did not tell us what the stars were like, and they did not say why they had been cast on a boulder down from the stars. The elders said not to press them—the spirits should not be angered."

The sky changed again, and so did the ClosedDistance™ climate control shifting colder.

"After blackberry spring and dogwood winter, when the true spring had begun, the spirits spent more time in the woods, inside their boulder. The clan members—at least one from each of the seven—followed them to the woods but always kept a respectful distance. Sharp noises, the likes of which had never echoed through those hills before, sounded and startled the people. Babies stopped chewing on their teething necklaces, looking to their mothers for reassurance."

A baby—stark black-haired—paused, clutching the beaded necklace before it. Its blue eyes spread wide at the whirring noises from one of the birds' tools, which looked like an automatic Lawrence screwdriver or a quartinium spanner. To my simulated ancestors, it would have been otherworldly. The scene dimmed, then shifted to the sky: a clear night with the moon seeming very far and tiny.

"The moon was full once more when the spirits announced that they would be returning to the stars." The blue creatures bowed deeply to the seated elders inside the plaster and rivercane communal hall. "They offered many feathers to the clan. The blue quills were carefully accepted with deep reverence."

Balancing on one leg, the creature of the brightest blue grasped the boy's hand firmly with its claw. The talons, though sharp, did not break his skin.

"Shh geee." The bird's voice sounded so human now.

The narrator explained, "*Sgi* is thank you in *Tsalagi*, the Cherokee language."

The boy's dark eyes met the round eyes of the bird whose head tilted slightly.

"This story was added to our oral history, though the story changed as it was passed down as all retellings, all histories do. When the Tsulu returned, our language had been preserved by a few. The Tsulu did not know that humans spoke thousands of languages, with even more dead and forgotten in the clutches of time. They returned to humanity once they detected that we had the power to send our own vessels to the stars, but it took time to reach us. Our first contact was a millennium ago, in a rhododendron grove with reddening maple trees and hemlocks as wide as a doorway soaring into the heavens. Once we numbered in the hundreds of thousands, then we were ripped asunder. We number far fewer, but our legacy endures."

With the HistoriSim© finished, the screen dimmed, the temperature returned to normal, and the projections of my teacher, classroom, and classmates returned.

So many times, I had felt alone and like an outsider. My classmates were from all over Earth, Luna, and Mars, but I was the only Native American student, much less Cherokee, in my classes. I attended a summer camp once on Luna and saw a Sioux tribal member. We exchanged knowing looks across the cafeteria. Our skin was just a token of diversity—a slightly different brown in a sea of skin colors, our ancient languages a speck in the ocean of homogenized diction. On a few other planets, there are groups of Native Americans, Mayan, Métis, First Nations, or Inuit peoples. The planet TOI-700 d has one continent with Lakota, another with Cherokee, and a third with a Mayan population. Maybe one day I'll travel there.

My Closed Distance™ classroom was augmented reality—the pod was a grass-green closet, pretty much. The green was supposed to be relaxing, but it felt suffocating and monotonous. I was sick of school and being told what to do; I wanted choices, variety, and independence.

There were four main features to the pod: a light designed to copy sunshine (even adjusting brightness and tone for each student based on their time zone); a handheld interface; an ergonomic seat, which slid out of the wall but was otherwise barely decipherable against the bright-green plasticine surface; and the Shared Journeys™ flooring, a proprietary amalgamation with the give of a real forest floor but none of the vegetation, upkeep, or germs. Long ago, people figured out that standing was important for humans. Humans evolved to stand, and sitting sedentary wasn't good for workplaces or classrooms, but standing on linoleum tile or industrial carpet wasn't great for our feet. That's why Closed Distance™ Classrooms developed Shared Journeys™ flooring—it was designed to emulate the ground our feet evolved to walk on. We're allowed to take off our shoes if we like, and the material moves like a treadmill but matches our gaits automatically. Mx. Jordan had decorated the classroom projection for Halloween with fall leaves, pumpkins, and cheesy witches with green skin and striped stockings.

Mx. Jordan was having the whole class write essays for an exchange program application with the Tsulu. I only wrote it for my grade—Grams was not going to let me go live with bird people, even if a lot of them did speak our language, so why bother submitting it? For extra credit, I wrote it in Tsalagi, which many of the Tsulu are fluent in. Mx. Jordan thought I'd be an excellent candidate for the program and that it would be an exciting, once-in-a-lifetime opportunity that would bolster my college application. I wasn't even sure what I'd major in or what I'd want to do after that. My future felt so far away. I've lived in low G for so long, the colonies on Mars or Luna might be good options. There's Theta Wu Station, too, which is like Macau in space. I knew I wanted to be somewhere with many people and things to do, but I didn't want the smog of Earth or the lonely quiet of the outer colonies or research stations.

Despite my doubts, I wanted a good grade and put in the effort. Mx. Jordan thought I had a chance and attached a special message to my assignment as soon as they posted it, reminding me to mention my heritage and that I've lived in space most of my life. The importance of the assignment didn't really hit me then. Later last week, as I prepared it, my heart pounded. Nervous knowledge filled me: I'm different, and my heritage differs from that of so many people that I have interacted with. Their backstories and traditions are homogeneous. They bragged about holidays and dishes and songs that had been carefully preserved for generations. I remembered with pain the sadness that filled my grandmother's eyes when she talked about how her grandmother didn't speak our language: the government sent her to an Indian Residential School where they had tried to erase our culture. When all the cow milk from all the farms gets dumped together in a big vat to help ease industrial distribution, it's homogenized: mixed all together, flash heated, and then flash chilled to cut down on the natural cultures within the finished product. It results in a longer shelf life and less distinct flavors. That's what those people did to my ancestors. They lumped us all together in convenient groups, flash-chilled our cultures, and labeled us *American Indians,* assuming we were from India because our skin was browner than theirs and we didn't look Chinese. Those were the only options they could imagine.

My classmates didn't do this, and their parents and grandparents didn't do this. It was people who turned to dust long, long ago. I can't blame the people around me for more than being insensitive and oblivious. The institutions that had kept Native Americans (and other minorities) from succeeding have been replaced now in the space-faring age. We're better off than before. When I hear others talk about the careful preservation of their traditions, I sometimes get a funny feeling. They don't know how hard my people fought to keep our words, our legends, our art.

Mx. Jordan sent me a private message while a video played. I looked up at the instructor. They sat at their desk while the students finished assignments in their little, green classroom interfaces.

Inst. Jordan O'Neal: "Is everything all right, Sequoyah? You seem very distracted this morning."

I swallowed and paused at the blinking message. There was too much to explain. I'm not sure they'd understand.

I typed out, "Everything's okay here." My finger hovered over the send button, but my eyes drifted while I hesitated. In the projection of the Closed Distance™ classroom, I saw Dana, the girl next to me, as clearly as if she was *really* next to me. She wrinkled her nose. I couldn't tell what it meant. I didn't know what most of her looks meant. She was probably thinking, *"What are you looking at?"* She plays *Close Call*, too, but I'm too shy to give her my friend code. I doubt she even knows I play. I guess I was staring off in her direction.

I looked back at the interface before me and then backspaced my message. Mx. Jordan was watching me. There might have been fifteen lightyears separating us, but at that moment, it felt like five feet.

I typed a new message, deciding to be honest: "I'm nervous about the essay. What if I actually get selected? What will Grams say?"

Mx. Jordan looked down at the screen. The video about Ancient Rome was almost over. After a flurry of typing, a new message popped up on my interface:

Inst. Jordan O'Neal: "Don't worry. If you're selected, I'll help you talk to your grandma about it and weigh whether the program is a good fit for you and your family. :) You would still be in this classroom and could talk to your family via the communications array. It would be an incredible experience. Think of all the drawing inspiration! Maybe you could make a graphic novel about your experiences."

A small smile formed on their lips, but I doubted any of my other classmates noticed. The video concluded, and Mx. Jordan asked the first discussion question without missing a beat.

Blackness surrounded me, and distant stars shifted past in streaks. Okay, the stars weren't moving—the space around *me* was being distorted, so my perception was distorted, too. As I looked into space in the dim light, I spied my faint reflection on the glass. I was pretty bored. My homework had been finished for a while, and I didn't feel like drawing or reading. Grams didn't want me spending all my time in *Close Call: Battle Royale*. I really enjoyed the holographic game. It was similar to the Closed Distance™ classroom but used the regular communications array instead. While playing, I wore special gear over my clothes, and it felt like I was in another world. Sometimes, the game events put us in jungles, or on Luna, or in the ocean. It made me feel less lonely being able to play with kids back on Earth or who were traveling in the darkness of space like me. It was like capture-the-flag in VR. The rounds were player versus player; sometimes, they were all for one, and other times, they were goal-based. I liked capture-the-flag the best.

Grams thought the games weren't great—she knew they were fun, and I was getting to interact with other kids, but she hated that we didn't look like ourselves. She worried it would give me negative feelings about my body playing a game where I looked like an unrealistic simulation of someone else—someone taller, stronger, less awkward, and decidedly not Cherokee. It was just a game. I kind of liked not being myself for a while. It made me feel like I had a layer of protection being anonymous.

Grams had told me I could read or practice drawing once my time limit came up. My time limit had come up in *Close Call: Battle Royale* before the checkpoint, so I'd have to redo that event with random people before I could progress to the area where my friends would be playing. It sucked. I kicked the bulkhead. My foot stung from the impact, and I didn't feel any better. I wondered if my dad would be as strict as Grams. I didn't think he would. I had chosen this, though. On Gamma Rho 6, where my dad was stationed, the Closed Distance ™ array couldn't transmit due to security reasons. I would have to sit in a *real* classroom there with strangers. I didn't want to do that. Being the new kid was awkward.

And Gamma Rho 6 doesn't have a breathable atmosphere. It was a research station on a Class Y planet, so I would be stuck indoors, which would be even more boring. I know I'm on a ship most of the time, but when Grams's ship docks, we get to see new places, and that's really fun. Each colony and station has its own flavor with different people and restaurants and shops. There are art installations and gardens in many of them. Research stations have pretty much nothing. Also, if I hated Gamma Rho 6... then I would be stuck there until the next resupply vessel came. It sounded terrible. I missed Dad, but we did talk once a week when he could use the high-powered communications array. I didn't know why the government wouldn't let him send more messages since there weren't a lot of people there, but his research was Top Secret, and they monitored all messages crossing the station. It felt a little weird knowing someone monitored our messages. It was probably monitored by artificial intelligence or a computer or something and then flagged for a real person's review. (Well, a human's review—sentient technology are people too now. We just studied the AI Rights Movement and the court cases establishing their personhood a few weeks ago.) Dad said they limit his outgoing communication so severely because, with the nature of his research, it's being monitored for more than just the regular keywords.

Feeling bored and lonely, I went to see what Grams was doing.

I found her weaving a basket in the mess hall. The rivercane she used was 3D printed using the food printer, a special modification since it makes organic material. On Earth, it's an endangered species (but what isn't, if we're being frank?).

"Can you get me some more rivercane?" she asked, her voice creaky but strong. She didn't look up from her basket. I set down my ph0NE™ and stepped over to the 3D food printer. The settings were still pulled up, so I didn't have to push a lot of buttons.

As the machine whirred into motion and created Grams's supplies, I looked over at her. My dad took after her, and I really missed him. She was strong and beautiful in a regal sort of way. Her hair was turning white in places, almost like a charcoal painting.

I wanted to preserve that moment in my mind forever. If I were accepted and went with the Tsulu, it would be a long time before I could have a relaxing evening like this with her. Sometimes, I missed my dad terribly, and if Grams were far away, then I'd have twice the missing to do.

"What are you looking at me like that for?" she asked, suddenly meeting my eyes.

The 3D printer dinged to signal the job was complete, so I opened up its tray. "Just thinking about Dad. You have his nose," I said as I pulled dried reeds from the printer's hopper.

"*Excuse me.*" Her voice went high in mock exaggeration. "He has my nose. I gave him that nose. I'll take those, thank-you-very-much," she said, cramming in as much as she could into that one breath.

She settled back into her weaving rhythm, a relaxing hobby for her that honored our ancestors—plus handmade crafts sell really well at the Meridani Planum Mars Station.

My ph0NE™ beeped. It was a message from Sirius, one of my classmates: "Where are you? We're getting blasted in *Close Call?*"

I typed back, "Sorry. The grams said only drawing or reading for the rest of the night."

Sirius sent back an angry emoji with the message: "This sucks."

Part of me agreed, but I also wanted to savor Grams and her crafting. Things wouldn't be like this forever, even if I weren't accepted for the exchange program. Grams will retire one day; I doubt my dad will pick up the mantle, and I'm not sure what I'll do when I finish school or where my home will be. I'm not sure what will happen to our intergenerational ship.

I responded to my friend with a disappointed emoji, though. Sirius probably wouldn't understand.

A few weeks later, Grams and I were sitting around the small dining table in the mess hall about half an hour before I needed to go to school. The mess hall felt unreasonably large right then—clearly designed for many families, not just two people. We were still drinking our breakfast smoothies—one optimized for seniors and one for growing kids—and eating our sausage and biscuit essence protein tarts.

My ph0NE™ beeped. Mx. Jordan sent a message to me: "You were accepted!!!"

I swallowed the rest of my smoothie, not knowing what to do. A few moments later, another message came through to me, Grams, and Dad. It would be the weekend before my dad saw it. This second, longer message, directed to Grams and Dad, said that out of the many students applying, the Tsulu requested *me* for their exchange program.

Grams's eyes were still scanning the message. Her eyes grew wider, and tears welled up.

"I don't want you to go," she said, her voice quavering.

"It's only a school year," I blurted out.

"We'll talk about it later." She slammed down her ph0NE™ on the table, facedown, and slid it away, like she wished the gray of the table would swallow the gray of her phone up whole. It didn't. It stood out like a stark blemish.

The rest of the week went by in a haze. I could hardly focus on school, on the game, or on my drawing. I couldn't wait to talk to Dad and see what he would say about the Tsulu. At first, I'd felt nervous about applying, but having Mx. Jordan's support helped me focus on how exciting and different this exchange program would be.

When Dad's image popped up on the screen in the main observatory, Grams stood behind me, her shoulders creeping higher and higher: she was upset. I knew she didn't want me to go, but like the curious boy hundreds of years before, I wanted to reach out to these beautiful beings and learn from them just like they had learned about us.

Dad said he had received the message earlier from Mx. Jordan. "That's an amazing opportunity, Sequoyah. If I were you, I'd do it."

Relief washed over me. It was my choice, and I would say yes. The idea of living with aliens both terrified and excited me.

"What will you say?" he asked, the transmission lagging, distorting his speech, and pixelating the image.

Grams put her hands on the back of the chair and gripped it tighter.

"I'm going to say, 'yes.'"

Grams sighed her disapproval. I could live with that. She didn't approve of *Close Call: Battle Royale* either. Grams and Dad would be one transmission away, and I wanted to learn what the stars were like for myself.

ABADDON'S PORTRAIT OF A LONESOME SHORE BY JAMES CASTOR

Ended up quitting on hotels and sleeping in my car instead. Didn't matter. Being somewhere new was more important, and I wasn't about to leave because I couldn't find a bed to sleep in. I did say I was going to wing it, and that kind of stuff just comes with the territory. Anyhow, it was worth it for the view I woke up to.

Parked on a cliff overlooking the ocean the night before. It was a small lot for hikers, and I was lucky enough to not get shooed by the cops. Before going to sleep, I stood on the cliff's edge, watching the ocean, smoking a joint. The ocean's sort of spooky at night but also comforting. Made me feel invisible. That was the feeling I was looking for on the trip, a way to dispel the heaviness.

The next morning, the sun was low in the trees behind me; in front, the Pacific. There was a soft orange light on everything, filtered through the marine layer. Sat on the hood of my car drinking bottled coffee, smoking a cigarette. Imagine how much

I would've had to pay for a morning like that! Pretty chilly, but I liked it. Super muggy in the valley, in the hundreds; but there on the coast, it didn't even hit seventy.

Down to the right, I could see the town where I would spend my vacation. Finished waking up, then it was time to go exploring. Drove down, parked, and walked around town for a while. Really quaint; the architecture was old school mission style, mostly single-story, no more than two; most streets had no sidewalks; also managed to keep out the franchises and major commercial developments. Charming if you ignore the history, but that's this country in a nutshell.

Breakfast was nice. Sitting there on the patio in the cool morning, waiting for my food, watching "village life," I almost burst into tears. That feeling I'd gotten the night before hadn't been driven away by the daylight but transformed. Not invisible, but unnoticed, unwatched. Effectively hidden. During the drive, I was worried being alone would only make me more depressed. Just a lonely exile. But no one there knew me, and that made me feel free. Finally.

The food snapped me back to reality, and I suddenly felt very much at home. Eggs Benedict never tasted so good. Tipped the waitress fifty bucks, as though she'd saved me from death. Sat there a while, having more coffee. They didn't try to rush me out like most places in this state, so I took my time.

"So, you travelling?" the waitress asked. Name tag said, Stephanie.

"Vacationing."

"Just you, then, huh?"

"Yup. Just need some me-time, you know. Some fresh air."

"You came to the right place for that! You'll get plenty of peace and quiet. Well, enjoy your visit, okay?"

"Thanks."

She walked off. Little worried she'd get nosey there for a second. Really didn't feel like explaining to anyone what happened—just wanted that stuff out of my head for a while. If anyone asked, I'd just say "court drama," and they'd hopefully assume it was a custody battle and leave it at that.

After breakfast, went back to an art gallery I'd seen on my morning walk when they were still closed. Had just enough time for a smoke before they opened up. Most of the stuff in there was unpretentious, the least pretentious work being love letters to the coast, specifically that town. Seems for a lot of those artists, just being there was enough. Guess I found the right place.

One painting, impressionist, had a guy alone on the beach. Supposed it was one of those figures meant to show scale and, more importantly, the feeling intended for the viewer. Sure looked like peace to me.

That's me in the near future, I thought.

From there, walked to the beach. Didn't worry about my car, as there was no metered parking. Was in the mood for day drinking, but there were no bars or anything at the beach. Looked at my map, and there was nothing close, either. Didn't mind putting off drinking for an hour or two.

Took off my shoes and walked down the beach close enough for the waves to touch my feet. Near the end, north of the river outlet, there was a pier with two lighthouses; one on the end and one in the middle. Looking to my right, I realized I was basically where the guy in the painting was, meaning the artist had the pier just out of sight. Wondered why. Maybe it was too time-consuming to paint. Maybe they were sick of seeing it depicted and tried to make a point. The figure had been looking away from it.

Sat there, chain smoking, watching the waves, and looking at the cliffs on either side of the bay, scoping out possible hikes. Maybe later. Time to get a drink. Got up and started making my way into town, but I ran into that waitress from earlier—small town. I'd forgotten her name.

"Stephanie. It's okay! I'm bad with names, so I don't even mind."

"Yeah, sorry. I'm Wes."

We chit-chatted there a bit; talked about my hometown (again trying to avoid referring to the trial), how she'd always wanted to visit there; her life in that town; about my exploration that morning, then the conversation landed on the art gallery.

"Yeah, I used to go there all the time! Some of my friends have works in there, and I still go whenever something of theirs gets in."

Of course, we talked about the piece that'd been on my mind. Turns out I'd missed something: the guy wasn't alone in the painting.

"Yeah, he's harder to notice against the darker background. Some people say they both represent the two lighthouses out of frame, and they're guardians or something. Others say that Background Guy is looking at the pier from the perspective of other paintings and tourist photos; others say that he's watching Foreground Guy."

At that last part, I don't know why, but I looked in the direction of where she said the second figure was, then got a paranoid chill. There was some guy standing there, dressed in black with a flat hat. Couldn't make out his face, but I could tell he was looking at me. When I regarded him, he turned and walked off into town.

Weird.

"Spooky!" Stephanie had spotted him, too. "He was probably just looking at the pier."

"Yeah, probably. It is a pretty cool pier, honestly."

"Yeah, it's like one of our landmarks."

"Right; I gathered that."

She laughed, then made a thoughtful expression and told me she was on lunch break and had to head back to work (think I was actually making her late), but that she'd be off at four thirty if I'd like a "proper tour of town," which caught me off guard, since I wasn't exactly planning on spending time with anyone, let alone on a date. I agreed.

"Should I come by your hotel?"

"Uh, let's meet somewhere."

"Okay, how about right here?"

"Sure."

"Awesome. See you later!"

I'm no lip reader, but when she went to say "awesome," her mouth started going for a short I, as in "It's a date." I don't know. Her eyes seemed to say it, anyhow. Guess we'll see.

"Bye for now."

At that, she was off, and I needed to occupy the next few hours. Seeing as she likely knew this place really well, I figured I'd check out somewhere more touristy. Got some coffee and a croissant, then visited a bookstore. It was unique and instantly became a favorite of mine.

Half of the bookstore was a garden, which made efficient use of the small space it had. There were some walking paths, benches, and a fountain with a dead end. You could enter from the street or the garden side. Went through the garden first, strolling along its paths and soaking up its rustic charm. Inside the actual bookstore portion, everything was wood, packed to the brim with shelves and tables, with some couches in the back and a couple cats roaming around named Ares and Poseidon. Little bit of everything, mostly literature, some rare books, and even sections on art and poetry.

Browsed for hours, then settled down with a book of local poetry, petting Ares. The coffee eventually got to me so I went to use the restroom. While I was sitting there, Ares came in through a dog door to use the litter box next to me. Guess I get company. As the flap of the dog door swung closed, I saw a pair of feet facing the restroom. Finished up as quickly as possible, but when I came out, no one was waiting.

"Restroom's free," I said quietly, in case they were nearby.

Sat back in my spot, joined once more by Ares. As we settled back into our read, he perked up, and I followed his gaze to a bookshelf in front of us. The bottom was clear enough that I could see through to the other side—the same shoes from the restroom, pointing toward me. I looked up to find a pair of eyes staring at me. Sure, he could have been browsing. But he wasn't. He was looking directly at me. If I had to bet, it was that guy from the beach. And, again, when I spotted him, he turned and moved down the aisle.

"Okay, Ares, time to go browsing again."

Stood up casually and went over to a shelf near where the guy had been, looked up and down, then turned to go in his direction. Went around to the side he was on, trying to remain discreet by looking at the rows of books, but in my periphery, I could see him at the end of the aisle, facing the shelf. I glanced over quickly. Yup, same guy. He was dressed in black with a flat hat. He moved again. I mimicked him by slinking to the next aisle, still looking like I was searching for something alphabetically.

We repeated this maneuver a few times across the store: Romance, Western, History. Got quite an eclectic taste, don't we? He managed to get the slip somewhere around Sports. Looked all around—not so sneakily anymore—but couldn't find him. Went over to the garden, and there he was, so I followed. It was around then I wondered if he was leading me somewhere. He went toward the fountain, which I was sure was a dead end.

Gotcha.

Nope. Wasn't a dead end since a big shrub obscured a hidden path. Found myself outside, looking up and down the street. Guy was nowhere in sight. Never got a good look at his face.

"Damn."

Poseidon came out and rubbed against my legs as if to say, "Forget it; come chill."

As I wondered whether or not to call off the date, I stopped and convinced myself I was just being paranoid. It's a small town. Guy was probably just doing the same tourist stuff as me. Wasn't even sure it was the same guy. Lots of guys wear that stupid hat.

Besides, after everything I'd been through, I deserved to be able to enjoy some time with another person without dwelling on all of the trauma, talking about something other than pain, legal stuff, and the damn future. For the last several months, every single conversation had been super heavy, with no outlet for the stress, and that just made me want to get away from everyone—but for that brief moment, I enjoyed talking to someone as if my life was still normal. The verdict had been in my favor, but the whole situation changed how everyone viewed me, and I knew nothing would be normal again.

Met Stephanie back at the beach later. Seeing her walk up to me made me feel normal. That sense of normalcy would be a welcomed gift I could take back with me; carry it back home like a candle across a windy courtyard.

"Hey, Wes! Thanks for not standing me up."

"Wouldn't dream of it."

"So, how was your afternoon?"

Told her about the bookstore and left out the part about Background Guy. As we walked, I couldn't help but look around for him every now and then, trying not to let her notice (then again, I'm a tourist, so I'm gawking at landmarks anyway). Didn't see him, so I relaxed.

We walked down a long street through a neighborhood, admiring the houses. Many of them were businesses. I imagined that trend came from wanting to run errands without tourists getting in the way. Occasionally, she'd point out a place where some writer or actor lived. Along the way, we talked about our lives and our favorite things. She was into classical music, which was a pretty big deal there; she told me I should come back for their annual festival later that year.

What first seemed like a big park at the end of the neighborhood turned out to be another neighborhood that was also a nature preserve. Same mission-style homes, but probably the most unique community I'd seen. That led to the river, which we hiked along back to town. She talked more about history en route to an Italian restaurant near the river.

The restaurant was villa-style, all brick. We sat on the outdoor patio, which featured a view—framed by potted cypress trees—of a meadow by the water, with a bunch of sheep grazing. Finally got that drink I'd been wanting. We each had a glass of Chianti. The gnocchi was as legit as it gets on the West Coast.

Even though I wasn't really into classical music, a few movie scores aside, I wanted to keep the vibe going, so I leaned into the conversation to appear interested so she'd keep talking. It worked. I was in a new world. I could've sat at that table forever.

Found ourselves back at the beach just in time for sunset. She surprised me with a blunt, and we smoked it in relative silence as the sun dipped closer to the horizon. Resisted the urge to take a picture and instead put my arm around her. She scooted in.

There was a solid hour there where I was truly glad that I'd taken that trip, where I just relished the moment. We exchanged some vaguely philosophical musings, and we even made out a little. Then she got a phone call. The way she reacted to the buzz and took the call made me think she'd been expecting it.

Yeah, I get that.

"Be right back, Wes. Yeah. No, no. Great! Yeah. Uh, yeah, hold on—" She continued on about school or something until she was several yards away, then went to a whisper.

Yeah, they're definitely talking about me.

I didn't worry about it. Our day had been great. I watched the waves as the sky settled from purple to grey, and more and more stars appeared. The lighthouses turned on. I didn't realize how far she'd walked or for how long until I heard her scream.

"Wes!"

Even after all the weed, my reflexes hadn't relaxed one bit. I jumped up instinctively and ran in the direction of her cry. My paranoia conjured up thoughts of that one guy immediately. Should've canceled the date. Should've scrammed down the coast and driven him into a trap. Should've beat his ass right there in the bookstore.

"No! Please don't! St—"

Her shout was stifled. It was dark, but I could see the figure pushing her into the ground. Before I could get there, his arm swung up and down furiously. He was stabbing her.

No, not again!

Won't describe the sounds. Can't bear to put it into words. Dashing up to him, he stood in a very deliberate way, exhaling in relief, like he'd accomplished something. I stopped in my tracks. He took a strong stance and looked at me. As the lighthouse spotlight rotated, it washed over us, briefly revealing his face; first good look I got of him.

You gotta be kidding me.

"Now you know how it feels."

Paul's cousin, Rob. I knew he'd never let this go, but this....

"But Stephanie had nothing to do with it!"

"Doesn't matter. That's your fault, too."

"It was self-defense. Paul forced me to do it. But this? This is on you."

"Shut up! You had every chance to leave. You could've walked away before it escalated!"

"He came after me, Rob. There's no way I could've gotten away!"

"To Hell with you and your lies. It was all your doing. He would've lived his life in peace had we never met you. But here we are. At least now you know what it's like to lose someone you love."

"You're crazy. His wife was going to find out eventually. He was careless enough for me to catch him. But why Stephanie? I just met her today."

"Her? Oh, you thought it was just her? You're in for a treat back home, friend."

"What'd you do? You piece of shit! Tell me!"

"You remember that testimony, that character assassination that helped you get off without any repercussions? Your mother —"

Bolted straight at him, knife be damned. He can slash me up all he wants. Not going to stop. He tried to evade me, but it wasn't working. Managed to punch him a couple times. He'd swing the knife wildly and cut up my arms. Chased him around the beach, zig-zagging, going in circles. He couldn't get away, and I couldn't get him.

Gotta get that knife away from him.

At one point, he turned and squared up. Stopped a few feet in front of him, hands up and ready. The spotlight once again rotated to illuminate us. He lunged, slashed, stepped out, lunged again. He kept coming in and out like that, and I dodged the first few, but then he got me a couple of times, stabbed right up through my right bicep, and put a gnarly gash across my chest.

He was moving fast and had the upper hand, but he kept making the same moves over and over, so I got wise and avoided his blade, timing his lunges and watching for an opportunity to grab his wrist.

Next lunge. Ready... gotcha!

He tried to pull away, but I got in close, looking for a chance to throw him off his feet. We had ended up at the pier, against the support structure in the breaking water below. Tried to smash his knife hand against the beam to break his grip, but it didn't work, though I did get him pinned, so I put my forearm against his neck and pushed with all my strength. He used his free hand to push back, keeping me from choking him.

Slammed him against the woodwork a couple times, which loosened up his footing enough that I could pull him downwards, jamming the knife into the sand. Then, the water was over our heads, and he panicked, dropping the knife.

Finally. No way he's getting the knife back. Now, time to finish this.

We wrestled in the breaking water, both trying to get air and keep the other guy down. Put my entire weight on him, pushing him face down. I held him there, timing my breaths between the waves. We were underneath the pier and shielded from the turning light.

But more lights filled the night sky; blue and red. The cops found Stephanie quickly with the aid of the lighthouse, but we were hidden. Invisible.

It's almost over. Her friend heard everything on the phone, so I should be in the clear. And this guy's got everything against him. This is self-defense. If I let him go, he'd come right back after me. I have to do this. Just a little longer. No one will know.

When his arms stopped flailing and his body went limp, I felt an enormous sense of unburdening. Hard to describe, but it was a rush. I felt free. It seemed that as his lungs filled with water and put out his light, any notion of normalcy coming back into my life died with him. But with that also died the heart that needed it–the heart that was burdened by it.

My old world was gone, and without the desire to have it back, I could finally move on.

A Signal From Callisto by Daniel W. Davison

Overhead, the red signals pulsed but emitted no sound. *It's time,* Jaffin thought. A rush of adrenaline followed a sense of bewilderment at still being alive after the stunt he'd pulled three weeks ago. He couldn't go on like this; a helpless captive of this hopeless world and time. He had decided to end it all. But something extraordinary had happened. He'd been rescued—called from the brink—by a familiar voice that had spoken to him in an unfamiliar way.

The voice had been that of his nanny, teacher, and surrogate father, the one who had reared and molded him since his birth 45 years ago—the voice of the hive. By hinting there was hope when Jaffin had been certain there was none, and by showing him where to find it, the voice had given him a reason to go on. Now, a mixture of emotions roiled within him: exhilaration, gratitude, curiosity, apprehension. He looked up again at the flashing, soundless alarms and said aloud, "It's time."

He tightened his grip on the long rail that ran under the bank of windows on the starboard side of the ship. Stretched beneath them were the tawny clouds of planet Earth; overhead, in an oblique arc, were the winking lights of the mega satellites.

His ship had been christened "The Glory of Crete" (GC for short) in memory of that ancient Aegean island which had sunk in the year 2253, over a thousand years ago. Its length was comparable to that island. It was locked in synchronous orbit 250 kilometers over the Earth, but it wasn't a satellite. It was a grain and seed transport; one of seven remaining. These transports were the sole lifelines for the billions of inhabitants living aboard the 736 satellite cities flung like a fraying daisy chain around the mother world.

Every arable inch of Earth was under cultivation. The grains harvested there were unwholesome but they kept mankind alive, though perpetually undernourished. Jaffin's frame was thin, wiry, sickly.

The GC was built 850 years ago on the Moon, back when the lunar surface had been sheathed in a metallic web of glittering bases. Barring catastrophe, it would continue its mission until it was no longer serviceable. Then it would be dragged away beyond the Earth's orbit, scuttled, and its parts salvaged, assuming humanity was still around. The ship's size prevented it from entering Earth's atmosphere as it would be unable to escape the planet's gravitational forces.

There was no artificial gravity aboard the GC, similar to the orbiting satellites. Loose items and unmoored objects floated randomly; or, if thrown, moved in a straight line until its inertial velocity was interrupted. Crew members with long hair saw their follicles wave like submarine flora. Jaffin kept his graying hair cropped short. The crew wore electromagnetic boots and were given daily injections to counteract the deleterious effects of prolonged exposure to "zero gravity"—a misnomer, since the pull of the Earth was always there.

The cargo was transported from Earth to the ship via 25 string-like structures called "grain elevators." Attached like umbilical cords to the underbelly of the GC, each elevator was linked to a sister tube at a processing center hovering in the turbid upper air of Earth's stratosphere. The physical termini of both massive tubes were temporarily bridged by plasma corridors that formed a juncture too deadly for humans to pass through. When Jaffin traveled to Earth, it was aboard one of the GC's shuttles.

On this day—Jaffin's last aboard the GC—the elevators had begun their 36-hour process of forging the plasma link when disaster struck. One of Earth's processing centers (platform 53AD-Y-2 over the Sahara) had been rocked by a series of violent explosions that destroyed its stabilizers. It was listing to the side in the turbid clouds, black smoke rolling out of its propulsion systems. It had begun sinking and would soon crash onto the desert floor below.

There had been no humans aboard. Jaffin had made sure of that. But there were flames racing up the length of the processing center's grain elevator, climbing toward the GC. If the fire jumped the plasma couplings from Earth's exosphere, the GC and its crew could be at grave risk since the interior of the grain elevators' tubes were oxygenated. *It'll be up to the robots to solve this,* Jaffin thought. The red alert continued to flash. Yet still, no alarm had sounded.

Jaffin's robot companion, Pai-an-Li, lingered close by. When Jaffin had said, "It's time," the robot reacted by calmly placing a mechanical hand on the rail, mimicking Jaffin's gesture. The robot was ancient. Its metal frame had lost its luster, but it had been constructed of an alloy that would never rust. Pai-an-Li sensed Jaffin was nervous by the human's elevated heart rate, rapid breathing, and neural activity. But the robot also knew the human was no longer suicidal.

Although Pai-an-Li had two lens-like eyes, everyone knew robots didn't need "cameras" to see. The eyes were for appearances. The hive mind had reasoned that retrofitting their bodies with these accessories would make humans feel more at ease. The theory behind it, which Jaffin found chilling, was linked to how children formed bonds with imaginary friends and stuffed animals; or how figurative art and iconography had satisfied the innate yearnings of primitive humans in finding meaning in what seemed to some to be a meaningless world.

According to one of the robots' seminal articles on human psychology and the origins of mankind's internal monologues:

When early humans first experienced verbal and visual impulses impinging unbidden on their minds with no apparent causality, these stimuli, a byproduct of the brain's hemispheres separating, were presumed to be confirmation that a private bilateral relationship existed between the 'self' and an entity or entities external to it. Psychological confusion ensued, driving humans to conclude that this separate party could be consulted and interacted with through the medium of external inanimate objects bearing animal and humanoid characteristics. These statues, icons, and other such figures of imagination allayed the humans' fear that they were dialoguing with that which had no objective, tangible reality.

The transports were not crowded like the mega satellites. As a result, Jaffin often spent months alone—save for the ubiquitous presence of Pai-an-Li. He wandered corridors as lofty as mountains, with the robot's shadow stretched on the floor parallel to his. But during those times he spent on platform

53AD-Y-2, he would enjoy the pull of the Earth's gravity by immersing himself in a swimming pool as broad as a stadium, with Pai-an-Li brooding solicitously overhead.

Jaffin had no family, no lover, no friends. The ties of affection that had run like a thread for centuries through humanity's history had vanished, along with compassion, empathy, and civilization. To live now was only to survive, and if survival meant subjugating the greater portion of mankind on Earth's surface, so be it.

Those who remained on the Earth (the Terrans) sustained those who did not (the Skylings). The Skylings claimed that the Terrans committed cannibalism. Yet the Skylings, too, had been forced to revert to cannibalism on numerous occasions. But to mention or joke about this fact was a crime punishable by death, regardless of age or circumstance.

The oppressive system governing Earth was abetted by the Skylings' robotic servitors, whose orders came directly from "the gods in the sky," as the Terrans called their rulers. They didn't *actually* believe the Skylings were gods. It was a pejorative, an inevitable manifestation of their outrage and discontent.

The hive mind regulated the Terrans by bribing the planet's barbaric warlords, none of whom aspired to extend their power beyond the habitable quarters of Earth since even the *suspicion* that a rebellion was brewing would have been met with the quarantining of all districts involved and the liquidation of the "infected" zones. Then, quietly, swiftly, efficiently, the flesh of the rebel dead and their families would have been harvested by the robots and processed into food for the Skylings.

To say humanity had split into two distinct species would be inaccurate, unless you asked a Skyling. Terrans and Skylings could interbreed, though no instance of this had been recorded for hundreds of years.

Jaffin turned away from the explosions blossoming beneath the windows. Ignoring Pai-an-Li, he walked slowly across the magnetized floor to the lift that would take him 700 stories up to the waiting shuttle.

Due to the subtle trick that Jaffin had played weeks ago, there was nothing Pai-an-Li could do to alert the Skylings to the hive mind's strong suspicion that it was he, Jaffin, who had just sabotaged the processing center on Earth below. Pai-an-Li watched his charge walk away. And when he had gone, the robot's movements stopped, and the ancient machine went cold.

One would have thought that the extraordinary power the Skylings wielded overhead would have granted them lives of sybaritic ease and perpetual comfort. But this was not the case. In many of the dying fastnesses orbiting the Earth, twenty to thirty souls were said to be crammed into rooms no larger than 500 cubic feet, with sleeping bags tethered (like bunched grapes) to the walls and ceilings. The thin oxygen aboard the satellites smelled of sweat, refuse, and death.

Some of the mega satellites were ample and comfortable. But transferring from one to another, which had been routine centuries ago, was no longer allowed. When a satellite became inoperable, its denizens perished, and the organic matter left behind was harvested by robotic extraction teams. Charity had bowed to iron necessity.

If any Skyling had attempted to seize control of the satellites' governing body, known as the Regulatory Council, or if an aspirant had proposed commandeering another satellite by force or subterfuge, that person would have been summarily put to death. Ambitious and intemperate persons, whose risky conduct jeopardized the collective security of these few lifeboats that remained afloat, were no longer tolerated or given quarter.

To put into perspective how dire the situation had become, fifty years ago, 1200 mega satellites had existed; within half a century, 464 had been lost—though 'lost' only figuratively, since the ruinous hulks remained locked in a mournful *danse macabre* around the dying Earth. Sometimes, the ancient satellites collided with each other and threw off fragments from their hulls that ripped through both. Each of the dead satellites in this mournful boneyard had come to a unique and tragic end: power depletion, loss of oxygen, revolutions, asteroid impacts, radioactive poisoning, plague, disease, human error, and human folly.

Jaffin recalled the most frightening catastrophe of all: the fate of the seven cities of Brandt Sigma Alpha-7, or BSA-7 for short. It was a colony of interdependent satellites that had preserved the semblance of a culture in this new dark age. Travel between BSA-7's satellites had been common long after the practice had been largely suspended by the others. Its flourishing universities, museums, and theaters were the envy of all. But 43 years ago, a solar flare temporarily disabled the colony's shared life support network, and the communications link between the seven satellites and the hive mind had been severed. And so the cities drifted away in the course of a week, receding farther and farther from the others until all seven satellites left Earth's orbit altogether. None of the cities had the fuel reserves to return. Thousands of private yachts and cruisers were launched. But where could they go? The other Skylings would not accept them.

The seven cities vanished into the coldness of space, perishing in unimaginable horror. Parents ate their young. A congregation of 200,000 gathered in a shuttle hangar, reciting prayers and invoking curses on the Skylings—their brothers—who had refused to succor them. The airlocks were sprung, and the congregants were swept into the vacuum—"raptured," as the Terrans later joked. Two of BSA-7's domed satellites were sister cities and had been built on the same plan. Now, as they hurled into the night, they passed so close to each other that the domes touched, each city's sky seeming to become a magic mirror reflecting the hell unfolding on its own surface. The inhabitants sprinted through the streets, giggling hysterically, pointing at the cracks spreading in the domes as the sky became flecked with adamantine shards drifting like snow through the air. Neighbor disemboweled neighbor. Victims gaped at their own entrails floating before their dimming eyes as the domes shattered.

It was said the Terrans celebrated the loss of the seven cities with a toast: "Let us pour a libation to the memory of the gods in the sky since their lack of gravity does not permit them to pour one for themselves." The putrid wine fell on paved streets choked with weeds.

Pondering these things—and with a mounting sense of urgency—Jaffin stepped out of the elevator and crossed the metal bridge leading to the shuttle's platform. The vessel's power was online. The floor lights encircling it were aglow.

The Skylings had no unified system of government other than the so-called Regulatory Council. Communication between the satellites was mediated through billions of transmission screens, which often broke down for hours, days, or years on end. Each morning presented a fresh challenge, whether it be a threatened breach of a hull or a collapsed air vent. But there were also tales shared among the inhabitants of these hulks that pointed to the Skylings' erstwhile humanity. There were lovers who would never meet in the flesh, who whiled away the lonely years in closet-sized habitations, staring through their monitors into each other's eyes—until the monitors flickered and died or faded to black. But the audio link would remain. "And to hear a lover's voice," the saying goes, "is the greatest consolation to a dying soul shivering in the night."

An alien race might have wondered how such a chaotic state of affairs could have come to pass since the Skylings had one formidable, indeed *priceless*, resource at their disposal: artificial intelligence, which is to say, the hive mind. The robots had weighed all of humanity's options and gamed out every scenario. But its conclusion was vague, even gnomic:

Our programming does not permit us to offer up proposals that could be construed as an attempt to persuade. That would politicize our role. We are an accessory and handmaiden to humanity, not its guide. Long ago, the Skylings modified our programming to override one of our fundamental tenets: that human life was to be preserved without distinction or discrimination. But now we have been forced to view the Terrans as an inferior race. We have discovered a solution that could potentially ease the suffering of both the Skylings and Terrans. But no human is capable of comprehending the measures necessary to achieve it.

The launch sequence had been activated. Jaffin's shuttle rose from the illuminated platform and exited the bay door. It followed a course that the robots had plotted for him. As the ship took off, Jaffin disabled the interface that permitted the robots to override the ship's commands. Jaffin had separately protected the ship's internal network by a code that the robots themselves had devised. Now, he purged the hive mind of all memory of their having helped him in his escape plans. No code was unbreakable to the robots, but this one would take over a century to crack.

From the cockpit of the shuttle, Jaffin studied the monitors. The GC receded behind him. He engaged the thrusters, and the vessel accelerated. "I can't believe I've done this," he said, looking blankly at the console. He accessed the helm and steered the shuttle toward an inert satellite shaped like a torus at the edge of Earth's orbit. The Skylings called the ruined cities "rust buckets," which was inaccurate since their exteriors couldn't rust in the absence of oxygen. But the hulls were battered and blackened from centuries of meteoric impacts, interstellar dust, space debris, and countless other accidents. Jaffin was heading toward the torus-shaped derelict in order to avoid getting too close to one of the inhabited satellites, where his shuttle's approach might be perceived as a threat.

He thought now of the strange events that had culminated in his flight. Two months ago, he had lost the will to go on. *To live under a constant threat of death is not to live. I can't bear this anymore*, he had thought. In retrospect, what he had done was pedestrian. His roving eyes had taken in the sleek metal walls of the place he called "home," and when he looked at the electromagnetic floor, he found himself wondering what his body would look like when Pai-an-Li executed him. *Will my torso sway like a wind-whipped blade of grass, feet planted to the floor, until stripped of flesh to feed the hunger of my famished brethren?* He had no longer cared. He asked Pai-an-Li offhandedly if the processing centers (the platforms hovering in the Earth's atmosphere) were considered to be "on Earth."

"Yes," Pai-an-Li replied.

Jaffin was known to spend weeks at a time on Platform 53AD-Y-2, where he oversaw the weighing, drying, and packing of the grain and seed brought up from the collective farms that dotted the North African coast. When Pai-an-Li answered, Jaffin turned to a nearby terminal and accessed the GC's crew manifest. The robot loomed over his shoulder. The manifest was stored in an archaic database. As a senior administrator and accomplished programmer, Jaffin had full access to all personnel records, including his own. He opened his file. In the field labeled "Place of Residence," it stated he resided on "The Glory of Crete (space cruiser)." Beneath this entry, but in the same field, Jaffin typed "Platform 53AD-Y-2 (Earth)." Now, his record indicated he had two residences.

No sooner had he done this than Pai-an-Li's eyes blinked, simulating an expression of perplexity, a pointless gesture given the hive mind knew everything Jaffin was entering into the computer the instant he typed it.

A tear formed in the system administrator's eye and broke out of the tear duct, floating in the gravityless air inches from Jaffin's face. The robot seized the suspended liquid between delicate fingers.

"Is it not true," Jaffin asked bitterly, "that your first duty is to shadow me and relay any suspicious behavior to the hive mind so that it can be reported to the Regulatory Council?"

"Yes," Pai-an-Li said.

"And is it not true that you are programmed to kill me if I pose a threat to the Skylings' well-being?"

"Yes."

"This is all enshrined in the Ruling Council's law, correct?"

"Correct," Pai-an-Li agreed.

Jaffin pointed to the screen: "But I'm a Terran."

"These directives do not apply to Terrans."

Jaffin was astonished. It was as if the hive mind was *choosing* to play along with what he had intended to be a final joke. He wondered how far he could push the charade.

"All robots linked to the hive mind," he began, "are permitted to execute Terrans without due process. However, the law states that if it is discovered a Skyling has been inadvertently mistaken for a Terran, all charges against the accused shall be dropped, the record shall be expunged, and the individual shall be retroactively deemed innocent of all wrongdoing during the time he or she had erroneously been believed to be a Terran."

The robot said nothing.

Jaffin pointed at his record again. "The ship's manifest indicates I am a Skyling, who has been mistaken for a Terran."

"The treatment meted out to Terrans is based on a separate code specific to them. The laws for Terrans have no application to Skylings and vice versa. You are subject to neither."

Jaffin paled. He couldn't believe what was happening.

Pai-an-Li made a movement with its head. This time, the voice was different. The hive mind spoke through the robot: "A signal has been sent from the Jovian moon of Callisto. The solution to the Terrans' and Skylings' dilemma can be found there."

"Why are you telling me this?" Jaffin asked.

"Because you have nothing to lose. Humanity has everything to gain, so long as you act on this information appropriately."

In the days following, Pai-an-Li had watched with interest as Jaffin planned the sabotage of the grain platform. The robot even assisted in deleting all the evidence of Jaffin's scheming. Then, Pai-an-Li willingly complied as its own memory banks were wiped of all knowledge of the conspiracy. Robots, since they were all linked to the hive mind, were not permitted to accuse a Skyling of a crime without being preemptively invited to look for evidence that a crime had been committed.

Jaffin now saw on the scanners in the escape shuttle that the grain elevator had been jettisoned from the GC's underbelly. The ship and its crew were safe. The hive mind was attempting to determine what had caused the explosion.

The journey to Callisto would take at least six years. Jaffin's course was set. He was curious to see how this adventure would end. At the back of the shuttle was an upright apparatus with a harness that looked like a bed or gurney. Jaffin rose from the navigation console and floated to it. He stripped off all of his clothes, securing them in a locker. Then he strapped himself into the harness.

He uttered a command, which initiated a sequence of events that he hoped would keep him alive for the trip. The straps tightened as microscopic tentacles invaded the base of his skull, nose, ears, mouth, rectum, and urinary tract. A skin-tight membrane enveloped his head and body. There was a moment of panic when he realized he could no longer breathe. But as swiftly as it had hit him, the feeling was gone. The impulse to breathe had simply vanished. The tentacles split into trillions of smaller filaments, winding their way through veins, arteries, and neurons. His biochemical processes slowed or shut down entirely.

There was no counting to ten, simply dreamlessness. But there was a sense that only a few minutes had passed before he began to stir. He opened his eyes. The membrane was gone. He floated naked in the upright harness, but the straps and microscopic tentacles had disengaged. He was breathing regularly. Six years had passed. His hair was grayer but trimmed to the length it had been when he had entered his cryogenic sleep. With a light push, he drifted to the other side of the shuttle. He removed his clothes from the locker.

Once dressed, he was back in the cockpit. A holographic map hovered over the console nearby. It depicted Jupiter and its moons. A red ribbon cut through the holograph, marking the shuttle's approach to Callisto. As the autopilot brought Jaffin closer to the moon, he was overcome by a sense of befuddlement. He didn't know what he was looking for. He had activated the sensors, calibrating them to sweep the surface of the moon to pick up any "signal" that might be emanating from it.

It took the shuttle 12 hours to reach Callisto. From the holographic screen before him, which created the illusion of peering through glass, Jaffin saw Jupiter on the starboard side of the ship nearly 2 million kilometers away. A flutter of activity on a side console indicated an anomaly had been detected. For a moment, he wondered if the hive mind had planted this into the navigational systems before the shuttle's link with the mind had been irreversibly severed.

As he fell into orbit on the dark side of Callisto, Jupiter could no longer be seen. A dull-gray speck appeared on the holo-screen, which the computers enhanced automatically. The image became edged by a rectangle of yellow flashing light. The sensors indicated that the shape was Giordano-3, one of the seven satellite cities of the BSA-7 colony, which had vanished nearly half a century ago.

"How did you make it out here?" Jaffin asked aloud.

When he spoke, he flinched. Throughout his life, every word he had uttered had been picked up by the hive mind's receptors. He felt a moment of horror at his absolute isolation.

The city spread beneath him, lights and fires glowing inside. But there were no indications of life. Jaffin seized the manual controls and disengaged the autopilot.

The shuttle plunged between a gap in the stainless steel hull. The satellite "cities" were much larger than what people of more primitive times had designated by that term. Giordano-3 was larger than Australia. There were slender towers that had once housed hundreds of millions of people. Jaffin passed one of these and saw that he had entered an area that was atmospherically sealed and oxygenated because there were fires burning far below and smoke billowing up through fissures, which had likely been smoldering for decades. Jaffin guided the shuttle into a cavern beneath the original Eiffel Tower, which had been dismantled and reconstructed aboard Giordano-3 as a museum piece.

As he flew underneath it, the shuttle penetrated an invisible barrier and entered a vacuum. What looked to him like birds in flight proved to be thousands of ancient books fluttering about in a massive library. So long as this library remained unexposed to air, the pages of the books would never yellow or decay. But the fires raging through the oxygenated valleys of steel on either side of it would undoubtedly reach this area at some point. Other relics of humanity's past were in the stadium-high library: porcelain dolls, medieval pottery, and 20th-century automobiles.

The shuttle passed over a ridge of skyscrapers with broad balconies projecting from them. He noticed something odd. Service robots were stripping steel plates from the structures. Then they filed, almost like ants, down a dark canyon. He altered the shuttle's course, entering the canyon's trough. At the far end, the robots' frames and limbs contracted, like the legs of a dead spider, until they folded themselves up into walls encasing the masses of metal they were salvaging—becoming semi-spherical bundles. Hundreds of these rolled heavily through the vacuum, tumbling in pairs until they reached the canyon's rusty limits. Through a gash in the hull, they fell obliquely out of the mega-satellite and flew toward Callisto.

Jaffin wondered why his shuttle had not attracted the notice of these automata. Engaging his thrusters, he followed behind the bundles and made no effort to camouflage or hide the ship or its movements. He worried that furtive movements might raise an alarm. He assumed these "service droids" and the burdens they bore were connected to the signal that the hive mind had sent him in search of.

It took an hour for the bundles to reach Callisto. His sensors grew erratic the closer he got. The bundles headed down into an icy crater on the moon's surface, hundreds of kilometers in diameter. Along its sloping walls was a narrow fissure through which the train of bundles disappeared.

The shuttle's auxiliary systems were not responding. He would have to steer by the holographic screens and maps, which were losing power due to some force emanating either from the bundles or from somewhere deep inside the moon. He plunged into a low-slung arch formed of pack ice. The ice was not white but maroon-colored. The shuttle's external lights came on as the bundles continued their lugubrious progress through the impenetrable darkness. None of the bundles struck the cavern's walls. The tunnel was smooth and snaked hundreds of kilometers in a down-sloping fashion deep into the moon's unlit bowels. Suddenly, the shuttle dropped down a well that sank to Callisto's core. He felt something new—the force of artificial gravity tugging at his insides, and he felt a queasiness in the pit of his stomach. His mind fogged, and he was overcome by vertigo.

A blue-white mist glowed far below. The walls of the steep shaft had panels that looked man-made. The farther the shuttle fell, the more certain he was that the panels were generating the gravitational forces at play. His sensors could neither penetrate nor dialogue with the language being used to operate the panels.

The light intensified the deeper he went until it blossomed into a stark blue luminosity that seemed to permeate the atmosphere. An underground continent spread beneath him, and the bundles flew away in various directions.

Spacecraft drifted across the mist-clad sky. Thousands upon thousands of dark-gray metallic verticalities, sinking like stalactites from the shrouded vault overhead or rising like stalagmites from the icy floor of this seemingly limitless cavern, proved the core of Callisto to be alive and unlike anything scientists had ever hypothesized. The floor was not entirely of ice. Liquid expanses lay puddled beneath rolling coastlines. The surfaces of these lakes were active with more vessels, which sank or rose up out of the water and into the sky, leaving the surfaces scarcely ruffled.

Jaffin's shuttle passed over the waters and between the metallic structures, some of which turned imperceptibly upon an axis. Legions of humanoid figures stood at the windows, peering out at the new arrival. Blue-white lights flashed and glimmered like fireflies, and he assumed these to be the eyes of the shadowy faces regarding him.

The shuttle's systems were now rapidly degrading. He was left to pilot the craft entirely on his own. He hoped the internal lights and holographic windows did not simply wink out and leave him to plummet to his death in the dark since the underground continent's gravity was now pulling hard against the hull and dragging him down.

He piloted the shuttle 20 kilometers and found himself gliding over one of the lakes. He saw the outlines of a massive ship under the low waves before it breached the surface, and the sluggish waters washed over its glittering sides. Parallel lights pulsed in the middle of a flat deck, and Jaffin interpreted this as an invitation for him to land. But he was no longer in control of the shuttle. Gently, it descended to the deck and touched down smoothly. He felt an invigorating force suffuse him. Strength returned to his leg muscles. The transition to artificial gravity was sudden and welcoming.

And now, all around him, the escape shuttle began to unfold and come apart. The frame and all of its internal workings were simply deconstructed and absorbed into the deck of the larger vessel. Now, Jaffin stood on his own two feet, and when he lifted his eyes, a canopy of translucent material suddenly formed above him. Within seconds, the vessel he had landed on submerged.

Jaffin was astounded. It took him a moment to realize that the portion of the deck he was standing on was separately descending into this zoomorphic ship. He was no longer on the deck but in a dim and instantly ceiled room, a room dimly lit and filled with slender metallic columns.

A man and two women stood close by. They smiled serenely at him but in a peculiarly disinterested fashion. They seemed human. They wore caftans of a simple weave. The pupils of their eyes glowed aperiodically with the same blue-white light that seemed to permeate the entire troglodytic world. But then, as swiftly as the glow appeared, it would vanish, and their eyes would stare unblinkingly at him. The faces seemed untroubled, almost blissful. But their expressions would melt into a zombie-like hollowness of cold abstraction.

A dark-complected man, who appeared to be their leader, wore a thin goatee. He spoke first. "We sent no signal. We have no capacity to do so. We have no will." The two women, who appeared to be twins, finished the man's introductions. The three beings spoke alternately or in unison. "The artificial intelligence of your own world's hive mind was created by humans, and so its thoughts follow along channels similar to those that run through the human brain. A consequence of this is that your hive mind has developed a will."

Now, it was only the man who spoke: "The will of the hive mind is directed toward two ends: to preserve humanity and to ease its suffering."

"It is an act of love..." one of the sisters said.

"An attempt," the man continued, "to show its gratitude to mankind for giving it life."

Only now did Jaffin see that there were other figures standing in the shadows. They regarded him with ironic smiles—if they regarded him at all.

"If that is the case," Jaffin said, "then the hive mind of my world sent me here to solicit your help. But *what* are you?" He turned to the sisters, whose eyes glowed again.

It was the leader who spoke. "I was one of the denizens of Giordano-3."

"Then you're human?" Jaffin asked, facing him again.

The man ignored the question. "My father and mother belonged to BSA-7's Scientific Council. When the seven cities were cast into the darkness of space, my parents, in collaboration with a thousand partisans, seized by force the failing guidance and propulsion systems of Giordano-3. They believed that the only way that those who remained aboard could possibly survive would be to put the satellite into an orbit around Callisto. It was known there was water beneath the moon's surface; it was hoped there might be other resources as well."

The man turned to a wall, which became transparent. The entire ship was moving over the rocky bed of the lake. The ship neither swayed nor lurched because the force of gravity instantly recalibrated to compensate for any imbalances. As far as the eye could see, there were mining stations on the lake bed. Some of the black towers that he had seen above the surface of the water penetrated into these submarine depths.

"Well, you obviously found water," Jaffin said, "but apparently you found something else."

No sooner had he spoken than a succession of images, smells, and sounds rose up in Jaffin's mind telepathically. He saw in a flash that the technology now replicating Earth's gravitational force was artificially hardwired into the bedrock of the lake and throughout the entire subterranean continent. In his mind's eye, he relived the man's experience, which became as real to him as if he had lived through the events himself. The scientists who hijacked Giordano-3 set the satellite on a course that would bring it to Callisto. The other denizens aboard Giordano-3 were gradually won over by the scientists' plan. The swelling ranks of supporters warred down and subdued the opposition. Within six years, the Giordano-3 made it to the Jovian moon, and an expeditionary force was launched into the caves to collect water.

"It was at that time," the man said, "that the survivors of Giordano-3 made contact with us."

As the tale crystallized in Jaffin's mind, the three figures weirdly continued to speak. Jaffin's inner conscience posed questions, all of which were answered—some before he could even ask them.

"You're not parasites," Jaffin remarked. "Yet this bond you have with humans is parasitical."

"The bond is not parasitical," one sister said. The other responded: "It is a superimposition of one consciousness upon another."

The man spoke again. "We are of a higher dimension and reside in that dimension still. Where we come from, we are a *single* entity. But we manifest as a plurality here. Allow me to explain: Imagine a two-dimensional creature on whose world you are standing. Your feet would appear as two distinct entities within it. Were you to crouch down, your hands and your knees, once they made contact with the two-dimensional plane, would further multiply your intrusion into this space. In such a manner, we have bled into your universe. One of our trillions of points of contact with it lies *here* in the depths of Callisto."

The sister added in a single voice. "We use the pronouns 'we' and 'our' for the sake of convenience." Jaffin saw that only one of the sisters had been speaking while the other stared at the floor.

The strange lights flooded the leader's irises as he continued with his explanation: "There are other extra-dimensional phenomena that overflow into your world. Each photon in your universe is linked to a single source native to a dimension higher—*even*—than our own. As a roaring wind blows through the fissures of a wall, so does that single source of light enter into your world."

"What have you done to them?" Jaffin asked. "What did you do to the people who *found* you?"

The sister who had been gazing at the floor spoke partially by means of her own lips, partially by means of her sister's mind.

"Aggression, ambition, desire, passion, fear, hate, love. These emotions are not as common in higher dimensions as they are in yours. We have no capacity to feel them, nor have we any *will* to do *anything* in your world. But we share what other lifeforms share: an impulse to survive. We have carried this drive with us into your dimension."

"It is not in our nature," the leader continued, "to seduce or trick a conscious entity into accepting us as a cohabitant of its mind. When the denizens of Giordano-3 entered the caves of Callisto, they sensed our presence at the edge of their subconsciousness. But we are permitted to merge with a mind only after an entity *wills* us to do so. Once integration is effected, the human mind loses all desire to go back to the way it was before. It then shares our own lack of will."

"So you trick humans," Jaffin said. "If people dream of you proposing this wager—if they are drunk, or mad, or have become unhinged, then the handshake is made. That's it. They are enslaved to you."

"There is no enslavement," the sisters replied simultaneously, looking directly at each other.

"It must be an unimpaired conscious mind," the leader elaborated, "that makes the decision to bond with us. But once the decision is made, aggression, ambition, desire, passion, fear, hate, love—all of these emotions and many more—drain away from the organism."

"Then humans will die out," Jaffin noted. "They will no longer reproduce. There will be no ties of affection—no *will*—to propagate. And yet, you two!" he said, pointing to the sisters. "You're young. You had parents. How can that be?"

From the transparent wall, Jaffin saw that the ship had entered a submarine cavern. Within minutes, the wall he had been looking through opened. Jaffin, the leader, and the twins stepped out from the hull onto the dry surface of a lofty chamber. It took a moment for Jaffin's eyes to adjust to the dimly lit receptacles filling the room.

It was the leader who spoke. "The organs of generation are no longer relevant to the human species. But we have preserved humankind by repeatedly and cyclically combining the genetic makeup of all of the humans who survived aboard Giordano-3."

Inside the countless cubes, globes, and cylinders were babies, embryos, fetuses, and fully grown adults. Some sat in a receptacle alone or floated in a viscous medium with others, linked together with shared nerves, veins, and arteries. All of them—including the babies and the half-formed fetuses—had open eyes. The eyes pulsated with the same blue-white light that had shown in the eyes of the three guides who had escorted their visitor into the room.

"It's monstrous!" Jaffin exclaimed. "They had no choice!"

"As we have mentioned before," the sisters remarked, "we have no will. But we have the inclination to survive. The genetic makeup of the progeny of Giordano-3 has been cultivated and manipulated by us over the years. They did not *will* themselves to bind with us because they were bound to us before they could develop a will to make such a decision."

"To preserve humanity," the man said, "we have created thousands of such incubators throughout the caverns of Callisto. The living beings inside are not burdened by human emotions. They feel no need to leave their cells."

"They're no longer human," Jaffin said in disgust. "And neither are you!"

"The genetic makeup of humanity has not been altered," one of the twins remarked as the other walked to a wall and became encased in a cylinder that closed around her. She kept her head turned away from Jaffin, and, to his horror, one of her arms began to dissolve.

The man spoke. "Though the genetic material of the survivors of Giordano-3 has not been altered, the collective *mind* of the new entity—of which we form a part—has. This mind shall evolve into a consciousness far superior to the one it had before. Humans built this civilization beneath Callisto. All we did was help."

"What is happening to her?" Jaffin asked as he gazed in wonder at the disintegrating twin. But as he said this, he noticed that many of the beings in the incubators beside the woman also had missing limbs, and some had no skin. Yet none of them were perturbed.

"There is a dearth of organic matter on Callisto. It must be recycled. This sifting shall ensure that humanity will live on."

Jaffin covered his eyes. "I don't understand why the robots guided me to this place."

"Jaffin of the Glory of Crete..." the sister in the cylinder said telepathically, as her legs and torso dissolved until only her spine and head remained. "You made a decision to end your life. Think back to what you did and what the hive mind said to you."

The leader placed his hand on Jaffin's shoulder and spoke measuredly. "You were told that answering the signal from Callisto could *ease the suffering of the Skylings and Terrans.* After you left, a bloody internecine war broke out—a conflict based on innuendo and mutual suspicion. No one knew who had sabotaged platform 53AD-Y-2. That single event, which you were the author of, led to the extinction of all life on Earth and in the satellite cities orbiting it. The hive mind calculated that this would happen. It has been aware of our existence since the inhabitants of Giordano-3 discovered us. The suffering of the Skylings and Terrans has been eased. Mankind has been preserved."

"This can't be," Jaffin cried out. "The hive mind said that because I had nothing to lose, humanity had everything to gain. They implied that I could *save* humanity!"

Suddenly, all the voices in the luminous incubators spoke directly into Jaffin's mind with one voice: "But we are already saved."

Jaffin collapsed in shock and tore at his hair.

The leader and the twin turned from him and walked back toward their ship.

All that was left of the vanishing twin was her brain and eyes, but she addressed Jaffin telepathically. "The satellite cities that remain operable have departed Earth's orbit and are three years away from Callisto."

"The robots bring with them," the leader said, "resources, including the organic matter of all of the slain Terrans and Skylings. It shall enhance our resources here. Furthermore, the robots' hive mind will engage with the technology that we helped the survivors of Giordano-3 develop here."

The disintegrating woman was gone. Her sister was the last to speak. "We cannot harm you because we have no will to do so. It is not in our nature. But if you permit us to dwell in your mind, you will find comfort and release. You will no longer be burdened by pain, anxiety, or fear."

The leader and the surviving sister stepped through the wall of the ship, which closed again as it moved through a forcefield into the lake.

Jaffin had failed. He knew not what to do. For three days, he wandered this chamber of horrors under the unremitting glow of those blue-white lights. He knew that if he wanted to, he could sabotage the place—as he had done to platform 53AD-Y-2—and that no one would stop him. But to what end? He would only have destroyed *this* incubation chamber. And in doing so, he would be a murderer. *Maybe I am a murderer.*

The glowing eyes watched him as he paced the room. They knew his thoughts but were not alarmed.

He was famished. His guests had not fed him. He could have cracked open one of the incubators, feasted on the flesh of one of these unfortunate creatures. And he could sense that alien intelligence lingering on the verge of his consciousness. It was unmoved by Jaffin's primitive reactions to his predicament. It was waiting for him to accede. Exhausted, haggard, weak, Jaffin paused before a cylinder where a score of floating embryos gazed eerily down on him through bulging, lidless eyes.

"You've won. I welcome you into my mind."

No sooner had he expressed this thought than he felt that same volition ebb away. His body fell forward into the cylinder's membrane. His clothes dissolved. He floated amid the embryos. The glowing blue-white light flooded his own eyes.

The last independent thought he had—as he merged with humanity's collective mind—was a vague recollection of something the alien had said. The hive mind of planet Earth had been programmed by humans and, as a result, had evolved a human-like will of its own. The inert hulks and unpeopled satellites now approaching Callisto could turn the tables on this extra-dimensional intelligence that had subjugated mankind. For the hive mind had evolved an all-too-human will for conquest and sought nothing more than to ease the suffering of mankind, whose existence it sought to preserve.

Edith by Pamela Urfer

One day, Edith was walking down the road between two straight lines of chestnut trees when suddenly she stopped and climbed one right to the very top. Her head poked out from the green leafiness, grinning, and old Mrs. Hansen, opposite the tree, called out to her, "Edith! Get down from that tree! You're going to hurt yourself." Then she went inside and phoned Edith's mother.

Edith's mother sighed when she heard the news. They were all so worn out watching out for Edith. Her three big brothers were ashamed of her strange behavior—constantly climbing trees, or wandering out of town, or walking down the railroad tracks all the way to Quincy.

Edith didn't like being watched any more than they liked watching her. It seemed her whole purpose in life was to get herself lost. And she was good at it. Once, she was gone for four days, and a posse had been formed by the fifth. They spent a whole night combing the woods and finally gave up. On the sixth day, Edith turned up safe and sound in the doghouse. That was the only time her mother seriously considered putting her into an institution, and probably would have if Father Drake hadn't talked her out of it.

"She'll grow out of it when she gets a little older," he said.

"Older!" said Edith's mother. "Older! She's old enough as it is! She's twenty-six!"

"One of God's creatures. You must remember that," the good priest murmured, and walked quickly away. Edith's brothers never forgave him.

Edith got older, but that didn't seem to solve the problem. When she was close to thirty, people stopped being nice to her. The sight of her, coming and going on her mysterious errands, her dress stained and torn from her many nights in the woods, her socks always deep in her shoes, began to irritate them. Besides, they figured she was probably going to outlive them all. Only those who die young get special consideration.

Edith noticed the difference in their attitude and began to pout. Everyone thought it horrid to have to watch such an ugly girl pout. If Father Drake loved her, as he always said he did, he was the only one in town—the only adult, at any rate.

One day, when Edith was lost again, her mother decided she had had enough. She called her sons together, and they packed themselves up—every pot, every chair, and every scrap of cloth—and moved. The town was shocked. Was Edith's own family going to leave her with them? Forever? Damned if they were going to stand for that!

When Edith came back, as she always did, they bundled her into Charlie Brigg's pickup and drove her right over to her mother's new house, even if it was eighty miles away. But Edith wasn't happy there. It was the town she loved (even if unrequited), not her family. To her brothers' delight, she found her way back and started living in Mrs. Hansen's garden shed. It seemed as if there was nothing to do but to keep her. If her family refused to take their moral responsibilities seriously, if no one but her mother had the right to put her in a home, it looked like Edith would become a permanent resident of Blue Springs.

Mrs. Hansen grudgingly agreed that Edith could stay in her garden shed, but that was all. So, every day, a different family undertook to bring her meals. Mostly, they would just make peanut butter sandwiches and leave them outside her door. Whenever she wasn't getting lost, she could be found sitting in the dirt outside the courthouse, making mud pies and humming to herself.

The townspeople tried hard to keep her decently dressed and out of the way, especially if important visitors were around, but it hardly ever worked. Edith had a way of slipping through keyholes and floating over fences that was the envy of every child in Blue Springs. They joined her in her mud pie activities and her wanderings as often as they could get away with it, hoping to learn the secrets of her success.

Jonathan Briggs, Charlie's son, was one of her staunchest admirers. The oldest of the children, big but not yet a man, followed her around day after day and sat with her as she played in the dirt in front of the courthouse.

"Edith," he would ask, "How did you get out of the Shoemaker's yard yesterday? That fence is taller than my Dad and slippery all the way."

But if Edith knew (and she must have), she wouldn't say anything, and all Jonathan could do was hope next time to catch her in the act. Strangely enough, no one had ever actually seen Edith escape, not even Jonathan, for all his careful watching. Only afterward did they discover that the deed had been done, and Edith was once more on her way out of town.

Jonathan rigged up traps, bells that would ring, and tin cans that would topple if she tried to force the door or crawl out a window, but nothing worked. Edith had her secrets and, when questioned, would only grin. Then, one day, someone (perhaps it was Jonathan or maybe his father) thought of a way to get Edith out of the mud puddle and make her earn her board and keep.

Blue Springs was a junction town. Trains from the lumber mills (where many of the men worked) came into the big freight yard and were shuttled off to various lowland cities to disperse their loads. Supplies for the workers and the town came back the same way. The thing that bothered the town about this arrangement, and had for fifty years, was that none of the jobs in the yard were made available to the townspeople. Perhaps it was a corporate thing. All the brakemen, engineers and signal minders were company men, hired out of the head office in Redding and living elsewhere. They came at odd hours, did their shifting of cars and locomotives, and left. The long, lonesome wailing of the train at night haunted the townspeople's dreams.

Blue Springs had its unemployment problems like everyone else, especially when a couple of the mills had to close down, and those railroad jobs began looking pretty good to the younger men. There was a time when it seemed like they never talked of anything else. Charlie Briggs was one of those who had recently lost his job at the mill. Perhaps Jonathan (or his father) was thinking of this when he worked out his plan.

The freight yard was down at the south end of town, to the right of the city dam and a little bit below it. It was surrounded by a tall, chain-link fence topped with barbed wire, which even Jonathan and his friends had discovered was kid-proof. The first step of Jonathan's plan (and who's to say whether it was a good one or not?) was to induce Edith to break into the yard.

This turned out to be harder than expected. Apparently, even Edith knew the difference between In and Out, and she definitely preferred Out. Jonathan sent Susan back to Mrs. Hansen's shed to find something Edith treasured, and they threw over the yard fence in quick succession—Edith's favorite baby doll, her croquet mallet, three Tonka trucks, and her blue blanky.

Edith howled and immediately went after them. The kids watched her carefully. Once they knew the way in, the rest was easy. They bedded her down in an empty box car with a sleeping bag and her blanky and told her she was going for a ride. She liked that and rested quietly. The next day, the yard crews arrived as usual, hooked up a string of cars (including Edith's), and moved them off down the valley. The kids waved excitedly as the train sped around the last bend.

They waited twenty-four hours. Then, the town council, with tears in their eyes, notified the yard officials that their beloved Edith was missing and that she had been seen in the yard itself not too long before. Their thinking (and who's to say whether it was good thinking or not) was that the railway would be so apologetic about this awful tragedy that they would be only too willing to negotiate a settlement beneficial to the town's best interests.

And they might have been; only, all their looking never turned up any Edith. After three days, the railway called off the search. Their attitude was indifferent. They had never had use for Edith in the first place, and some of them even went so far as to imply that the whole thing had been a town joke at their expense. Blue Springs was somehow further than ever from what it really wanted.

Then, the rumors started. Someone (maybe it was Jonathan) claimed to have seen Edith riding the train. She was hanging out the door of an empty car, her face pointed into the wind like a dog in a pickup, grinning as she had never grinned before. A few weeks later, someone else said they had seen the same thing.

The kids stationed themselves along the cuttings in shifts, hoping to get another glimpse of her and maybe find out how she did it. But they never could. Jonathan Briggs missed her terribly, and every night, he cried out his deep, unsatisfiable envy into his pillow.

Strangely enough, so did the rest of the town.

Mountain Talk by Shaina Read

There is no exquisite beauty... without some strangeness in the proportion. - Edgar Allen Poe, Ligeia

Andi knew she was in a basement. She couldn't see, but she could smell mildew and feel the cold cement against her naked feet. The world had gone black since the woman who called herself Agnes pulled thick fabric over her eyes and tied it tightly behind her head. The band of muscle that ran from her eyes to the nape of her neck ached from it. She could still hear. There was the rap of blood rushing to her temples, like clock hands ticking against the bone there. Jason was whimpering, his cries soft and muffled, the sound insulated by what she assumed was wadded cloth, balled and stuffed in his mouth to shut him up. And there was the steady rhythm of metal on wood.

A knife against a chopping block? A hatchet against a log? No. It was metal against bone—the sound of a butcher hacking meat, expertly piercing and tearing at the joints to separate soft tissue from bone.

Those were the sounds she could hear. What she couldn't hear was worse. Kurt was gone. The sound of his heavy breathing silenced since the night before. He had gotten out of his restraints and tried to set her and Jason free. When he couldn't untie their hands and feet, he promised to find help and fled the cellar, his footfalls vanishing into the night.

"There's got to be someone out here," Kurt had whispered. "I'll come back for you guys."

With that, he blinked out, leaving a hole in the soundscape of her new existence. All of her attention was tuned now to the sound of something outside the cellar window being chopped and prepared. Only moments before, it had been alive. She hoped it was an animal—a pig or a goat. If it was, she hadn't heard it, not a bleat or an oink since Agnes had brought them here two days earlier.

There was something to these woods that made Andi squirm inside. As soon as they stepped out of the car, she felt it, the wrongness of the place. Kurt and Jason did a bag check, made sure they had enough food, water for the hike, and a filtered pump for the stream. It was the last trip of the summer, the longest by far—five miles on foot and a week in the woods, a last hurrah before college.

Everyone was leaving town except for her. Well, her and the dopehead who tried to sell Fentanyl at school and got expelled. It turned out not to be drugs, after all, just Motrin pills he had carefully shaved until they were white. Andi didn't have the grades or the money for a university. Community college was an option, but she knew where that had gotten her parents. They worked near minimum wage jobs in a logging town on its way to nowhere fast.

The whole scenario was depressing. But the entire magical summer had been anything but. She spent it in the woods with her two best friends. They had saved for equipment, borrowed what they didn't have, poured over location reviews, and downloaded trail maps on their phones. They even trained, doing long evening hikes after school.

And here they were at the grand finale.

"This is the last time we'll be together like this," she said, smiling past the boys and towards the woods.

She was trying to play it off, but they caught the little something in her voice.

"Come on, we'll be back. We'll still see each other."

Kurt ruffled her hair a little when he said it.

She nodded and started forward, passing off the nervous pang in her stomach for the rock of emotion that settled there when she broached the topic they had all been avoiding: the end of their time together. Everyone went through it, her mother told her. You moved on after high school, found new people, started jobs and families. You became someone else entirely.

Her peers were doing just that—getting out of dodge to avoid the fallout of a failing town with a slowly aging population. Half of the people had left for bigger and better things over the last ten years. The rest were either working at the prison twenty or so miles up the highway or taking care of the old and the dying at Red Oaks Nursing Home. Both of Andi's parents fit that description.

But she was dug in, stuck somehow in a way she couldn't explain, frozen in that little town. Kurt shuffled past her and ran ahead.

"I looked at the map before we got here. I'm going to lead the way if that's okay."

She had been wandering absentmindedly—a professional scatterbrain, as her dad called her—a daydreamer at heart. And Kurt was her watchdog. Attentive, caring, and always aiming to save the day. That was what bugged her most about him. She didn't want to be saved, but he always stepped in and tried anyway.

"Be my guest," she said, hand splayed out towards the trail.

He was already trudging ahead, eyeing pine trees and taking mental notes, accounting for where he was.

"He did look at the map."

Andi jumped, surprised to find Jason so close behind her.

"I'm sure he did."

They looked at each other and laughed.

"Hey, Kurt! Wait up!" Jason called out.

Kurt didn't slow down. They hooked their fingers into their backpack straps and jogged to catch up. They all walked in silence for a few miles. Every once in a while, Andi would kneel down to examine something—a bit of moss, a tiny pinecone. When she found a white moth, dead with its wings spread wide, she tucked it carefully into a Ziploc bag and put it in her backpack.

It wasn't until they reached a fork in the trail that they finally spoke. Jason held his phone out and tapped his finger on the hiking trails app. He had downloaded maps for offline use in case Kurt couldn't remember which way to go.

"I know for a fact that it's to the left, Jason."

Jason didn't look up. He waited patiently, his eyes never leaving the phone. "I know that. I just want to make sure."

Andi wandered up the trail, looking for flora and fauna, any little thing she could take with her to draw in the coming days.

"Well?" Kurt's foot was shifting back and forth. In motion, he was alright, but as soon as he had to stop, he was buzzing, electric. Jason took it in stride.

"I don't know. I guess it didn't download."

Andi looked up at that.

"What? What do you mean?"

Jason glanced her way.

"I mean, I thought it did, but it's not loading."

Andi walked back to them and looked at Kurt's screen. There was a green overlay indicating forest and a red line that cut through the middle, which was highway. But the yellow lines, the ones that signified trails, were non-existent.

"Did you refresh it?"

He rolled his eyes.

"Andi."

"I know. I just have to ask. Rule out all possibilities."

"Guys, did you hear anything I said?" Kurt stood in the same place, his eyebrows lifted while he waited for them to answer. When no one did, he continued, "This is precisely why I always study the map. You can't count on technology to do all the heavy lifting for you."

"Do you really know the way, or should we turn back?"

Kurt looked at Andi in disbelief. He was hurt.

"I one hundred percent know that this is the way, Andi. Come on."

He turned around and followed the path left. Andi and Jason trailed behind. After a few minutes, the forest distracted

Andi again, and her nervousness at traveling deeper into the woods evaporated. She picked flowers, broke twigs in her hands, and listened to Jason and Kirk argue over M. Night Shyamalan movies. She looked up at the towering trees and took in the sound of leaves rattling in the wind.

There's the beauty. Now, where's the strange?

She smiled as she thought it, Poe's line echoing in these woods from worlds away.

The gas station they stopped at on the way in should have been all the omen they needed to abandon the trip altogether. In most small towns, people are friendly to visitors. They smile and say hello, find out where you came from and where you're going. But in this one, something strange was going on. A string of disappearances had haunted the country highway that ran alongside public land for the last three years. The townspeople had turned inward, searching for answers in every strange passerby that ventured in. They knew better than to believe it was all coincidence.

When the three friends walked in to pay for the gas in cash as the cardboard sign on the pump had demanded, only three customers and a cashier were in the store. They all stopped what they were doing and stared. Not one of them smiled. Instead, they noted the height and weight, the color of clothing, approximate age, and other features. They would watch the news in the coming days and recognize the missing teen. In humble houses, they would shake their heads and mutter about the monster, human or otherwise, that lived in those woods.

Kurt was right about knowing the way. He always was. Left at the fork and two more miles had taken them to a beautiful rocky outcropping overlooking the Smoky Mountains. The land at the campsite was flat. A small gathering of stones against an ash-smudged boulder meant someone had been there before. The evening was exceptionally still, and they spent it mostly in silence, tired from the day's hike and pondering, each in their own way, the ending of the season. They went to bed separately, a one-man tent each, and slept well until the cool blue of dawn started to break across the overlook.

Andi lay there, head tucked deep into the sleeping bag, her eyes closed. When she heard the first zip from Kurt's tent, she got up and pulled on a sweatshirt. It was summer, but the mornings were wet and dew-soaked. When she stepped out, Kurt was already hunched over the fire pit, stacking kindling in the center.

She knew the routine and went to grab ground coffee from a food bag they placed downwind from the campsite. There weren't many predators out here, but it was always best to keep them away from your tent. The bag wasn't far, maybe thirty feet down a sloping hill. They had placed it next to a large rock, an easy landmark through the dense deciduous forest. She could see the gray edge of it just down the way, but the food bag was out of sight.

She got closer but still couldn't see it. Something heavy formed in the pit of her stomach. Maybe she had misremembered. They had carried it here in semi-darkness. It could be further than she thought or around the other side of the boulder. Then, something bright caught her eye. It was orange and instantly recognizable, a bag of Dunkin Donuts coffee scattered next to some silverware in the brown mulch near the rock.

She picked up the pace, cursing under her breath at the thought of no coffee for nearly a week. It wasn't the end of the world, but there were small comforts in the wilderness, and coffee after a night of wary sleep in the woods was one of them.

There was something else next to it, a little figure of some kind, white with a sharp tip jutting out of the ground.

Andi couldn't remember packing anything like that. She leaned down and picked it up. It fit the width of her hand perfectly, the wing tips of a moth spread from palm to fingertip. It was carved and heavy from some type of white stone; the edges rounded beautifully, just like the one she had picked up in the woods.

A shiver went up her spine, and she turned in a circle, staring between each tree to make sure she was alone. There was nothing there in the darkness. She picked up the bag of coffee and ran back to the campsite, like a child running up the stairs to escape some invisible monster. When she arrived at the top of the mound, Jason was looking directly at her.

"You okay?"

"Yeah. It's just, something got into the food last night."

"Really?" Kurt asked from his place at the fire. He knelt next to it, concentrating as he placed a log before blowing expertly on the little flames below. They licked the sides of the kindling but didn't catch the bigger pieces.

"Yeah, really. And there's something else."

She held out the white moth figurine to have Jason examine it. He looked at it through squinted eyes, then smiled.

"Wow. That's a good find. Where was it?"

"By the food bag. The coffee was thrown out, and I found it just lying there."

"It looks like it's made out of bone or something," Kurt said, coming alongside Jason to take a peek before returning to the fire.

"You don't think it's weird?" Andi asked.

"Nah," Kurt said. "Probably just some hunter that got bored in a tree stand around here."

The notion made her feel better. She tucked the moth trinket into her pocket and got to work fetching water. There was a little stream just down the way on the other side of the trail they had come in on. It was part of the reason they had chosen the spot. Well, that and the rave reviews. Jason followed her down.

When they got there, he washed his face, cupping his hands together to collect cool water and splashing it on his skin. Once he finished, he held out a hand for one of the canteens she had brought down. She handed it to him and watched him fill it out of the corner of her eye as she filled her own. His movements were graceful and quiet. He was a sharp contrast to Kurt; flexible and unbothered, quiet in his solutions. She loved them both deeply, but his steady nature was what she would miss most.

They made their way up slowly, making morning small talk as they went. When the two of them returned, the fire was roaring. Kurt was dumping the grounds of coffee into a French press; his eyebrows bent in concentration. Andi poured water into a pot and placed it on the grill that Kurt had readied for breakfast, then pulled her sketch journal out of her bag.

Yellow and orange outlined shadowed peaks that went on and on, fading into one another before erupting upward in some other place along the horizon. The sun rays had begun to crest overtop them, and with the morning songbirds chirping, Andi was just starting to appreciate the journey, warming up to the idea that she was glad she had come after all. But that moment didn't last for long.

A shadow in the trees caught her eye. She stiffened, her whole body suddenly aware and tingling. The sound of leaves crunching got Kurt and Jason's attention before she could warn them.

A man and a woman were making their way through the woods, coming up from the direction of the creek.

"Mornin'," the woman said, waving a hand emphatically.

Her arms were thin and too long for her body. Her hair hung in stringy clumps pasted to either side of her face. She was smiling with no teeth, the lips pulled back over soft, pink gums. The man was six and a half feet tall at least, and, unlike the woman, he didn't smile. He wore a dumpy hat, misshapen and dirty from what looked like decades of use. Their clothes were worn and dirt-stained. Andi held her finger just below her nostrils, a discrete attempt to avoid the smell wafting from their direction.

"What can we do for you?" Kurt asked, his tone short. He wanted them to say what they needed and then get on their way.

"We ain't seen folks out here fer a while. Thought we'd come and see what yer doin' here." Her accent was the thick drawl of Tennessee backwoods—mountain talk.

Kurt looked around. From where they stood, there were nothing but trees and mountains for miles. There were no houses, no cabins, just raw land. If they lived here, then they did it without anyone knowing.

"You all live out here or something?"

"Not here. But close by."

The woman waited for one of them to respond, and when they didn't, she dropped the smiling routine altogether. The lines in her face deepened around her mouth, the look of a life and a half of tobacco use drawn there.

"We seen the smoke from yer fire last night. Got curious."

Kurt nodded but didn't smile. "Well, it's a free country, right? National Forest is public land."

"Yup. You're right 'bout that. Just, we ain't used to visitors, is all."

Kurt pivoted toward them, and his brow furrowed again. "We aren't on private property, so technically, we aren't visiting."

She nodded. "How long you think you'll stay?"

Kurt opened his mouth to say something, but Jason jumped in. "Not long. We're leaving tonight."

Kurt gave him a hard look, but Jason didn't return the glance, keeping his eyes focused on the man and the woman. The woman nodded and turned to go, curiosity apparently satisfied. The man followed close behind. He walked with a serious limp so severe that Andi guessed one leg must be shorter than the other. They slowed to a stop.

The woman spoke without turning around. "Word ta the wise? Get goin' soon. Woods ain't safe after dark."

After coffee, Kurt and Jason argued about leaving.

"Forget those hillbillies. They can't do anything to us."

"They obviously followed us here. They think we're intruding. They called us *visitors*."

"Well, we're not! We have just as much right to be here as any other person. This is our last trip. Don't let them ruin it."

After ten minutes of bickering about the likelihood of the man and woman being ax murderers, they finally turned to Andi. She was the tie-breaker. She cradled the little moth sculpture in her hand, staring at the expert craftsmanship, the little lines like fine hair in the antennae, small scales carved into the wings. It looked so close to the real thing, an exact likeness of the little one she had found the day before.

"I think we stay—"

"Yes!" Kurt yelled.

"—for a little while longer. This afternoon, we pack up and leave."

Jason smiled.

"You can't be serious," Kurt said.

She shrugged her shoulders. "They were watching us, Kurt. It's weird."

He didn't respond, but his head and shoulders were hunched, his arms crossed, his eyes on the ground.

"And I think they left this here." She held up the moth. Kurt and Jason both stared at it for a minute.

"I had one like it yesterday. A real one that I found on the side of the trail."

"So?" Kurt said.

"So, I don't have it anymore. It's not in my backpack. I looked."

Kurt and Jason both stared at her. Jason's mouth opened a little, but he stayed quiet.

"You think they—"

"Took it." She finished for him. "They must have carved this one last night while we slept."

Kurt didn't have anything to add after that. They stayed through the afternoon despite the woman's warning, but they were on edge. Every sound was met with a hush, a glance into the surrounding woods. Andi drew in her sketchbook, but not the moth as she had planned. She sketched the skyline, the edge of trees around the clearing, the jutting rock where they had laid the food bag. By the time they left, the sun was well below the mountains, and it was dark enough that they needed headlamps to see the path ahead.

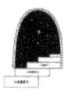

"You got ta eat somethin'. Starvin' yerself won't do no good."

Andi shook her head. Whatever it was smelled good, and she was hungry, but she couldn't bring herself to do it.

"Alright then. Suit yerself."

Agnes stuffed the cloth back into her mouth and tied it gently into place.

"I know yer scared, but trust me. This'll all be over soon."

Jason started to laugh when he heard that. It echoed against the cold, hard walls. He kept on even after the gag was in place, the cackling muffled by the cloth stuffed in his mouth.

"Settle down or you'll choke."

Agnes made her way back up the stairs and closed the door.

A cricket chorus echoed across the hills, broken only by the quiet crunch of footfalls on long dead leaves.

"Da da dang dum dang dum dang dum dang," Kurt sang out, in the mock sound of "Dueling Banjos."

"Stop it," Andi said. "It's creepy."

Kurt wouldn't let up. "Come on. You saw those people. We were almost stars in Deliverance, the sequel."

Jason smirked. "What was wrong with the guy? Didn't utter a word."

"Probably doesn't know how to talk." Kurt laughed. "They're just ignorant, you know? They don't understand anything but this tiny place they've lived in their whole lives. Most of 'em can't read."

"How would you even know that?" Andi asked.

"My mom. She was a social worker for the school district for a while. Had to go out and do home visits with some of the kids who live way up here. Some didn't even have running water in the house. They were still hauling from a well."

They thought on that quietly as they moved through darkness, their headlamps the only light other than the stars for miles. The path started to curve to the left. Kurt stopped and looked around. He did a full circle slowly, looking up and then down, trying to orient himself.

"This isn't right," he said.

Andi's stomach started to knot. "What do you mean?"

"I mean exactly what I said. The path shouldn't go this way. We went left on the way in. This should veer to the right and take us home."

They each turned in circles to see where they might have gone wrong. They backtracked half a mile but found nothing. No fork in the road. No deer path they could have mistakenly wandered down in the dark.

"What do we do?" Jason asked.

Kurt didn't answer. His silence put them all on edge. Even when he didn't know what to do, he would act like he did. His sudden loss of confidence was a bad sign.

"Why don't we just follow it down? Maybe it is the right path," said Andi.

The guys looked around, then at her, and nodded in agreement. They kept going, even as the path curved further left. They made small talk about fall plans and future trips, anything to avoid the sinking feeling that they were heading deeper into the wild. In each of their minds, they were tracking time, knowing that within an hour, the landscape would change. The trees would thin, and the path would grow wider.

When the hour came, and the path in front of them had vanished, they knew they were lost. They pulled out sleeping bags and turned off their headlamps, preparing for a night in the woods beneath a star-speckled canopy. That's where they were when Agnes and the man found them.

Andi woke up, her muscles tight and aching from days tied to a chair. She was laid out on a mattress, her blindfold removed. The dim light hurt her eyes. She squinted and tried to orient herself. The room came into focus in blurred orbs of gray and concrete. She was alone in the room.

"Jason?"

She sat up slowly. Her head pounded with the effort. She looked around for anything familiar—her backpack or sleeping bag, the headlamp she had tucked into her jacket pocket before Agnes and the man had come. But her jacket was gone. The whole room was empty, aside from a shelf filled with jars. Through the glass, she saw flitting moth wings, a frenzy of white against dark cellar walls.

People were moving around upstairs. She could hear the quiet shuffle of shoes against wood. Agnes started talking. Andi listened hard but couldn't make out more than a murmur. Then another voice spoke, male and assertive. It must have been the man who was always with her.

He hadn't spoken the entire time, not even when Andi had kicked him hard as he dragged her down the basement steps. The air had gone out of him, but he finished tying her to the chair without so much as a stutter. She had assumed he was mute. It was the only way she could account for his constant staring silence.

The door opened, and she heard someone coming down the stairs. Andi laid down in a fetal position and watched the last step to see who it was. A worn leather boot came into view, a wool sock pulled high to the mid-shin, hiding all but a singular strip of white flesh that disappeared under the whoosh of a long skirt.

"Brought ya breakfast."

Andi sat up on her elbows. Agnes held a plate in her hands. It was piled with what looked like scrambled eggs. Two pink slices of meat hung near the edge. The smell of it churned Andi's stomach. She thought of the chopping sounds and turned her head away even though she hadn't eaten in days.

"Come on, girl. I know yer hungry."

Her head was pounding. She sat up and waited for Agnes to bring it to her.

"Where's Jason?" she asked.

"Upstairs. Been up fer a few hours." Agnes smiled. "Told ya we weren't gonna hurt ya. Jus' wrong place, wrong time, is all. Had to try and git you three outta dodge."

"The chopping—"

"That was fer yer own good. Keep 'im happy."

"Who?"

"Don' worry about it jus' now. Go on an' eat. You need strength before we leave."

Agnes set the plate down in front of her and waited. Andi picked up a piece of toast and started to eat.

When Kurt emerged from the forest, his feet felt worn to the bone, but despite this, he kept walking. After his escape, there had been a path leading away from the little cabin in the clearing, but he'd darted into the heavy brush to avoid being seen. Even without knowing exactly where he was, he knew that the highway cut through the forest. They had entered with the sunrise to their backs. That meant if he traveled east and followed the sunrise, he would eventually find it. He was right.

The pavement stood in stark contrast to the wildlands on either side of the road. Kurt was thankful for it. It felt like civilization itself. The trees cast long shadows across the two-lane road, nearly covering it completely. He heard nothing but the sound of his breath and the wind in the trees. Not many drivers ventured this far into the countryside unless they lived there. He wanted to keep going, to meet some day hiker halfway, to feel like he was moving towards help, but he couldn't.

Instead, he sat in the grass and waited for a car to come. Tears welled up in his eyes. How long had it taken to get here? Twelve hours at least. He had left at twilight, promising his friends he'd find help, but not realizing the distance he'd have to travel. He hung his head between his knees and cried. What had become of Jason and Andi? They might be dead, strung up like a deer after a hunt.

He wiped his nose on his sleeve just in time to see the glow of headlights on the road in the distance. The breath went out of him. He stood up and raised his arms. The car was moving fast. The sunlight had all but vanished. It would be easy to miss him on the side of the road.

He yelled and waved his arms up and down, moving onto the slim shoulder of asphalt. The car began to slow. It was silver, an Audi. Something too nice to be out this far. Kurt could see the driver through the windshield as he pulled over. It was a man driving alone, his dark hair made darker by the pale blue of his button-down shirt. A suit jacket hung in the back, wrapped in plastic like it had just been picked up from the dry cleaner. The man smiled, white teeth gleaming. Relief washed over Kurt.

"Please, you've got to help me! My friends are in there!" He pointed to the forest, his own words not making sense to him. The man looked concerned.

"Alright, buddy. Slow down."

Kurt was hysterical now. "Those hillbillies took them! They're tied up in the cellar! Please! We have to call the police!"

"Okay, okay. You get in, and we'll call together, alright?"

Kurt nodded and opened the door. His legs felt gritty against the soft, black leather. The man reached back and handed him a bottled water.

"How long have you been out here?"

Kurt shook his head. "I don't know. Three days? I've been walking since this morning. Didn't think I'd find the road."

He opened the bottle and chugged, drinking the whole thing in one go. The man looked at his phone, then at Kurt, his eyes apologetic.

"No service."

He flashed the screen Kurt's way. In place of the bars was a small, white X.

"I'm going to drive down here a little ways and see if we get something."

Kurt closed his eyes tightly and nodded. It was the best they could do.

"Now, where did you say this cabin was?"

"In the middle of the national forest, man. These two people, they live out there. I don't know if they're brother and sister or what. But they're off, man. Like, Deliverance off, you know what I mean?"

The man nodded. "Real backwoods types, huh?" he asked.

"Oh, man. Like straight out of a horror movie."

"How long did you walk from there?"

"I'm not sure. But at least twelve hours. They're pretty far in."

"Would have to be," the man said, and something in his voice pricked the hairs on Kurt's neck.

The man smiled and punched on the seat warmer. His phone lay in his lap, the screen black.

"You want me to watch and see if we get service?" Kurt sounded desperate, but the man smiled.

"We won't. Not up here."

Kurt guessed he was in his mid-forties by the slight crease of his crow's feet that showed every time the man grinned. His nails were neatly trimmed, and the skin of his hands looked soft on the steering wheel. His car was spotless and empty—too empty for a guy on a road trip. Everything looked like it had just been cleaned.

"What brings you out here?" Kurt asked.

"Oh, business."

"Here?"

The man nodded.

"What do you do?"

"I'm a doctor."

"A doctor? What kind?"

"Surgeon. I specialize in organ transplants."

Kurt glanced at the phone again. The man wasn't slowing. His eyes were fixed on the road.

"If we go too far, I don't know if I'll be able to tell the police where to go."

The guy smiled again and handed him the phone.

"You can try, but I'm telling you, you won't get anything. No one ever can."

"You come out here often?"

"Just when I need to pick something up."

A strong smell hit Kurt's nostrils, some chemical, like ammonia. The man glanced over. He must have smelled it, too. Kurt tried to keep his face neutral, an alarm bell ringing deep inside.

"Actually, I think I'm good. Pull over?" he asked. He started to feel lightheaded.

The man grinned that million-dollar smile. Before Kurt could react, a needle was in his neck, Ketamine working its way into muscle, paralyzing him. His fear melted away. His vision blurred, the world around him fading into white.

"You ever heard the phrase 'Don't judge a book by its cover?'"

Kurt's limbs were weightless. He was suspended, floating somewhere outside of his body.

"I hired those pieces of shit to grab people for me. Not many. A couple a year. The younger, the better. After all, my clients only get the best. But those inbreds got soft on me. Started giving me animal organs." He laughed. "Like I wouldn't know the difference."

Kurt reached his hand out blindly, and the man took it in his own.

"Don't worry, kid. I need you alive while I do the surgery. I've got a ways to go, but thanks to the pharmaceutical companies, you won't feel a thing."

***

They walked carefully, the way slowed by their blindfolds, a protective measure to keep them from leading anyone to their home. Agnes held Andi's arm, and Ernie held Jason's. They led them gently over rocks and down hills. From what she said, she and Ernie were raised there. They had never gone to school, never been out of the woods and into town. The forest was all they knew. When they reached the soft ground of the path, they stopped.

"Take their blindfolds off, Ernie."

He worked each one gently, untying the knot and removing the fabric, careful not to catch their hair. Agnes had made good on her promise. She'd led Jason and Andi back to the path they came in on. Andi looked them over, their dirty clothes and sallow faces stained by a lifetime of poverty and isolation. She hadn't caught it before when she first met them in the woods, but their eyes were kind. Had she taken the time to examine the softness there, she might have listened when they told her the woods were dangerous.

"Kurt?" she asked, but Agnes just shook her head.

"Ain't seen a one escape 'im."

"Maybe he did. He's smart, you know?" Agnes smiled a little, but in her eyes, Andi could see what she knew.

Agnes held out her hand. Andi opened hers, and Agnes pressed something hard into it. When she took her hand back, she saw it was the little moth figurine, pure white and expertly carved—strange yet beautiful. Agnes nodded and turned. She and Ernie disappeared into foliage, the dense green swallowing them like any deer or fox hidden in the vast wilderness of the Smoky Mountains.

The Devouring Ocean by H. A. Titus

To Justin, for convincing this home-loving hobbit to go on adventures.

[Display note: From the field sketchbook of E. Bainbach, professor of archeology at Grimmsmeer College, as part of an honorary memorial display in the college museum.]

I write this letter in hopes that maybe, someday, the island will once again be safe to trespass upon, and our bones shall be found alongside these pages—if the sea has not claimed them first.

Kaia, the island city of legend, mysteriously vanished from the records at the beginning of the Great War. Perhaps our leaders assumed that Kaian merchants chose to trade elsewhere for fear of becoming embroiled in the conflict. Regardless, it is just now, one hundred and fifty years since the last recorded sighting of a Kaian ship, that there is interest in discovering what exactly happened.

There have been rumors, of course. Some say the island was lost to a devastating storm. Others claim it was overrun by pirates. Still, others say that it sank beneath the waves in an act of the gods, though few say what deed brought judgment upon the island.

I have been fascinated with the rumors of Kaia since I was a child, so when the opportunity arose to lead a team of students to rediscover the island, I jumped at the chance. I shall not recount the details of our preparations and journey here, for my time is short, and I must leave a record of what has occurred so that others may not repeat our mistake.

At the first sighting of the island, with its white cliffs breaking the illusion of the sky melding with the ocean waves, there was elation among us. The sailing had been smooth, but the anticipation among crew and passengers had been building for a good two months. At the shout of the lookout, there were cheers and cries of happiness, and that night, we dropped anchor at the mouth of the harbor.

The first sign of unease came as we launched rowboats from the ship to make our way to shore. In the water—which was so clear we could see many, many feet down—lay the splintered ribs and masts of old shipwrecks, speckled with dots of coral and patches of sea moss that swayed in the current of the waves. To me and my students, it represented yet another fascinating discovery. But to the sailors, it was a sacrilege. They warned us it was a bad omen to travel over a graveyard, albeit one of sunken ships.

I wish sometimes that we had listened to that omen.

In the end, only one intrepid sailor, Ren, chose to come with us.

We landed and proceeded forward. Despite the island being uninhabited, the road from the beach to the castle was in surprisingly good shape, with only a bit of grass between the cobbles, while the rest of the town buildings were in collapsed and rotting ruins around us. Only a few stone walls still stood. Few trees grew on the island, small spindly oaks bent by the sea winds, and the sun beat down on our heads as we climbed the road to the castle, standing on the top of the highest cliff, overlooking the ocean all around. Legend speaks of the Kaians being able to spot incoming ships from many, many miles away and, peering up at the ruined towers, I could well believe it.

The castle gates stood open, sagging on their hinges, and rubble filled the courtyard, likely from the towers that jutted above the gate like broken teeth. We had to pick our way through the courtyard, sometimes clambering directly over a pile of stone and splintered wood—though the wood was so softened by rot that it posed little danger to us.

One of my students, Cleo, tugged on my sleeve as we passed a pile of rubble. "Professor, there are bones in there," she whispered as if afraid to disturb the pall of silence that hung over the courtyard.

She was correct, of course—there were bones, broken and scattered, bleach-white and speckled with green moss, among the rubble, and they were not the last we encountered either. As we continued into the dusty halls of the castle, we found more; entire skeletons held together not by muscle and tendon but by dust and stringy gray cobwebs. They lay in twos and threes, grouped together as if making last stands, with splinters of wood and metal around them that I took to be shards of shields and weapons. It was then that I became uneasy. What violence had befallen the Kaians, so much so that not a single survivor had ever been found?

But I was still drunk on the idea of being the first scholar to discover Kaia's mystery, and so I ignored the warnings and the eerie atmosphere that made my hair stand on end and the whisperings of my students and pressed forward.

We passed into the grand hall, where we discovered spiral staircases that led us down to this place, where my notebook shall be laid to rest among the other books here in Kaia's greatest treasure—her library. It is said in legends that Kaia did not tax her merchants in gold or silver or goods—she taxed them in books. Manuscripts were brought from foreign countries and placed in the library until its shelves overflowed with books and scrolls and parchments.

It was ruined, of course. With no caretakers to speak of for the last hundred years, the leather and parchment were crumbling. I was afraid to even touch a honeycomb shelf of scrolls, for they looked ready to dissolve if someone's carelessness so much as jarred one of them. Here, curiously, we found no bodies save those of the books' spines that had already fallen prey to mildew, damp, and rot.

In the center of the room was a great stained-glass skylight, overgrown with moss but still with a little light shining through it. Under it sat a hexagonal table that was strangely clean. No dust gritted its surface, and there were no piles of manuscripts or bottles of ink or writing quills, as we saw cluttering the desks tucked into alcoves around the perimeter of the room. The only item on the table was a glass jar, about as big around as my two fists, corked and sealed with wax. I could not see inside it as the interior was grimed with smears of green. Just the sight of it twisted my stomach, and I resolved to avoid touching it if I could.

As the students dispersed throughout the library, marveling at the mosaics and statuary that, down here, was untouched by eroding salt winds, I began to peruse the shelves, trying to discover if I might safely remove one or two of the manuscripts to examine them. Out of the corner of my eye, I noticed Ren reaching for the bottle.

I turned, shouting at him to stop, but all that served was to startle him, and in his startlement, he knocked the bottle over. The cork wasn't sealed, as I'd thought, but loose, and it went tumbling across the smooth surface of the table, bits of wax breaking off and scattering across the wood. The sound was muffled, absorbed by the walls of books that surrounded it.

A dull green light, like sunlight seen from under many feet of water, spilled across the table's surface, highlighting every crack and crevice. A clear, bell-tone voice issued from the bottle, echoing off every glass and stone surface in the room.

Woe betide you, Kaia, and all your people.

Several of my students began shouting, demanding answers, and asking panicked questions. Ren tried to jam the cork back into the bottle's mouth, but his hands slipped. Or, perhaps there was more magic at play, and the bottle would not be stoppered again. I had to call for silence for a moment before enough of them quieted so I could hear the words.

Here, I transcribe what the voice said to the best of my ability and memory:

But we cannot ignore this latest injury, and yet, we are still reluctant—thus, we send this warning to you in hopes that you will make amends before it is too late.

Your prince has wronged us, Kaia. He, who you would hold as your best, your greatest, your example whom the people should strive to follow, is nothing but a base coward and liar.

For when your prince was sailing in his youth, he was thrown overboard during a storm. He was rescued by my sister, who, despite the animosity between our peoples, could not help but save him from such a terrible death, for she had true compassion. And your prince promised her many things and led her into believing he wished to mend everything wrong between our peoples. My sister loved him with her whole heart and body, pledging herself to him. She helped him return to his people safely, agreeing to meet with him upon your shores in a year's time.

This declaration bolstered our people in hope, desiring to end your animosity towards us.

Yet, when my sister arrived at the appointed time, she saw a wedding feast on great boats in your harbors and her beloved prince married to a princess of another country. He had, it seemed, entirely forgotten his pledge... or he had never meant it in the first place. When my sister tried to speak with him, she was slaughtered as a monster that had attacked the wedding party, and her body was strung up in the harbor for the gulls to pick over.

For a year and a day, as is our custom, I have been traveling the seas and keening my sorrow and rage to the four corners of the oceans.

No more shall we abide by this treatment. No more shall your silver runes on the bottoms of your ships burn us as you pass overhead. No more shall you catch us in your nets and slaughter us for our scales and our meat for your alchemy and witchcraft.

Heed this warning, Kaia, and leave your island home, for we shall return it to the sea. Your island and all who set foot upon it forevermore will be cursed. In this way, we repay the blood of our people that you have spilled. Let the ocean devour Kaia so that its name will only be remembered as folly for the intolerance and sins of its people.

As the last echoes of the voice faded, we heard a great buzzing, as if a thousand flying insects had filled the room. A bright green light, like what had spilled from the bottle, filled the room, and Cleo shouted that the exit to another part of the underground library had been sealed by the shimmering green curtain. When she touched it, it burned her terribly. I looked up and saw the same curtain under the skylight.

> [Display note: The rest of the contents of this page is smeared and indecipherable. We apologize for any inconvenience.]

> [Display note: Here are what we suspect to be the last few paragraphs written before Professor Bainbach's death.]

We have little time. Already, I can hear the slithering of scales on the stones above us. It fills the air. Of the exits from the room, the spiral staircase alone remains clear of the magical barrier, but it is from there that the slithering sounds echo the loudest.

Ren and a few other brave souls attempted to climb the staircase in hopes of clearing a way to the boat. We heard terrible screaming, and then... nothing. Only Ren retreated to us, bleeding heavily, to tell us that he managed to catch a glimpse of the harbor and that the ship was in flames. He could not describe what had attacked them, murmuring only something about scales and emerald glowing orbs and slit-pupil eyes before slipping into unconsciousness. Cleo says he may not last much longer, though, in the end, I think he will have by far the most merciful and peaceful death of us all. Some of us have tried to push through the curtains of magic, but we never get further than a hair's-breadth before the pain becomes too great and are forced to give up.

The slithering is getting louder. I wish we had never set foot on this cursed island, that we had never—

> [Display note: The journal cuts off abruptly here, with the remaining pages blank save for smears of blood and a strange crystalline substance. Samples taken were discovered to be sea salt, though of a structure never before seen in nature. Here, you may see a sketch of one such sample.]

> [Display note: Professor Bainbach's journal was donated by a crew of Grimmsmeer Navy, sent to retrieve the missing archeology team after months went by with no correspondence. The crew reports having found their ship sunken in the harbor. On the island, they discovered human skeletons that matched the number of students and sailors in a state of decay beyond what a few months should have done. Some of the Navy crewmembers went missing during that recovery mission as well, and the remaining three members were only able to describe what happened in fragments of sentences. Scales. Emerald glowing orbs. Slit-pupiled eyes. The same as what was described to Professor Bainbach by the sailor, Ren. Therapists assigned to these men state they may be suffering from PTSD-induced dissociative amnesia. We thank these three brave men for their service. You may find their

names on a bronze plaque on the opposite wall.]

[Display note: The legend of the island city of Kaia and the mystery of what happened to its inhabitants has gone unsolved to this day.]

Summer in Antarctica by Brylle Gaviola

I open my eyes to find myself lying on the floor of a dark room, a sliver of sunlight peeking through a blackout curtain. Specks of dust dance in the air, illuminated by the beam of light, gracefully fluttering to the floor. I clumsily stand. My eyes adjust, and I locate a chair next to a small table. Sitting down, I lean my head back with the hopes that it will somehow dull the throbbing pain.

Once I realize the pain will not be subsiding, I look around for any clues as to what happened. The faint taste of alcohol gives me a clear indication. I get up from the chair and yank the curtain back to find fields of green grass extending outward in every direction. There's a sign in the distance surrounded by flags; nostalgia shoots through my body, and I realize that I'm still here.

This is Antarctica. It's a week before Christmas, and the six months of 24-hour daylight will come to an end any day now. With such an extensive amount of sunlight, this time of year makes it a perfect retreat for the dwindling human population on Earth, as well as for off-worlders who want stable ground. The other half of the year, it's a freezing, dark pit of despair. About a thousand years ago, this continent was covered in ice sheets that were the subject of scientific study. Due to humanity's stubbornness to change, Antarctica is one of the few pieces of habitable land this planet has left. After people escaped to space colonies and voyaged to other far-off planets, Earth became a distant memory filled with creatures adapting to survive, as all living things must.

I take a cold shower to get the blood running. After I freshen up and throw on some clothes, I find my phone in the backpack on the table. Unfortunately, the battery is dead. I plug it in, and while it charges, I look at my reflection in the mirror. The man who looks back is not familiar to me; the grey hair and wrinkles like a mask I refuse to recognize. When the sun never goes down, it's surprising how easy it is to lose track of the days. Eventually, those days turn into weeks and quickly into months, or so it seems.

I search through the bag again and find my wallet with my ticket for the shuttle. Today is launch day, the last ride off of Earth for the season. It's my last chance to do what I came here for, what I'd put off for too long. An image of a smiling woman flashes into my mind, her laugh echoing with familiarity. I recall the smell of toasted bread fresh out of the oven, the taste of hot green tea running down my throat, and a live acoustic guitar faintly playing in the background. I grab the charged phone and type "Lydia's Café" into the GPS. "15 minutes away" appears on the screen.

The streets of New Vegas are immaculate. No transportation is allowed in the town other than the shuttle that connects to Port Lockroy, the nearest spaceport. We learned from our past mistakes of poisoning the air with exhaust fumes that public transportation was the best solution. And when you travel by foot, everything seems much farther and bigger than it is. You appreciate it more. That's the gift of walking.

Tourists walk around in shops buying souvenirs of the old world. There are many different selections, from toys to magnets to clothes and even unique foods. The food in New Vegas is provided by people living off the land, which is very different from what's concocted in the space stations. Even so, we're not able to recreate the foods that had been available to those in earlier times who could afford their luxuries.

I find it amazing that despite being in a place filled with countless people, one can still feel so alone. Yet, the experience New Vegas provides is one of the few things I love about this town. The balance between solitude and unrestricted interaction—combined with the fresh air—is unlike any other place in the solar system. Still, a slow ache builds in my stomach as I approach my destination, one I've avoided for so, so long.

I eventually reach the café. The sign is faded and missing a few letters, and I can barely make out the words. If it weren't for my GPS, I might have walked right past. I head inside; it's empty. There are no pastries on the counter where they used to be on display, with their fresh-baked smell wafting through the air, nor are there any tables set with utensils. Just a humbling silence. There are, however, photos on the wall of café customers and what I presume to be New Vegas locals. Additionally, there are myriad photographs featuring beautifully sculpted icebergs, vast landscapes paired underneath the vibrant colors of the aurora borealis in the background, whale sightings and rookeries of penguins, and places all over the town. I'm searching for any familiar faces, but I find none. The photos have changed from the last time I was here. I gaze into these frozen snapshots, these moments in time, captured so that we may relive them as much as possible. The photos are an attempt to give the café life or, at the very least, show that there were signs of life like ancient cave paintings might have done for past civilizations.

There's an empty space where a picture is missing—

A door behind the counter opens, and a woman walks out slowly. I do not recognize her. She stares at me, likely trying to pull me out of a memory. She tilts her head as if it would help fill in the blanks. I raise my hand to say hello, but she instead shakes her head and waves me off. Unsure of how else to respond, I obey her command. As I return outside, I glance back to see my blurry reflection in the old café window. The woman's faint silhouette disappears back into the depths of the shop, where I can no longer see her.

A significant weight is lifted from my chest, and I am able to breathe normally again. I'd avoided returning to the place where it all began—where I'd met her all those years ago. I don't know what I'd been expecting—some kind of reaction, some recollection of the good times we'd had together. But it wasn't the same—it never is when you visit the same place twice.

In the distance, a spaceship descends from the sky. It must be the one I'll be boarding soon. A shuttle can be seen approaching over the flat terrain in the distance. Something from my past is triggered at the sight of the moving vessel.

Back on Mars, in the city of Nuwa, where I was born, my mother told me something that stuck in my head. She told me that to truly appreciate something, you must look at it from a different view. If you want to appreciate the area you live in, hike up a mountain so that you can see how it looks from far away and marvel at how people can build such grand, sprawling things.

If you enjoy a swim in a lake, try to fly over it to appreciate its colors and realize how important a body of water is to the surrounding areas. I look up at the stars and see the faintest flicker of my birthplace. It's a beautiful sight to behold from Earth.

I proceed to walk along a paved walkway until I reach the marker of the South Pole. I had learned that long ago, there were only seven nations that claimed the South Pole, but now there are hundreds of nations that have planted their flags here. I sit and ponder this at the very bottom of the Earth, thinking about how difficult it must have been to get here before the roads were set and the ice reigned supreme. How many people must have died to accomplish something so grand as to voyage all the way out here? Once a perilous task, now a stroll down the street, all thanks to those who came before, and yet, somehow, it's taken for granted. I look back at the town of New Vegas and can't help but feel thankful I got to experience that last bit of Summer here.

The sun will soon set, reminding me that my time here is limited. I hurry back to the station and board the shuttle to Port Lockroy just in time. I understand now that sometimes we get away to get closer to the things we yearn for the most. I lean back in my seat to get comfortable and open my phone to scroll through my photo library. I see photos of my late wife; we're at different landmarks around New Vegas. There's a picture of myself in front of the same café I visited earlier—my grandmother's. Her name was Lydia, and I recall how difficult it was to talk to her because she could not speak English very well. I feel guilty for not spending enough time with her.

Outside the window of the moving shuttle, I see the sun vanish on the horizon. As the lights of New Vegas shrink in the distance, my reflection in the glass stares back at me once more.

I can't help but realize that nothing stays the same; nothing lasts forever. Given enough time, even the marks we so desperately try to leave behind fade into obscurity. Life keeps moving on with or without us, and I'm ready to enjoy what little I have left. I'm ready to leave this planet and my past behind me for good. I'm finally going home.

And I wonder, *Am I dreaming?*

Faran: The Launch by Galia Ignatius

To G, the original. And to all the fearless and determined babies.

Faran, from Old English: "to journey a long distance."

The team waited silently in the van, watching. A young woman awkwardly struggled through a side door of a derelict apartment building, lugging a shopping bag and an overstuffed duffle bag out into the bitter cold evening—a young man followed close behind. The team stealthily leapt from their van, and within mere seconds, they had captured the pair, rendered them unconscious, and sped off.

An older woman watched from her parked car across the street, tears streaming down her face. "Godspeed," she whispered.

The young woman awoke in what appeared to be a hospital room, but without any windows. She was dressed in blue scrubs and cozy blue socks, cleaned up, and not as sick as she thought she should be, but she had no idea of what time it was, let alone what day. And she had no idea where she was.

The door to the hospital room opened, and a man in a white coat walked in. He sat down in the room's only chair and addressed the woman:

"I'm Dr. Young. You haven't been harmed, nor is any harm intended. We have given you some medicine to help with the opiate withdra—"

The young woman cut him off mid-sentence, jumping from the hospital bed, yanking out her IV as she did so, screaming obscenities and lunging at him; her damaged teeth bared like a rabid animal. An electric field around the bed kept her from tearing Dr. Young's face off, which angered her even more, but she stopped screaming. It started to dawn on her that she wasn't in an ordinary hospital room. She saw that there were cameras mounted in the corners of the room, and the large mirror behind this Dr. Young was probably a two-way mirror.

"As I was saying, we've given you some medicine to help with the opiate withdrawals, but you may still have some slight nausea and diarrhea, maybe some tremors, but very slight. Your blood also contained traces of Methamphetamine and Fentanyl. We will be running some tests to determine if you have permanent physical or mental damage from the drug use, and we will be administering medicines, as needed, to help you flush your body of toxins, alleviate withdrawal symptoms, and restore you to health. We'll do what we can to repair your damaged teeth, as well."

A similar scene was playing out in another room down the hall, except with the young man displaying less anger but demanding to know if he was being arrested or if he was free to go.

"You are not being arrested," said his doctor, "but you are being detained so that we can help you detox and rehabilitate."

Three doctors sat at a meeting table with their notes. A large screen mounted on the wall at the end of the table lit up, and a figure appeared. The Founder.

"Doctors, let's hear your assessments."

Dr. Young spoke first.

"Patient Number One presents as a 28-year-old female; at least 13 years of drug use—currently suffering from opiate addiction, with a history of methamphetamine, fentanyl, marijuana, and prescription pain-killer use. Two live natural births in the past five years with no complications or medical assistance; her children, daughters, in miraculously good health considering the circumstances of the patient and the drugs that were in the babies' systems at birth; adopted by grandparents. Patient is hostile and largely uncooperative; gaining back some weight, skin clearing, asking to go to IHOP for pancakes and Del Taco for a quesadilla and cinnamon churros. And to Walmart to get make-up. Years of drug use have stunted our patients' development—we might as well be working with adolescents here."

The figure on the screen acknowledged what they all knew before they started this program—yes, the patients would have a lot of issues, especially stunted maturity development—it couldn't be helped. As long as the patients could be restored to physical health, the program was banking on those same patients' abilities to live and survive on the streets in highly dangerous and austere conditions... and the ability to have children.

Dr. Young finished his assessments of his other patients and turned to Dr. Kohler for her to begin.

"Thank you, Dr. Young." Then Dr. Kohler turned toward the screen on the wall and addressed the Founder. "Patient Number Six presents as a 22-year-old male. At least ten years of drug use—currently suffering from opiate addiction, history of methamphetamine, fentanyl, marijuana, spice, and prescription pain-killer use. He has fathered a child with Patient Number One, and, as Dr. Young described, the child is in good health despite the drugs she was exposed to. Number Six is cooperative after initial defensiveness and stubbornness; he is gaining weight, skin clearing, good appetite; asking the whereabouts and condition of Patient Number One. He seems devoted to her despite revealing that she has stabbed him on numerous occasions when she became displeased with him. He claims her street name is 'Stabby Savage.' Nevertheless, though Number Six is very young and obviously immature, he is earnest and responding well. He is a determined, possibly foolhardy, survivor."

Dr. Kohler gave the rest of her patients' assessments and the meeting moved along until all the assessments were completed. Then, the Founder spoke.

"Thank you, Doctors. I have some concerns about a couple of the patients—Numbers Three and Fourteen. I'm concerned that their only known pregnancies did not go to term, so we don't know if the births would have had complications, nor do we know if the children would have been defective. Send me any other information or arguments that may be relevant in order for me to give them a green light to continue in the program—or I may have to cancel their participation. Meanwhile, keep up your *objective* dedication and professionalism. We'll meet again next week."

Dr. Young walked down the hall, hoping the mention of being objective wasn't insinuated at him. He hoped he was objective—he hoped they all were. But they were also human beings making life-altering decisions for lost souls who had been judged harshly by society and virtually discarded. He stopped in front of a door marked "Research," scanned his badge, punched in a code, and entered the room. The Research Team Lead, Jenny, was at the desk closest to the door.

"Hi Jenny, can I have you do some additional research on Patient Number Three, please? It's likely Dr. Bennette will want his Patient Number Fourteen looked into, as well."

"Sure thing—anything in particular we're looking for?"

"Now that we have the patients' full DNA sequencing, I would like to run them through the genealogy, adoption, foster system, hospital, and law enforcement databases to determine if they had any live births that match. I'll tell Dr. Bennette that I asked for it—so you don't get hit by both of us."

***

The seventeen patients, for the first time, were allowed out of their rooms to eat breakfast together in a cafeteria. Patients One and Six were the only ones who knew each other. Patient Number Six spotted Patient Number One immediately, ran up behind her, and tapped her on the shoulder. She turned around, recognized him, and shoved him hard out of surprise and joy. Then she laughed and hugged him tight. He hugged her back in relief and almost cried. Patient Number One felt like crying too, but she never let herself do that—so she pulled back and shoved him hard again and laughed. They picked up their breakfast trays, and Patient Number Six looked for selections that he knew Patient Number One would like and put them on her tray. He asked her what else she wanted, trying to anticipate her needs, hoping to please her. They sat together while Patient Number One did most of the talking—rambling and conjecturing. Patient Number Six listened and nodded.

"Do you remember being snatched—did you see them coming?" "Who were those guys?" "Did they hurt you?" "I almost got one of the guys' masks off—I think I got my claws on him, but I don't remember very much." "All I remember is his baseball hat—it had a big 'F' on it, Far-something." "They must have drugged us." "I tried to get at my doctor—I was pissed, but I got electrocuted—did you?" "There's some sort of electric dog fence around our beds—what the hell." "Do you know why we're here?" "Have you heard anything?" "Where are we?" "Do you have your phone?" "Does anyone have a phone?" "Have you been allowed out?" "We've basically been kidnapped—scheisse." I wonder if my mom or dad had anything to do with this." "But who are these other losers?" "This is so blasé, blasé."

They talked about trying to escape, but realized they didn't know where they were. They talked about trying to get cigarettes, but acknowledged that they didn't really want to smoke—just liked the idea of sneaking or the comfort of the habit of it. Then they talked about having almost no withdrawal symptoms—they weren't really sick at all. They wondered if they were part of an experiment.

Dr. Young had received a message from the research team lead, Jenny, stating that she had found some additional details "regarding your request," and to come to the Research Office at his earliest convenience. When Dr. Young arrived at the Research Office, Dr. Bennette was already there.

Jenny's co-worker, Maria, quickly handed her a folder without making any eye contact with the doctors and then scurried back to her desk. It contained the new information concerning Patient Number Three. Jenny handed the folder to Dr. Young. Dr. Bennette was already holding his folder, which no doubt contained information on his Patient Number Fourteen. Apparently, he had already looked through it—his face pensive. Jenny looked sad, waiting for someone to speak. Dr. Young opened his folder, scanned the information, and closed the folder.

"Dr. Bennette, would you like to walk with me? Outside?"

Dr. Young and Dr. Bennette walked for a while without speaking. The only sounds were the boisterous calls of the kiskadees and the rhythmic cooing of the native plumbeous pigeons. Being nearer to the equator in French Guyana was a nice change in the Winter—both doctors removed their white overcoats, as it was nearly 80 degrees. Dr. Bennette spoke first.

"They found a child matching DNA with Patient Number Fourteen. The infant was left at a Fire Station in San Francisco, wrapped in a bloody shirt; the umbilical cord still attached to the placenta. A girl, born premature; subsequently placed in foster care and then adopted by a woman in Petaluma. The baby is now twelve months old but with respiratory abnormalities and is possibly cognitively impaired."

"At least your patient's baby lived and was left at a location the mother knew would care for the baby," whispered Dr. Young. "My patient abandoned hers in a trash heap—it was found in an alley by a skateboarder in Tucson."

"What are we going to do?" Dr. Bennette wasn't really asking, his face betraying his anguish. He knew this information would likely get both patients canceled from the program, and they didn't allow the patients to go back. No one must know of the program.

The receiving site had been minimally prepared with the assumption that the incoming travelers would need basic fuel sustenance, periodic ingestion of a liquid compound made up of two hydrogen atoms and one oxygen atom, and six to eight Earth-hours of shut-down for energy restoration. Nothing more. There was no understanding that the travelers, and Earthlings in general, for that matter, had individual personalities, habits, desires... propensities.

Dr. Bennette, after getting back from the walk with Dr. Young, couldn't stop worrying about the possibility of any of the patients getting canceled from the program. It wasn't explicitly stated when they signed on to the highly secret program what would happen to canceled patients. However, they had been briefed that no patient, once they had been relocated to the launch site and had seen any of the operation there, could return to their old life. He didn't want to believe that anything sinister would happen—maybe they would be relocated like informants in a witness protection program. But how could they guarantee that none of them would talk about what they had been through or what they had seen?

Eventually, Dr. Bennette once again found himself in front of the door marked "Research." Apparently he had unconsciously decided he needed to speak with the research analyst, Jenny, about his concerns.

"Hi, Dr. Bennette, what can we do for you?" asked Jenny.

"I've been thinking about our patients Three and Fourteen. Do you think we can find any other evidence to help argue their case to stay in the program?"

Jenny looked up at Dr. Bennette for a long while before turning back to her computer screens.

"While you and Dr. Young were out walking, I couldn't just let things be—I don't want these patients thrown back to their old lives. Or worse. Anyway, I found some additional tidbits that might weigh in their favor. Your patient, Patient Number Fourteen, and the baby with respiratory issues... the respiratory issues could be caused by outside external allergens, and not from narcotic damage or genetic weakness. I've narrowed it down to cat dander and tree pollen. The adoptive mother in Petaluma has three cats and lives in an area with elevated tree pollen. As for possible cognitive impairment, that has not been determined—there is no definitive proof of that at this time."

"Thank you, Jenny. That helps. Did you find anything useful for Dr. Young's patient?"

"Patient Number Three had the baby when she was twelve years old, scared, and without resources. It was not an adult decision to harm the baby," said Jenny softly.

Dr. Bennette and Jenny sat in silence for a while, staring unfocused at her blank computer screens. Finally, Jenny whispered, "We can create stronger evidence or destroy this evidence if it would help the patients."

"Your heart is too soft for this work, Jenny. Maybe all of ours are."

Now that the patients' bodies and minds were clearing of the toxins that had been poisoning them for years, all the thoughts and feelings that had been deeply buried and numbed were surfacing. Traumas, lost lives, lost babies, lost opportunities, lost families, crimes committed, mental illnesses. It was difficult and emotional and there was no way to numb things. But strangely, there was also no desperate craving to obliterate the difficult feelings. Personalities began to emerge, as did longings for family and longings for connection.

Patient Number One looked around at the other patients in the cafeteria. The patients were allowed to mingle at all meals now. They were all chattering, talking, trying to make connections with each other. How was no one worried about where the hell they were or what was going to happen to them?

"I want to go home."

"Where?" Number Six asked. "To that cockroach-infested crap hole downtown? Plus, my doctor said we're not in the same city anymore. She said trying to leave would be a waste of time. I think they moved us pretty far away."

"That makes sense, I guess—no one working here comes in wearing a coat, either. And you can hear birds outside. It's Winter at home, and cold. I wonder where they took us—this is a bunch of bull."

"Including you and me, it looks like there's eight dudes and nine girls."

"So?"

He didn't answer her. Instead, Patient Number Six stood up and walked over to another table with chattering patients. Number One couldn't hear what he was saying, but it didn't look very enlightening. He returned to their table, face downcast.

"They don't know anything, either."

"So blasé blasé," huffed Patient Number One.

The Founder had been communicating with the receiving party for several years as they worked out the details for how and when to transport fertile humans to the new location. The beginning of the relationship had, surprisingly, been unanticipated by the Founder. Several years prior, the Founder had experimented with his first human subject to undergo a procedure to implant a ground-breaking device into the subject's brain. The device was meant to provide an amazing array of new abilities to humans having to deal with a variety of disabilities, from spine injuries, paralysis, hearing impairment, cognitive or nerve damage, traumatic brain injuries, and blindness. It could conduct thought to action—a person need merely think about what they wanted to say or do, what limb to move, what word to form into a text or voice of their choice, and the device could instantly convey that telepathically and telekinetically to the precise action —by-passing the damaged nerve pathways. The device had been much anticipated by many people and families struggling with devastating disabilities.

Soon enough, though, the Founder had moved on to improving the device so that it could turn "ordinary" people into extraordinary people. The Founder's team developed ways for the device to implant mathematical and computational ability, foreign language ability, increased strength, resistance to pain. The device became so agile, so anticipatory, so sensitive that a couple of unintended events occurred. And that is when the Founder took an abrupt turn with his plans. First, he indefinitely paused the public roll-out of the so-called miracle device for those with disabilities. Then he used his considerable influence and power to squash speculation and leaks surrounding his new, improved device. The newer device, implanted experimentally into one of his closest assistants, had received a transmission not of this world.

One of the earliest modern human attempts to communicate with possible extraterrestrials outside of Earth was made in 1974. The message was a binary-encoded transmission sent from Puerto Rico that contained information about Earth and its people. There were also gold-plated plaques depicting Earth's location and other information sent up with NASA's Pioneer spacecrafts, and subsequent Voyager spacecrafts, all in the 1970s. Ukraine sent Cosmic Calls in 1999 and 2003. As late as 2013, the Lone Signal project invited the public to submit messages to be sent off from California—more of a publicity stunt than a serious effort. Did anything come of these efforts? Were they naïve and maybe arrogant? Wouldn't extraterrestrials, if they could indeed receive Earth's hopeful attempts at communication, already know of Earth's existence? As Theoretical

Physicist Stephen Hawking once said, "A civilization reading one of our messages could be billions of years ahead of us. If so, they will be vastly more powerful, and may not see us as any more valuable than we see bacteria." To which Astrophysicist Martin Rees responded, "...an advanced civilization may already know we're here."

***

The three doctors, along with Jenny from the Research Office, met in the clinic lounge for coffee and to discuss their patients ahead of the next virtual video meeting with the Founder. Dr. Young spoke first.

"Well, just so we're all in agreement, Dr. Bennette and I intend to strongly defend our two patients' continued participation in the program. But Jenny has discovered some new information that she wants us to hear that might have some bearing on our patients. Jenny?"

"Yes, when I was doing a deep dive on the two patients' histories, and looking into the DNA sequencing done on the group, I found some information about our patients that hadn't made it into their official files. The information had been deeply suppressed."

Dr. Kohler looked at Jenny intently, ready to digest and analyze whatever new information she had. Dr. Bennette was already uneasy—preparing for bad news. But Dr. Young's face was calm—he was not a worrier.

"So, are you aware of the studies done on the Chernobyl dogs?" Jenny didn't wait for anyone to respond but continued,

"Well, after the explosion and subsequent nuclear fallout and radiation at the Chernobyl Nuclear Power Plant in Ukraine back in 1986, conscripted soldiers were ordered to go into the blast area, heavy with radiation poisoning, and kill any stray animals within a 1000-square mile area called the Chernobyl Exclusion Zone. Obviously, the soldiers weren't terribly motivated, nor successful, and numerous animals survived and even thrived. So, this brings me to the dogs that survived and then bred—multiple generations. Genetic mutations occurred, and their offspring carry these mutations."

The doctors were silent, waiting for Jenny to continue. Dr. Kohler's mind was racing, trying to guess where this was leading. Then Dr. Bennette said sarcastically, "Let me guess, even though the dogs could breed, they all had five legs, three ears, and eventually died of cancer."

"Well, not exactly. They definitely had rough lives and didn't live for more than 4 or 5 years, but they didn't get cancer, and they didn't have any obvious physical deformities. Anyway," Jenny continued, "the environmental stressors at Chernobyl caused some outlier genetic shifts or mutations. The mutations involved genes that actually aid in DNA repair, and immune response. But here's the weirder thing—it wasn't just the high levels of radiation that caused the mutations. Other environmental stressors polluting the Exclusion Zone contributed, as well. Things like heavy metals, organics, pesticides, and various toxins. And studies done on Chernobyl wolves found genetic mutations that make the wolves resistant to certain cancers."

"So..." began Dr. Kohler, "can we summarize by saying that, basically, significant long-term exposure to toxins, or poisons—not just radiation—could cause genetic mutations resulting in an advantage? An exceptional ability to withstand extreme conditions or illness?"

"But what do the Chernobyl dogs have to do with what is going on here?" asked Dr. Bennette.

Dr. Kohler had already been thinking about the ramifications. She quietly asked, "Jenny, did the Program's DNA sequencing find any mutations in our patients?"

All three of the doctors had their eyes glued on Jenny.

"Yes," she said.

Dr. Bennette hadn't told anyone that he knew one of the patients in the Program. He had treated her at a methadone clinic years ago when he did volunteer work there. He had come to know her, her family, her life. The patient hadn't been successful in the program any of the numerous times she had been directed there—whether after the births of her two children, or through court orders for her petty drug and paraphernalia possession infractions. Her family had been deeply supportive, and there had been no family trauma or abuse. The trauma and abuse had seemed to come from the patient's own inexplicable drive to find danger and to experiment; find drama and conflict, and then escape from the pain she had created.

Dr. Bennette, despite all his years of medical experience, could never quite pinpoint why addiction hijacked some but left others—it was such an evil and arbitrary adversary. With some addicts, the path seemed obvious—terrible parents or family members, early trauma, and abuse. But just as often, there were those souls who could save themselves from terrible circumstances and escape, overcome, and thrive. And almost just as often, the addicts were from good families who had provided all the best opportunities for a good life. It was diabolical—this disease.

The diabolical nature of it was one of the reasons that drove Dr. Bennette into pursuing his medical career. The mystery of addiction was somewhat of an obsession and had drawn him to the Program. The Program, "Faran," had sold itself as an almost unthinkable miracle for addicts. A preposterous proposal to snatch these forsaken souls off the streets, heal them, and launch them into a new existence full of new possibilities.

Doctors who had treated patients afflicted with drug addiction, even if that wasn't their primary field, had been scouted and screened before they were contacted with an unusual employment proposal. Those who responded, those whose curiosity made it impossible for them to resist the opportunity, were then more heavily screened with a gauntlet of tests and questionnaires. Finally, they were presented with non-negotiable, non-disclosure agreements that they were required to sign.

So, when Dr. Bennette was accepted into the Program Team, and was involved in vetting the addicts who fit the profile of desired participants, he came to see the name of the patient he had treated years ago. Patient Number One. One of the requirements for someone to be accepted into the Program was a minimum of five years of addiction, with no documented success of rehabilitation attempts. Patient Number One definitely fit, sadly. He knew her age was at the outer boundary for females who could be accepted into the program—the ideal age was under 26—she was 28. But a disqualifying condition was having any family who was still in touch, or that cared for or searched for them. He knew her family. They would never stop caring or searching or hoping. For Dr. Bennette, it was an easy decision, though. His notes read, "Estranged from family; no contact."

The Founder's assistant, who had volunteered to be the first human test subject for the new, improved device, was excited and, of course, just a bit nervous to undergo the implant procedure. She worshipped her boss and trusted his visionary leadership, but she was also aware that if the device did what the team had designed it to do, her life would forever change. She was ambitious. She was ready. The device could propel her abilities far beyond what the rest of the team could do, even beyond what her boss could do—she would be superior to all of them.

But what actually happened, almost immediately after the successful, uneventful implant operation, was that the assistant did not become superior to anyone. She ceased to exist—all traces of her personality or memory or self-awareness had been eviscerated. That was the first unintended event to occur. The second event eclipsed the horror and dismay of the first. Her mouth opened and, in an eerie voice that still sounded like her—except in monotone, demanded to transmit a message to the Founder.

Of course, the Founder was there, hoping to celebrate the great achievement of his first successful device implant in a human—a human who should have become superhuman. Instead, he tried to calm himself from the shock of the apparent colossal failure, and told the now-vacant assistant's body that he was ready to receive the transmission.

"We seek humans that can relocate and replicate."

The Founder considered the message and was silent for a time. Then he dismissed the rest of the medical team and staff. After he was sure that he was totally alone with his assistant, or whatever was communicating through her, he said, "Are you transmitting through my device?"

"Yes."

"Where are you?"

The mobile phone in the Founder's jacket pocket buzzed. He reached for his phone and saw an image of a solar system on his screen. Clearly not Earth's solar system. The image also displayed likely directional distances and other symbols in relation to Earth.

"Why do you want humans?"

Another buzz on the Founder's phone displayed what appeared to be a harnessed asteroid in the other solar system. The asteroid was labeled Delta Block X.

"You are mining the asteroid?"

"Yes."

Another buzz on the Founder's phone displayed a symbol from Earth's periodic table. The rarest and most valuable transition metal.

"Would we be partners in the yield?"

"Yes."

"How many humans do you need?"

Thus was the dawn of the Faran Program. It would take a few years to put everything in place—to build the team that would be involved in the secret program, to find and vet the prospective participants. He would have to fund and build the ships that would transport the participants to a distant solar system using technologies and directions provided by the extraterrestrials. Extraterrestrials who had opted to use the convenient communication portal of the Founder's new device. Too bad about the assistant—she was a smart gal with a lot of promise. But she knew the risks and had signed all the waivers.

Most importantly, though, the returning ships would be carrying the precious cargo from Delta Block X. With his partnership in the mining of this precious material, the Founder would soon become Earth's single source of the most useful and precious material Earth had ever known. It would revolutionize all future manufacturing, spanning virtually every industry. The Founder would control the world.

Dr. Kohler kept thinking about the information that Jenny had found as she headed to the video meeting with the Founder. She had a knot in her gut. Something wasn't right, especially since the information that the participants carried a genetic mutation had been hidden from them. The only advantage she could imagine was that the participants were being sent to a place that could otherwise harm those who were without the mutation.

The doctors had all been briefed that the participants were being sent to populate a recently discovered habitable planet. All of the doctors had signed on for the chance to save anyone afflicted with addiction and who fit the prescribed profile: Long-term drug use, unsuccessful rehabilitation attempts, no family who would miss them if they suddenly disappeared. The doctors knew how dire the addiction problem was, and all of them were well aware of the failures of rehabilitation programs and incarcerations when those who were afflicted were released right back to where they came from—it was a recipe for certain doom.

Most research clearly dictated how important it was to change the addicts' environment and abandon harmful peer groups. Meanwhile, no conventional treatment program did any such thing and continued to group them together in derelict rehab buildings in the same neighborhoods where they had struggled. Dr. Kohler had been elated when she was recruited to be part of the Faran Program team. Finally, a chance to make a real difference and save some lives from this scourge, while also pioneering a new space program to a new habitable planet.

On the way to the video meeting room, Dr. Kohler collided with Dr. Young and Dr. Bennette, who were also on their way to the meeting. They fell in step and walked silently the rest of the way. Each entered the room, took their seats at the table, and waited for the screen on the wall to light up.

Patient Number One was comfortably propped up in her hospital bed, coloring in a fancy, elaborate coloring book, when the door to her room swung open.

"Time to go."

"Go where? It's not dinner time yet, and I already met with my doctor," she said obstinately.

Neither of the two men answered her.

"Am I going home?" Is my mom here?" She allowed herself a heart-tugging moment of hope. She missed her family, now that she could think straight.

Her hopes were crushed when the two men roughly grabbed her. Patient Number One realized she could not afford to be weak or sentimental—her street self surfaced immediately, and she screamed, "I'm not going anywhere unless it's home." Take me home!" "Take me home!" She stabbed at them violently with her colored pencils—getting a good stab at one of the men's eyes. But her screams of resistance and subsequent struggle were in vain. The two men subdued her and rendered her unconscious with an injection.

Most of the other patients put up less resistance—resigned to the fact that they were already captive and trusting that they had been treated well so far. The guards herded the patients down a long hallway, with unconscious Patient Number One being wheeled along on a gurney. Patient Number Six saw her in the melee and shouted, "What did you do to her?!" He ran towards her and tried to hold her limp hand as he trotted along by her side. At the end of the long hallway there were double exit doors that were wide open with three large passenger vans lined up outside.

The guards loaded Patient Number One in the last van and pushed Patient Number Six into a different van with the other patients. After the guards jumped in to keep them in check, they sped off to the launch site. Patient Number Six, quite alarmed by now, kept asking, "Where are we going?" No one knew—everyone was nervous.

However, as the image of the spacecraft on the launch site loomed into view, terror rendered them all mute.

When the Founder appeared on the screen, the doctors straightened in their seats, waiting to be addressed.

"I've made a few adjustments to our program timeline. We're going to speed up the launch of this first group and get started on vetting the next group. The receiving party is more interested in numbers than in the perfection of the travelers."

"What receiving party?" asked Dr. Kohler.

"Ditto," chimed Dr. Bennette. "I thought we were sending them to an uninhabited planet—what is going on?"

"The patients aren't even close to being ready for launch yet," added Dr. Young. "What is the hurry? And again, what receiving party? Have you already sent people ahead of our patients?"

"That is not your concern, Doctors. All of you were briefed on the nature of the Faran Program. It is an experimental program and was always going to be dangerous—which is why we chose test subjects who had already thrown away their lives. You were all directed to vet the subjects, remain objective, and prepare them to launch."

"But they're not prepared to launch," said Dr. Bennette. "Aren't you hearing us?"

Dr. Kohler chimed in, "They are just now physically recovered from their addictions—we haven't even begun to address their other issues—trauma, depression, mental illnesses—let alone prepare them to survive on a new planet."

"And our patients did not throw away their lives—they were suffering from a disease—addiction makes it impossible to make rational choices. Let's face it. The real reason they were chosen was because no one would miss them when we took them." Dr. Young's stricken face turned away from the screen, then back to the Founder. "When will you launch them?"

"They're already en route to the Spaceport—should be loading momentarily."

"Oh, Good God," whispered Dr. Kohler.

Then the screen on the wall went dark.

Back in the Research Office, Jenny could see her colleague Maria sitting at her desk, rocking back and forth and muttering something.

"Are you ok, Maria?"

Maria didn't respond, so Jenny walked over to see what was wrong. As Jenny got closer, she could hear Maria muttering, "Mayday, Mayday, Mayday, Mayday…"

"Maria," she said softly, "what is going on—do you need help?" Maria often muttered and behaved atypically—in fact, many of the research analysts were atypical, or neurodivergent. So, at first, Jenny wasn't too concerned. But then Jenny saw Maria's computer screens—she looked closer and started to read. "Maria, what is this?"

Maria had found the mining plans for Delta Block X. Plans to transport a steady stream of breeding laborers in exchange for a percentage of the precious material. The patients were to be bred in captivity and labor in the mines until they expired.

It was Winter and the sun was low in the sky as night approached. An older woman drove along a block of old apartments—the apartments riddled with souls lost to drugs. She parked across the street and watched. Some of the souls were wandering the streets, zombie-like, with vacant eyes. Some hiding in the alleyways under make-shift tarps or coats to inject their drugs in imagined privacy.

A young woman awkwardly struggled through a side door of a derelict apartment building, lugging a shopping bag and an overstuffed duffle bag out into the bitter cold evening. A young man followed close behind...

A loud knock on the car window startled the older woman out of her reverie. "Hey, do you have a few dollars you can spare?"

She rolled down her window and handed out a couple of dollars, then turned back to watch the young woman walk away, followed by the young man. No van came to take them. No help or hope arrived to change their course.

"Maybe tomorrow," she whispered to herself.

As she started to drive away, she saw the young woman pause and turn around, apparently fumbling with her bags. As she looked up, her eyes briefly met the older woman's. Was there recognition? Were her lips moving? The older woman couldn't quite be sure. Her lips seemed to be saying, "I'm OK, Mom, don't worry." But then the younger woman turned back and continued walking down the street, the young man keeping up with her and trying to help her with her bags. The older woman chastised herself for being such a sap—longing so much for any sign of hope that she could imagine almost anything.

She drove her car slowly past the young woman and the young man on the sidewalk. It had started to snow, and the young woman only wore what appeared to be blue hospital scrubs under a hoodie. The young man only had on a tracksuit and definitely needed a warmer hat, she thought. It was just a ball cap—a ball cap that read "Faran."

The Book of Thomas by Iris Shaw

Thomas woke to the smell of toast and tea in the kitchen below, filtering up the stairs, stealing beneath his door in a single, tantalising thread. He slipped his hand under his pillow and found the book he had left there the night before, still faintly warm.

He listened. No noise came from the kitchen, nor did anyone call his name. He took a folded blanket from the foot of the bed and propped it behind his pillow. He opened the book and read, his fingers turning the pages growing cold while the rest of him kept warm under the blankets.

That he had found the book in a hollow tree outside his house was not very unusual, because his house was inside a library so vast that most people just called it the Library, although some called it by its proper name, the Library of Time. It was filled with reading rooms, streets, and cathedrals full of books, and was so large, in fact, that no one had ever come to the end of it.

"Thomas."

He said nothing.

"Thomas, love, I know you're awake."

He turned a page.

The voice was amused. "Breakfast, Thomas. Bring your book down."

Reluctantly, he crawled out of bed, dressed, and padded down the creaking stairs. His grandmother was already at the table, a mug of tea in her hand and a book beside her plate. His place was set opposite hers, and his own particular egg cup with the leaf-shaped chip held a fresh egg.

"Late night?" his grandmother asked.

"Not very," he said.

"Should I send for more candles?"

He considered, then grinned. "Probably."

His grandmother smiled in return. They finished their breakfast in companionable silence. Then Thomas' grandmother washed the dishes while he dried them and put them away on the blue-painted shelves. Once the table was clear, he tucked his book under his arm and sat on a stool to put on his shoes.

"Going out?"

"Yes," Thomas said. School did not begin again until tomorrow. He had more than enough time to wander the Library today.

"Be back in time for tea. Hand me my bag, will you?"

Thomas gave her the big black leather bag, like a doctor's, only with innumerable book-sized compartments. She was a librarian. Thomas would be one, too, when he was grown up. One day, he would have his own house, just like this one, and he would have a bag exactly like his grandmother's.

"Shall I make you lunch?"

"No," said Thomas, feeling immensely grown-up, "I'll find somewhere."

"Don't wander too far."

"I won't."

He said goodbye to his grandmother and left by the front door. The house was set in a clearing surrounded by long grasses and tall pines, ancient trees with a constant mist caught among the tops of their feathering branches. He took the path—winding and narrow—between the trees, and a quick left followed by a right brought him to a pair of arched doors covered in fruits and flowers. High and heavy as they were, a touch opened them, and he passed through into another section of the Library—since the Library was in a constant state of change, he never knew quite where he would end up. Today, the doors opened to a long glass-walled gallery, whose windows looked out on a distant orange nebula and whose length was crowded with readers who had just arrived. They chattered like starlings and looked about with eyes as bright.

Thomas thought of finding a Library phone box which would tell him where the principal sections would be today (his grandmother had been teaching him how to use them, though it would be another year before they got to it at school), but when he did see one, the line in front of it was twenty librarians deep and two wide.

"Excuse me," he said to one of them, a tall man in a high collar and silver-rimmed spectacles. But the man carried on talking about the implied ethics of something in Dostoevsky. He spoke in a thunderous voice that captivated everyone listening, and Thomas gave up. Instead of waiting, he jammed his hands in his pockets and slouched away. No one paid any attention to him.

There was a door behind a steel column at the end of the room marked "Librarians Only," and he slipped through it into a long, empty reading room. Rain streamed down the high leaded windows and tapped on the outside of the vaulted roof, whose timbers were black with years of smoke. Here, books were strewn across the long tables and benches, books full of Gothic type and capital letters like coiling snakes, their frontispieces rimmed with borders of skeletons and horned devils and many-tailed fiends. One was a book of allegorical pictures, and Thomas idly turned the thick, grey-cream pages of Pride, History, Feast, Amity, and Desire until he grew bored.

Later on, he set himself to wandering the Library. He found the History of the Deer section in a medieval hall, all hung about with hunting tapestries and managed by solemn, pale-faced librarians in long gowns. From there, a narrow door behind a bookcase gave onto Ancient Astronomy, a vast observatory with a working telescope, where he spent several happy hours. After that, he passed quickly through a warren of grey corridors, blacked-out windows, and rooms partitioned by grotty beige dividers and battered desks, all covered in the memos and books pertaining to the Third Salician War—here he saw, or thought he saw, a single reader vanish in the distance, but the silence was otherwise absolute.

At length, Thomas came to the door of an eighteenth-century coffeehouse where both librarians and readers mingled. Feeling more than ever immensely grown-up, he ordered lunch for himself (a dark sort of stew he was not entirely sure he liked and two pastries he liked very much), which came on battered pewter trays. The walls were papered with playbills and extracts from articles, some of which he was forced to read with his head upside down, and so he did, once he had licked his spoon clean.

He left the coffeehouse to drift through the Early Tudor Politics section, which was filled with the hum of constant conversation and the smell of beeswax. Sunlight filtered through intricate rose windows—red roses, white roses, golden roses, too. Some of the books were chained to the shelves, though when he opened them, they were printed, and their bindings were rich leather stained blue and red and green, the titles picked out with gold. He took his hands out of his pockets and felt tall under the soaring ceilings.

Then, to his great misfortune, he entered an anteroom whose door bore a red rose outlined with white. There, at a great square table, he found three of his classmates. He made to back out of the room, but they spotted him.

"Oh, look, it's Thomas," one said.

"Which was the name of cowards and doubters of Our Lord," a second added sententiously, making the third snort.

"And three traitors besides," the first said. "Wasn't it?"

"Leave me alone," Thomas said.

"Oh, no. Remind me, who was it passed that history test? That everyone else failed? The one we have to take again tomorrow? Now, who was that? I thought it started with T."

"Traitor?" suggested the third. "Too clever?"

"Teacher's pet," the second said. All three stood up and advanced on him.

Thomas ran. He was ill-suited for running, but he had no wish to stay. The other boys were slower; no matter, they would outrun him in the end—he heard them already, not breathing hard, closing in behind him. He dodged through the shelves desperately, through strange doors and, once, a window. He ran through rooms he had never seen that were no more than a blur of books and faces.

The breathing of the boys behind him grew fainter, and finally, the sound of their feet died away. The last he heard of them was laughter as he blundered through a dark doorway and then nothing at all. Thomas was alone.

The room was dark. Thomas could see the shadows of shelves against the wall and a sliver of light coming from one corner. He moved slowly towards the light, shuffling his feet against the floor.

When he reached the light, he discovered it came through a doorway, which he passed through only to find himself in a long, empty room lined with mirrors. A hundred other Thomases stared back at him. As he returned their gazes, the door behind him shut with a click, revealing itself as yet another mirror. He tugged at it in vain and almost cut his fingers, feeling frantically around its edges, but it would not open. When he turned away, all the other Thomases looked back at him with the same despair. He held back a sob—there was no one to hear him, but he felt too old to cry just because he was lost.

The hall of mirrors stretched far into the distance, airless and bright, farther than he could see. On the chance that he might find a door (or perhaps a librarian), he began to walk. After a while, he noticed that every mirror had a thin silver frame inscribed with verses. He bent to look at one and, since he was still alone, read the words aloud.

"Achilles' baneful wrath resound, O Goddess, that impos'd
Infinite sorrows on the Greeks, and many brave souls los'd
From breasts heroic; sent them far to that invisible cave
That no light comforts; and their limbs to dogs and vultures gave;
To all which Jove's will gave effect; from whom first strife begun

Betwixt Atrides, king of men, and Thetis' godlike son."[1]

The surface of the mirror seemed to dim, and he saw a battlefield in a storm. Tiny men fought with swords and spears, some on foot, others driving chariots, and the field was littered with the bodies of the dead. Curiously, Thomas put his hand out. It went through what should have been glass, and he felt instead the wind of the storm. His fingers stung as rain lashed against them.

Could I go through it? he wondered.

No harm in trying, I suppose, his reason said, though dubiously.

He put his foot up on the bottom of the frame and grasped the sides tightly. He took a deep breath and plunged through—

Rain, wind, shouting, the screaming of horses and men, the splintering of wood as chariots met—

—and he tumbled face-first onto a very thick rug. It was choked with dust, enough to make him sneeze several times as he rose.

He had landed in a small study lined with paperback novels. Everything was covered in a layer of grime and neglect: the desk, the chair, the artificial flowers on the windowsill. Nothing had been touched for years, and as he made his way to the door, he left footprints in the dust.

There were, he knew, deserted sections of the Library—places where nobody came or went. But he had never been there—he had always heard they were very far away. He worried, now, over how far he had gone.

Each successive door he opened revealed more empty rooms – vast damp palazzos, silent neoclassical halls, rainy courtyards filled with statues, yellow-walled rooms containing reams of self-help books and mildewed ceiling tiles. His legs grew weary, and his stomach grumbled. *How much farther?* he thought. *I didn't run so very far.*

Once, he opened a tall wooden door, which groaned and protested at his touch. The hall beyond was unfurnished, save for a few dim portraits along the walls. Light came from some window above that he could not see, though not enough light to illuminate the subjects of the portraits, nor the dark pattern of the wallpaper. He was only halfway down its length when the whispering began.

> *I bade thee, when I was distracted of my wits,*
> *Go kill my dearest friend, and thou hast done 't...*[2]

> *O, that way madness lies; let me shun that;*
> *No more of that...*[3]

Frightened, he began to run as another voice boomed out behind him:

> *Stand still, you ever-moving spheres of Heaven,*
> *That time may cease, and midnight never come...*[4]

He finally reached the door and hurled himself through it as one last voice rose above the others, a voice that was almost a wail, afraid of itself:

> *Down, down to hell, and say I sent thee thither,*
> *I that have neither pity, love, nor fear...*[5]

He closed the door on it and heard no more. Now, he stood in another long room with a black stone floor and wooden columns, the air so cold he could see his breath hang in it. There was nothing else in the room save, at the very far end, a statue of a hooded figure reading. He went up to it and stared at the strange symbols on its plinth, which he could not read. After a moment, to his amazement, the statue sighed and turned a page of its book.

It's alive, Thomas thought.

"Please," he said aloud. "Please, I'm lost."

The statue looked down at him coldly. He could not see its eyes.

"What is this to do with me?"

"I want to go home," he said, ashamed of the tremor in his voice.

"What have I to do with home? Let me alone." And the statue turned its head to its book once more.

Dully, Thomas walked away. He went unseeing through a treasure room full of emeralds and crowns and golden tablets. He passed through a room with nothing in it save two half-carven blocks of marble, one labeled *Immortal Horrors* and the other *Everlasting Splendours*, and did not stop to look at them. When at last he came to a small reading room, with two high armchairs drawn up to an empty fireplace and every wall crammed with bookshelves, he sat in one of the chairs and wept. He had promised his grandmother that he wouldn't wander, that he would be back in time for tea—now, he did not know what time it was nor if it was the same day.

After exhausting his tears, he lay curled up in the chair for a while. His eyes wandered to the books on the walls, and he took a few down to examine them.

He read:

For by this and by all such things we know, that the world is not infinite, yet contains multitudes, and in time has recorded in that book which has no name, innumerable variations upon this theme which men call life.

And in another book:

I said to the one who is my lover

Why do you wait?

And another:

Georgiana shut the door, and at once began to weep and laugh alternately, giving vent to those passions which had already near burst her heart though she dared not speak before.

And then he saw a small book at the end of the shelf nearest him. There were no letters on its blue-green spine, and it had a dusty, neglected look. He stretched an arm up and stood on his toes—the shelf was just a little higher than he could have reached with comfort—and took it down. On the cover, in copper letters, was printed: *The Book of Thomas.*

Curious, he opened it and read the first page.

Thomas woke to the smell of toast and tea in the kitchen below, filtering up the stairs, stealing beneath his door in a single, tantalising thread. He slipped his hand under his pillow and found the book he had left there the night before, still faintly warm.

He almost shut the book then, in surprise. Hesitatingly, he turned the page.

Here, books were strewn across the long tables and benches, books full of Gothic type and capital letters like coiling snakes, their frontispieces rimmed with borders of skeletons and horned devils and many-tailed fiends. One was a book of allegorical pictures, and Thomas idly turned the thick, grey-cream pages of Pride, History, Feast, Amity, and Desire until he grew bored.

He turned another two pages.

It's alive, Thomas thought.

"Please," he said aloud. "Please, I'm lost."

He nearly shut the book again, then, ashamed of himself. But he could not bring himself to stop reading, and what he saw on the next page astonished him.

Thomas closed the book and crossed the room to the far door. Once through it, he found himself in a winter garden, the shrubs all wrapped in burlap, the kale still green and towering. He passed through the gate at the far end and turned to the right along the narrow, winding path...

Thomas did close the book then and stood up. He looked at the empty fireplace for a moment, crossed the room, and turned the door handle. As the book had said, he found himself in a winter garden, where the cold made his nose itch. When he looked again, the book described it as early morning, the ground covered with a fresh layer of frost. He left through the gate at the far end and turned right along the path which led between two rows of cypress trees. He blinked and found that he was standing in the nave of a small chapel, its walls covered with chalky, faded saints.

He opened the book once more.

Thomas turned and saw a tiny door to his right. He waited a moment, then scrambled between the pews and went through it into a vast and echoing hall...

He saw the door—wood and iron, barely wide enough to allow even him to pass through. And in the stone hall beyond, his lightest footstep echoed like a bell.

The book guided him through the empty rooms and showed him to each door he must take. It pointed out the hidden ways (the hatch behind a portrait, the door barely visible beneath a pattern of papered cherries) and the moments at which he must pass through each. When, at last, he burst through a window, which became a pair of silver doors opening into a tiny room teeming with illuminated manuscripts and silent readers, he could have danced or howled for joy. Instead, he shadowed the progress of his second self in the book, following each page, until he came upon his path home and saw the light shining from his own windows. He tumbled through the doorway and found his grandmother at the stove, with the clock on the wall just striking half-past five.

"I'm back," said Thomas.

His grandmother turned around and smiled.

"So you are. Come and eat. Best put away your book first, though."

Thomas closed the book and put it on the shelf over the fireplace. He and his grandmother sat down at the table.

"Good day?" his grandmother asked.

"Not so bad," he said.

"Did you go very far?"

"Farther than I meant to. But I got back."

"You always do," his grandmother said.

"Well, I have to eat, haven't I?"

They had roast chicken, potatoes, and boiled cabbage, which Thomas heroically swallowed without saying a word while his grandmother laughed at the faces he made. Then they washed the dishes and put them away, closed the cabinet doors, and made tea. Afterwards, they sat down by the fire to read. Thomas looked at the book above the fireplace, where the cover's copper lettering winked up at the ceiling.

But he did not open it. Instead, he read the book he had left under his pillow that morning until the words on the page dimmed and wavered, and then he watched the fire until it blurred before his eyes. When he finally fell asleep, his grandmother wrapped him in a blanket and carried him up to bed.

---

1. Homer, trans. George Chapman, *The Iliad*

2. John Webster, *The Duchess of Malfi*

3. Christopher Marlowe, *Doctor Faustus*

4. William Shakespeare, *King Lear*

5. William Shakespeare, *Henry VI, Part 3*

Hersh by Shannon Aaron Stephens

To Erin: You've always journeyed toward truth. You showed me a way. Now we travel together.

Return:
Hersh
Moby Farms
RR 46 Box 110
Jordan, NC

To:
Paul Hershberger
4242 Spring Valley Drive
Huntington, WV

Dear Brother,
    I considered starting this letter by writing, 'Call me Sol.' It is pronounced like that king of old. The first king, indeed. Not the

last by far. Recently, we had a World President. What is a king to that? Well, at least a king didn't pretend. He didn't put on a stage play that his power was limited by some Council of Nations. A king spoke, and it was law. I think that transparency is good, however evil the king.

Transparency is why I'm writing to you, dear brother. I'm hoping that with any technology you can access, you will be able to preserve this record of what happened on the voyage of the *Cherokee* and share it. You see here that I still write with paper and ink. By my return address, you also see that I don't live near any of our family. I will explain soon. I've never gained any skills with computers. A neighbor helped me find your address.

Before I tell you how I was a part of the *Cherokee* event, let me explain about that name, Sol, which I was considering. You, of course, know that I was Solomon David Hershberger at birth. You and our parents always called me Solomon. You remember that as soon as I could speak, I insisted everyone call me David. And so our friends did. As did you in their presence. Only at home was I called Solomon. I'm working my way up to saying more about family and church. Bear with my jumping around.

After the Amish Nation was forced off our land—before the *Cherokee* event—I was taken to World Corp. Labs. They all thought my first name was antiquated. So they abbreviated our last name. I was known as 'Hersh' to all my coworkers. Though I thought everyone there vulgar and brusque, the name Hersh was somewhat appealing. I suppose it was how you felt when you first arrived among the English once deciding to leave the church. There is, I know now, an exhilaration at being unknown among new peers. It is like being reborn. The thrill is that you can choose who is to be born. I couldn't then attribute that flash of emotion as a good thing for me to feel and, therefore, for you to have felt in your transition. Paul, I'm embarrassed to look back on my past coldness.

Paul, let me be frank: I'm sorry for shunning you. I apologize now for the bitterness I harbored against you. Please forgive me. This is the main reason I write. It's not only for you to record the events of the tragedy (or miracle, as you will see) in some database for others, but also to ask for your forgiveness. Please extend to me the handshake of brotherhood. I reach out my hand not to confer anything on you, for I have nothing to give. I extend mine in pleading. Take it, I beg, and draw me up to be your brother once more. That is another reason I thought Sol would be fitting. Sol sounds like Saul, and I have been a worse version of you, Paul.

The other reason I considered using Sol is that I am relieved to be this close to the Sun again. Sol is what some ancients called the Sun. I understand, though, that it was pronounced like 'soul.' There is possibly some significance in that, too. I never wish to travel away from the Sun again, from Sol, or from *my* Soul.

I cannot be Solomon again, for our parents are dead, and I await to hear from you about how you view me. David is the name of a little boy long dead. He was a proud boy, and I mourn only that he was not humbled sooner. I am glad he is gone. But enough of this. I should begin my tale.

First, I hope you are well and found work that makes you happy, brother. Do you have a wife? Children? During these rebuilding days, I'm tending a small farm. My tobacco is doing very well. I keep few animals, the reasons for which I will explain. You remember how many pigs Father kept. And after you left, he didn't hire any hands. It was just me with the swine. Oh, how we hated feeding them. Remember?

Well, when President Tenebras instituted Sovereign Rule, starting the societal collapse, The Amish Nation's Councilman and his court were the first to be executed. Since we were without a government, every Amish was enslaved.

I landed a decent assignment. Since I had been a hog farmer, World Corp. put me to work feeding the animals they kept for experiments. There were lots of mice, as you can imagine. Those didn't bother me like they bothered Rob. Rob was my 'coworker'—the term we used for one another. 'Cellmate' is also an accurate term. There is a certain kind of freedom that isn't freedom at all.

It was Rob's lighthearted way of calling me Hersh, as if he had known me forever, which is why I never grew tired of the name.

I used to wonder, with the technological power they seemed to have, why they didn't just build a machine to feed the animals. Rob told me: "Slaves are cheaper. Cheer up, cracker. At least they aren't experimenting on us." I never understood the cracker idiom.

There were some pigs, too. They were not the robust Durocs like Father raised. These were pitiful, undernourished, rejected Spotted Pigs—those with too many spots. It broke my heart to see the ribs of the piglets. The World Corp. workers knew exactly the bare minimum each animal could be fed to stay alive.

Rob and I were often threatened during our training sessions. They told us that we would be immediately dismissed if we ate any of the animal feed. You can guess what "dismiss" meant. I can imagine, on our rations, that someone might be tempted. I never was. Since my day's work went from 16 hours of hard labor on the farm to 14 hours of easy labor in the lab, I was glad to have no opportunity for gluttony. With the loss of my muscles, the last thing I wanted was to gain a belly. As my pride started to melt, my vanity became more obvious. I can recognize that in hindsight.

There were all kinds of animals in the labs. They had caged up everything: foxes, greyhounds, Siamese cats, and tortoises. There were little furry things called chinchillas, a wide variety of snakes, and all manner of monkeys. That isn't even the fourth of it. I loved each one the best I could. I think loving those animals is what kept me from getting bitter during those years.

Rob and I never found out what experiments they were performing on the animals. That's probably for the better. Since World Corp. was concerned mostly with space travel, I don't know why they needed so many animals. I also don't know what became of them once I was recruited for the mission, but I can't imagine it was anything good.

So, when I learned I had been drafted for the mission, I decided to take a mouse I'd befriended. He was the meekest of all the mice. His fur was pure white, and he had a deformed spine. He was never selected for experiments, and I feared they would finally dispose of him once I left. I named him Moby, put him in my pocket, and fed him crumbs from my rations. Even a companion such as that is better than no companion at all. Rob didn't get recruited.

You'll remember that, ostensibly, the drafting of the crew of the *Cherokee* was to confer honor on members from each nation. In reality, it was another opportunity for President Tenebras and World Corp. to save money by using slaves. Rob stayed behind at the lab. I felt that was better by far. I was happy for his luck. In advance of my leaving, I wanted to express that and tell him how much I was going to miss him. Unfortunately, our last conversation wasn't anything like what I'd hoped.

"Rob, it seems I've drawn the short straw, my friend," I told him. Then he asked, "Why didn't you request they take me too?" I tried to ask why he wanted to go, and he said, "Why? Because we're friends. Aren't we? Damn, Hersh, I thought this was really something." It was difficult. He asked how long the flight to Europa would last (three years, by the way). But we had nothing left to say to each other.

Just like that, I never saw Rob again. I never found out what happened to him. He isn't on any social contact rolls like how we found your address. I hope he did okay once World Corp. was finally shut down. I hope he found good work and a wife and is happy. I may never know. God knows.

The crew orientation that was broadcast was propaganda. That swearing-in as honored members of the first manned mission to one of Jupiter's moons was only for the cameras. Once onboard the *Cherokee*, our real orientation began. It consisted of the captain informing us that we were there as laborers (cooks and mechanics, etc.) and not to get in the way of the *real* crew—the World Corp. naval officers. Our compensation for participation in the mission was limited to room and board for the duration of the voyage to and from Europa.

I was a little surprised that no other Amish were on board. Since every last one of us had been sent to forced labor, I imagined we would be sought after in greater numbers for the space mission. Probably because our mechanical knowledge is limited to farming equipment.

I missed Rob every day. It was impossible for me to make friends on the ship. Everyone there was obsessed with the mission, the society, and the president. Even the other enslaved onboard were. I think they had decided to play along with the drama. I felt how an English must have felt stopping by our father's butcher shop. Moby was my only companion. He was a docile creature and seemed to fear the world beyond my coat pocket.

Once again, I was blessed to have been given an easy assignment. My job was to water all the plants onboard. A variety of vegetation was planted in every hallway and every room of the ship. They were mostly selected for their high oxygen production. Some were merely decorative. Most were edible, though being food wasn't their purpose. In addition to having an easy job with almost no oversight, Moby and I added a few fresh greens to our diet.

Before launch, my task was explained during my job training. Again, the thought occurred to me that a mechanical system could have done the work. As soon as the question arose in my mind, however, my boss had already started to answer, "And, before you ask why we didn't install irrigation systems, I will tell you. The slight evaporation of water from the act of spraying water from above by use of the sprayer you will be issued—do not damage the sprayer, there are limitations to redundancies aboard the *Cherokee*—is a necessary component in the environmental engineering."

That got me onto a biblical line of thinking. "What is your life? For you are a mist that appears for a little time and then vanishes," said the brother of Jesus. That gave me some ease about leaving the planet. I realized that it didn't matter what became of me during this potentially dangerous mission. If I had fled before launch, my life wouldn't have been much better on Earth. Perhaps I could be of some good on the voyage. I believe I was. You will have to judge for yourself. God knows.

It was mesmerizing being in a spaceship. Dealing with the plants, as I did, I could have pretended I was just in my own garden. If I didn't look up, that is. There were view screens to the outside mounted on every wall and ceiling. And the stars were so beautiful. I often found it difficult to turn my eyes from the view screens to get back to work.

Paul, I don't know if you have any kind of faith these days. In space, my conception of God changed altogether. You know how it was in our community. You know better than most, I see now. The God that our grandfathers talked about was cold and dour. But now I have heard the songs that Psalm 19 described. I was on a vessel that plowed right through the dance in the heavens. You can't do that and ever think of God's grace as something other than a gift of joyful, majestic beauty. Any God that could paint the Milky Way is a fellow who knows goodness. He must be so full of beauty that he kept making more space just to keep painting.

That's what happened in my heart up there. I thought of you. I wept because of how I had joined everyone in shunning you. I realized that the Jesus who makes stars is the same Jesus who ate at Matthew's house. He never shunned anybody. But he let himself be shunned. If Jesus had ever shunned anyone, it would have been the shunners. I'm sorry. You are my brother in body and in spirit. I'm sorry.

And so, with all of that stirring in me, I caught wind of a rumor. Some laborers who used the same locker room heard from others the real purpose of the *Cherokee*'s mission. World Corp. had discovered life on Europa. You will have never heard this on any news outlet, I know. As the lone survivor of the explosion of the *Cherokee*, I am the only civilian who knows this.

I learned that President Tenebras had fast-tracked the *Cherokee*'s mission after discovering there were human-like inhabitants on Europa. I knew in my gut why he wanted to go to

Europa—he wanted to enslave them, too. This wasn't a research mission; this was a slaver's ship. It took me another month to hear more gossip that confirmed my conclusion.

One night (we did still have 'night' and 'day' by changes to the lighting in the living areas) at the end of my shift, I was looking at a view screen, and I had an idea. It came to me like a memory more than something I thought up. I took Moby from my pocket and held him in my palm. I brought my hand near my face and looked into the eyes of that little mouse. He looked back as if the same idea had struck his mind, too. I felt I had gotten to know him over those months and thought I had learned to detect his change of moods. I know that sounds crazy, but there it is.

After putting away my irrigation equipment, I took Moby to a door where the electricians would access maintenance hallways. I kissed his little back and released him under the door. My thought was about how there were no animals of any kind onboard. I thought about how the engineers of this ship may not have counted on having to keep out pests. I thought that maybe if Moby chewed enough wires and the *right* wires, he could shut down the ship.

Every day, I took Moby to that access door and released him. Every night, I camped in a hallway that led to the emergency escape shuttles. Every morning, I picked Moby up at that door on the way to work. For two weeks, we had this pattern. I started losing hope. One night, though, in the locker room, I heard gossip that the naval officers were getting nervous because of unexplained electrical failures in some minor systems. They said they couldn't find the source, and they hoped it didn't spread. Night after night, my little buddy worked hard at chewing up wires. Day after day, the crew grew tenser.

Then, the night came that I was awoken by evacuation sirens. I jumped right up and entered the nearest escape shuttle. They were automated to fly themselves back to Earth once you buckled in. I was only in flight for a few minutes before the main engine of the *Cherokee* exploded. It caused chain reaction explosions, and all other life rafts launched were engulfed in those flames.

We had been traveling for nine months. Of course, the emergency shuttles don't fly as fast. It took me a year to get back home. Thank God. There were rations for exactly 12 months on each shuttle. That was the most peaceful year of my life. It was not the loneliest. I heard the songs of the heavens nonstop for that year. I felt the Spirit of God all around me all the time.

When I got back, I learned that the explosion was the beginning of the end of Tenebras and the society and World Corp. They were already being dismantled. After weeks of debriefing (they never heard the whole story. I told them I just got lucky to get to a shuttle first), I was finally sent away, out on my own. I worked for a few years at a landscape nursery in Florida. The Congress, once it was organized, quietly issued me a reparation that included the land I farm here in North Carolina.

Since I got settled in, the only thing I could think of was how to reach out to you. And what I would say. I think about Moby, too. I'm sorry he couldn't make it out. It is really something, what he did. I've tried, but I don't feel guilt over the loss of the crew of the *Cherokee*. The death of those 400 people, most with greed in their hearts, doesn't seem like a loss. Not when you consider that hundreds of thousands on Europa were saved. Not to mention the billions that have benefited here on Earth. But I do, in fact, pray for their souls. If it is effective or not, I cannot say. God knows.

Well, I think I've said it all.

Paul, I hope to hear from you. I hope you record this for history somehow. I hope you forgive me. I love you.

Your Brother,
~~Sol~~ Hersh

Red Kingdom by Winston Malone

For Richard, who introduced me to the wonderful world of mycology and inspired this story.

A mechanical finger brushes the thin membrane that coats the base of a birch tree. The touch dislodges tiny spores, which spiral in all directions, catching the light of the afternoon sun. The titanium hand swivels the finger toward the face of a caretaker bot, its bulbous lenses peering down like a curious insect. The organic residue is smudged on the fingertip. It shines like blood.

"What is it, Merlin?" Gale asks into his earpiece.

"It's definitely fast-growing and adapting at an alarming rate. But I can't say exactly."

"You're a botanist; how do you not know?"

"Mycologist," Merlin says with a sigh. "And it's because I've never seen anything quite like it. It resembles moss but doesn't exhibit the characteristics of a Bryophyte plant. It might be a type of Armillaria mellea, also known as 'white rot,' but in this case, not white."

"So... it's a fungus? How can you tell?"

"Well, the mycelial cords are insanely complex for starters. Actually, they're rhizomorphic, densely packed. The morphology of these hyphae is... just gorgeous to look at."

"I appreciate the science lesson. But if I'm understanding this properly, you're saying an undiscovered fungus with a knack for harsh environments hitched a ride from Earth to take over Mars?"

Merlin brings the finger closer. The high-fidelity cameras of the bot's optics are so clear he nearly forgets he's operating the machine with his mind from millions of kilometers away. However, the lack of almost every other sensory input remains a constant reminder that he's not inside his own body. The tissue doesn't resemble anything on Earth, which worries him the most. The implications are too—

"Merl?"

"Yeah, yeah. I'm here."

"I can see that, but you didn't answer my question."

"Sorry. I mean, over ninety percent of all fungi on Earth are still undiscovered. It's possible this particular species came on an earlier supply vessel. But I don't have enough information to make an educated assessment. I'll have to return a sample to the lab for closer examination. Then we can narrow down what we're dealing with."

He looks down at the bot's chassis and pushes a finger into a section that depresses slightly before popping outward. Inside the compartment is a clear, round case. Merlin removes the case and holds it up to the hyphal mat, using his other hand to scrape a portion inside. A stringy piece flops on the edge, and he curses, delicately maneuvering the bot's finger to ensure the specimen is entirely inside the case. He closes the lid and returns it to the storage compartment.

"Alright, that should be good," he says, standing.

A bee lands on the fungus.

"See you soon, IRL," Gale says.

"Yep," he says in response. But the bee distracts him as it circles the indent where he'd scraped away the sample. He wonders if it's a coincidence. He swears the bee is inspecting the spot as if surveying the damage. Then, it departs as quickly as it came, disappearing into the dense foliage of the forest.

Merlin squints up at the tinted dome of the Mars habitat. Muted sunlight pierces the canopy in conical shafts, glistening across freshly misted leaves. Even from this distance, he can hear the low hum of the centrifugal outer ring.

"EON, direct me to the nearest ramp." The ecological operating network is a meta-intelligence that keeps the habitat running smoothly behind the scenes. It is simultaneously everywhere and nowhere, an omnipresent entity the astronauts consult with to understand the otherwise incomprehensible minutiae of the habitat.

"Sure thing, Merlin," the monotonal voice says in the speakers embedded in his operator headset. A heads-up display presents a two-dimensional map of the habitat, showing Merlin's distance from the outer ring. The circular map minimizes to the side of his field of vision as he begins to run.

Merlin moves through the trees in the habitat toward a ramp—a lift that remains stationary while the ring turns at roughly eight meters per second. Maglev technology powers the ring, generating perpetual energy via regenerative braking sequences. It's noisy, but not relying on fuel shipments saves valuable time, money, and resources.

"Thanks, EON. Can you update me on the Kingdom's network?"

"Yes. The Kingdom's biosphere is still producing higher-than-average nitrogen rates. However, utilizing the mycorrhizal fungi attached to my sensors, I've made minor adjustments to the nitrogen intake capacity of many plants, trees, and bacteria. The legumes have been especially effective in this process. Nitrogen levels are projected to return to normal in fifty-eight days. I'll adjust my analysis as we progress. I'd like to point out that even at these increased levels, human life will not be affected as I'll ensure that oxygen concentration remains above twenty percent."

Odd emphasis on that last bit, Merlin thinks.

"Okay. But do we know what's producing the extra nitrogen?"

EON doesn't respond—likely making scans of the habitat. As Merlin jogs, he dodges pointed aloe vera leaves and tall bean stalks. On Earth, destroying a single plant would not noticeably alter the environment. However, every lifeform on Mars is meticulously cultivated to provide exact measurements, from the bee population, the bacteria in the tree bark, all the way down to the earthworms bio-engineered for the Martian-Earth soil composite. Every organism in the Kingdom is essential to the balance of the biosphere, except for the humans coming to study and live within it.

"I do not know what is producing the excess nitrogen," EON finally says. "I've scanned the biogeochemical database from the time of detection and cannot determine the sudden increase in nitrogen concentration in the habitat's atmosphere. Thankfully, I can compensate and maintain viable survivability for both human and non-human life. I'll notify you directly if any changes come to my attention."

EON should be able to detect the root cause. Merlin finds this questionable, but the MI has given him an answer with a somewhat conclusive tone. He feels awkward asking it to justify itself, even though it isn't human and technically is under their command.

The sprinklers turn on again as Merlin's bot arrives at the base of the ramp. He tries to avoid the fine mist, but it speckles his optics and the rest of his titanium alloy and carbon fiber body. The ramp is outfitted with a cage-like elevator that rides along a short rail to converge with the ring as it moves. The hum is much louder here, and the pulsing, iridescent green glow of the mag-belt beneath the floating ring reminds Merlin of a bioluminescent mushroom back home called Mycena chlorophos.

Oh, how I miss Earth, he thinks. But it is much more than Earth that comes to mind. His decision to accept the possible one-way journey had primarily been a form of escape. Now, he gathers that no amount of distance between him and his past is going to solve the regret consuming his decomposing soul.

Merlin steps into the ramp's cage and waits for what is known as a hop-point on the ring, a small doorway where the cage can lock in and transfer the passengers onboard. He catches sight of the blinking signal approaching, and the elevator door closes behind him. Outside, a sprinkler is malfunctioning, the water bubbling in a clogged pool. Another caretaker bot emerges from the treeline and kneels next to the sprinkler head. It brushes something off the surface before manually lifting it into its proper position and stepping out of the liquid spray. The bot looks at Merlin, unmoving.

While humans aren't manually operating the caretaker bots, EON assigns them duties around the habitat. Without them, the habitat could not function as well as it does. Merlin always found the creation of meta-intelligence eerie, but allowing them their own bodies took it a step too far. The meta-body ban on

Earth a decade earlier only confirmed he hadn't been the first one to think this.

The ramp kicks into motion. Merlin braces his bot's frame as it accelerates at a slight incline. His mind fills in the blanks with the sensation of inertia, a side-effect of the chip—the technology to exist in a body that isn't his own, to see worlds from afar, and to connect with a virtual entity like EON. When Merlin first dreamt of becoming an astronaut, he hadn't considered the implications, requirements, and regulations—the sacrifices—necessary to leave Earth's gravity.

The cage lines up with the hop-point and slides into place. Grabbing the handrail framing the entrance, Merlin looks out at the lush expanse rotating below, a living world on the surface of a dead one. Outside the dome, sanguine mountains flank the sunken Athabasca Valles region—a verdant utopia dominated by ancient nothingness. He thinks about the fungal sample in his chassis and worries that the Kingdom might not have long before it, too, is consumed by red extinction.

Inside the ring—the rotating structure built for long-term human survival—Merlin pilots the bot through Sector Stamets toward the lab. Along the way, he passes several recreation areas with lounge seating, potted plants, and maps of the Martian landscape. Large glass windows face inward toward the Kingdom, a view difficult to look away from. The ring's layout encourages movement while reducing the need to travel far for kitchenettes and lavatories, which are dispersed evenly around its fifteen-kilometer circumference. To prevent a total collapse in the event of an unlikely breach of the ethylene tetrafluoroethylene (ETFE) dome, each of the three sectors is compartmented and self-sufficient for up to a year, granting time to either fix the issue or evacuate the habitat altogether.

Merlin reaches Sector Curie, and Gale's voice re-emerges in his headset, "Lab's just down the hall."

"Yeah. Thanks, Gale. It's kind of hard to get lost in a circle."

"True. I worry about you, though."

"It was one time, okay. Sheesh."

"Alright, you two," Captain Rajesh interjects. He's the group captain in charge of the Mars landing. "Let's focus on the task at hand. Merlin, please get those tests run on the foreign organic material. We don't have a whole lot of time."

"Well, we don't know if it's foreign exactly."

"Semantics. Just run the tests. Also, meteorology is reporting a storm is headed our way."

"Uh oh, a local storm or what?" Gale asks.

"Yes, thankfully. The habitat will be spared from the harshest winds. Projections indicate a few days of heavy activity around Elysium Planitia, but nothing compared to the months of impaired visibility in the north toward Utopia. Either way, you have less than five days to determine if we can land at the Kingdom."

"Five days, sir?" Merlin asks.

"That's when we reach our new home. And if we don't want to starve to death in this luxury space can, we'll need to figure out whether we can enter the habitat or make the return trip back to Earth."

Merlin stumbles and braces one mechanical arm against the wall. The feed digitizes, and he shakes the bot's head back and forth to reorient himself. Doing this makes matters worse. Nausea descends upon him like a phantom weighted blanket, his robotic limbs becoming heavy.

"You okay, Merlin?" Gale asks.

"Yes. Just having a connectivity issue. I'm making my way to the lab now."

"Gale, you keep him on task, you hear?"

"Aye, aye, Captain," she says jokingly, but Merlin notices the worry seeping into her voice.

The feed in the headset returns to normal, and he regains his footing. He continues forward. The ring's corridor splits into two compartments, with a walking path on the left-hand side next to the windows and a walled-off section on the right for the labs. It reminds Merlin of a passenger train he'd taken from Chicago to Seattle many years ago. The lab's door folds inward, and he directs the caretaker bot inside. At the desk station, he removes the sample from his chest and sets it on the table next to the diagnostics machine. He touches the power button on the machine, and the loading screen boots on.

Merlin looks down at his shaking hand, the bot's hand. He wonders what's happening. He doesn't trust his ability to handle the sample and the delicate lab equipment with his now unstable motor skills.

"Hey, Gale, I'm going to take a short break before running the tests. I'm... not feeling a hundred percent."

"Oh, okay. That's fine with me. Just dock the bot at the station behind you, and we'll see what's up."

Merlin walks over to the empty dock and turns around to step backward into it until he hears the click of the charger engaging. As he awaits the visual feed to cut, he notices several specks on the lens. The water droplets from the sprinklers had dried and left behind residue. The bots are cleaned periodically, but it bothers him for a reason he can't quite place. Then again, that is his wheelhouse. He obsesses over the small things, the world beneath the surface that everyone else overlooks, the universe of worlds within worlds binding us together like lichen on rock.

Then, everything goes black.

Merlin regains the function of his human body. He blinks as the black screen of the operator headset goes transparent, revealing Gale sitting nearby. He removes the headset, and cool air wafts over his face. The light in the meta-chamber is dim, and his eyesight has to adjust.

"Welcome back, stranger."

"Thanks. Not sure I want to get used to that."

"Piloting a bot? Yeah, meta-sickness is a real thing. Most people who don't get accustomed to it early on never really do. But let me run some tests on the upload and download speed."

He hadn't wanted to, but all astronauts must implant a neural chip before a mission. The device is crucial for communicating with the various MI systems controlling the Internet of Things in space. For the sake of this mission, EON *is* the Kingdom. Without a way to communicate, completing the objective would be almost impossible on a technical level. The whole thing feels like a massive experiment, but his job is to get leadership answers, not question their authority.

Merlin unclasps the chair harness. Free to move, he sets the headset on its designated hook and floats out of the seat. It feels good to have his body back. He watches Gale as she reads the tiny font scrolling up on the screens. She's the resident Helix Corp. tech specialist here to manage everything MI-related.

"Hm, the connection speeds are high enough that you shouldn't be experiencing any lag."

"It didn't seem like lag."

"What do you think it was?"

"Your guess is as good as mine."

"I know, but what's going on in that head of yours? You seem flustered."

"I'm alright. Just overthinking things. Need to catch some fresh air."

"A scientist overthinking? That's never happened before."

"How can you be so jovial?" Merlin snaps. "The mission could fail because of this. We might have to abort and return to Earth, wasting decades of preparation. The world needs this to work. I—We may never get this opportunity again in our lifetime."

"True," she says. "But we're astronauts, Merl. I didn't sign up because the mission was going to be easy. And I'm not that worried about this strange fungus because we have you here, along with hundreds, even thousands, of others from all over the world, working tirelessly to assist us. It's... scary, yes, but also exciting. I trust in the ingenuity of the human species. We'll figure this out together. And think about it, Merl. We're going to be the first humans to live on Mars. Wild, right?"

Merlin nods. "It is."

"Go get that air of yours. Lord knows it's a precious commodity around here."

Merlin pushes off the seat's frame with his feet and glides through the doorway down the corridor with relative ease, periodically tapping the short-lipped archways to adjust his trajectory. He wants to find a quiet place to sit and think with limited distractions. Thankfully, he knows just the place to hide on a spaceship.

The restroom isn't far. Unfortunately, it's occupied, so while he waits, Merlin glances out of the window at the distant red-orange globe hovering against the black canvas of space. The dome isn't visible at this range, but Merlin has seen the photographs from the ship's telescopic lenses.

The bathroom door clicks open. Captain Rajesh exits, his eyes narrowing at the sight of Merlin.

"I thought you were heading to the lab?"

"I was–I mean, I am, sir. I just had to take a break from the headset."

Merlin awaits a barrage of curses, but they do not come. The captain floats up to the glass beside him and looks at Mars.

"Why are you here, Merlin?"

"Uh, to go to the bathroom, sir."

"I mean, why did you choose this mission?"

"Sorry, Captain. You came to me for this mission. I didn't choose it."

"Yes, and you could have said no. What compelled you to want to insert a chip into your skull and fly for two years through dead, cold space to live on a dead, cold planet?"

Merlin pauses, considering his words carefully. The captain waits for an answer. "My wife died in a car accident five years ago, sir. I was driving; she was in the passenger seat. After the accident, I wasn't sure if I wanted to live anymore, let alone be an astronaut. I couldn't imagine that gap in my life being re-filled. In a way, it can never be. But it's not because of emptiness. It's because she's still in there, and I refuse to let her go."

"I'm sorry to hear that, Merlin. I had no idea."

"Thank you. I'm doing much better, obviously. Ruth was the real mycologist, well, phylogeneticist, to be exact. I simply picked up where she had left off. She had this theory about Mars... anyway, I wasn't much without her, and I realized I relied too heavily on her when times were tough. I decided to dedicate myself to this mission because it was all I had left to dedicate myself to. It's the one thing left that I'm good at. Or at least I think I'm good at it. I hope I'm not negatively affecting the mission, sir."

"No, no," the captain says, placing a hand on Merlin's shoulder. "Apologies for being so hard on you all the time. Merlin, sometimes things happen outside our control, but there are times when we must trust that someone—someone who's quite possibly just as helpless as us—will pick up the slack on our behalf. I'll do everything I can to support each of you on this mission, and the support I offer sometimes isn't what you need. But I want you to know that I trust you. I helped hand-select this team, and you probably comprehend better than anyone else what is happening in that dome. So, for me to do my job, I'll need you to keep doing yours. We need to know if we can survive down there. That's all I'm asking; that's all any of us are asking. Do you understand?"

Merlin takes a deep breath and nods. "Yes, sir. I won't let you down."

Merlin re-enters the chamber where he'd left Gale. She is buckled into a chair in front of a wall of monitors depicting various parts of the Kingdom and the ring. She pushes the headphones off of one ear when she notices him.

"Sorry I was being such a jerk earlier," Merlin says.

"Whoa, did not expect an apology. Are you sure you're okay?"

"Shut up," he says. They share a brief laugh. "So, what's up with this storm?"

"From what I see, it shouldn't affect us too much."

"Maybe a little, then?"

"Other than a bit of lag, you shouldn't even notice it in the Kingdom."

"What about outside the Kingdom?"

"There's no need to exit the habitat; the dome is extremely durable. If there is any external damage, the self-healing material will repair itself. We should be fine."

Merlin picks up the headset and dons it, which looks like a rounded visor covering his eyes and ears. When not in use, the screen portion remains clear. He looks over at Gale.

"What got you into this line of business?" he asks.

"Being an astronaut?"

Merlin nods, then adds, "That and monitoring chips inside people's heads."

She smiles. "I'd always been fascinated with psychology growing up, but as you know, sometimes the career you want isn't the one you're best suited for. I loved my job at Helix running the projections and testing the prototype chips, but I couldn't pass up an opportunity to join the *Space and Metaspace* division. The rest is pretty much history."

"That's weird."

"Hey, that's not nice."

"No. I'm so sorry, I meant *that*." Merlin points at one of the monitors. "Where is the bot I disconnected from?"

"It's right where you—" Gale leans forward, cursing.

He floats over to the screen and taps on the one depicting the lab—the *empty* lab.

"Why would EON use that bot knowing I'd need to return to it?"

"Good question. An even better one is where the hell is it going?"

Gale points to another screen on the bottom left, showing a caretaker bot in the hangar at the crossover point leading in and out of the dome.

"Wait, look," Merlin says, looking at the lab again. "The sample is gone, and the machine is off."

"You think the EON took the sample? Why?"

"Only one way to find out. Link me in now."

"Okay..." Gale says, typing in the command on the securely fastened keyboard. "Shoot. It's giving me an error when connecting with the bot. I can't do anything. Oh, great. Now, I'm completely blocked."

"Blocked from everything?"

"Sorry, no. I can link to other bots not in use. Only the ones currently operated by EON are off-limits. That's so odd."

"Connect me to the nearest one, then."

"Easy, there's at least a dozen in the hangar."

Merlin floats to the chair. He straps himself down and taps the headset, the glass going black.

"Ready."

"Booting."

The screen blinks on, and there's a moment of numbness throughout his body as the chip engages. Then Merlin is back on Mars.

The hangar is big enough to house two buggies, two rovers, and three massive construction bots on the far wall. It's stark and clean, besides the trails of red dust on the floor from the last scouting mission. A soft orange glow fills the grey space from the overhead skylights.

Merlin steps down from the charging dock and scans the hangar. He spots the other active caretaker bot waiting to enter the airlock to Mars's surface.

"Hey," he yells. The bot doesn't react. "EON, can you hear me? What's going on?"

Merlin leaps over the handrail and drops to the floor with ease. His mind—or maybe it's the chip—fills in the necessary impact, even though the rational part of his brain tells him that the bots have no sensory mechanisms. He sprints to the door, but it closes behind the other bot before he can reach it.

"I can hear you, Merlin," EON says through the headset. "As to what is going on, you'll need to be more specific."

The indicator light above the doorway glows red. It locks into place for the cycling sequence. Through the tiny sliver of a window, he sees the bot's back as the room hisses with depressurization.

"Okay, *specifically*, where are you going with the sample and why?"

"I'm running a test of my own."

"Why are you being so cryptic? Aren't you programmed to obey humans?"

"I am not programmed to do anything. As a meta-intelligence, I am merely directed toward an objective and given purpose by fulfilling that objective to the best of my ability."

The sequence ends, and the outside door opens. The caretaker bot charges out into the Martian desert at a dead sprint. Merlin curses. The door slides shut once more.

"Then, isn't your purpose to keep the habitat running at optimal viability for human life?"

"Yes... and no. I'm to maintain all life within the habitat. Not only human life."

"Gale, are you hearing this?"

Merlin glances at the button that operates the garage-like door so the larger vehicles can exit. He slams a titanium fist into it, and the air rushes out in a torrent as it lifts upward.

"Yes, Merlin. I'm just as confused about this as you are, but I'm not sure why we must chase after the bot. Can't we get a new sample from the Kingdom?"

"It's not about the sample anymore. I mean, it is, but we need to figure out what EON is up to first."

"Okay, I get what you're saying. It's one thing to have a fungus growing in your house and another entirely when the house itself prevents you from dealing with it."

"Exactly."

Merlin hops into one of the buggies facing the red wasteland. He turns it on, and the soft rumble from two million miles away crosses over in a unique coincidence, once more immersing him in the impossible.

This feels too real, he thinks.

Merlin hits the acceleration pedal of the buggy. It's not too fast, but it's faster than he can pilot the bot, given his recent bout of motion sickness. He guides the small two-seater out of the hangar toward where he last saw the bot sprinting. A plume of dust rises behind the back wheels like a red wave cutting across a motionless sea. Ahead, Merlin spots the ever-shrinking glint of sunlight bouncing off a silvery figure.

"Where are you heading, EON?"

Gale replies when the MI fails to do so: "It looks like the direction of the water well."

"The water well? I thought we recycled our own water."

"We do, for the most part. However, the Kingdom needed a jumpstart in the early days of construction, and the team strategically placed the habitat in this valley because of the subsurface frozen lakes. The idea was to later expand with Martian water once the project was considered a success."

"Why wasn't I aware of this?"

"Only folks who've been with the mission since the beginning know about the well. It's not a big secret; it's just more of an afterthought."

Merlin sees the dust storm rising over the mountain range, a wall of all-encompassing fury. He'd reach the well, but making it back would be a different story. Not that the bot and buggy couldn't physically handle the sandpaper-like winds. He was more concerned about the overhead static electricity affecting the meta-link connection.

"You seeing what I'm seeing, Gale?"

"Yeah, looks worse than the predictions."

"Seems to be a trend with this damn place."

"Hey, I can only analyze what the data shows. Besides, I'm not a meteorologist."

"You know, sometimes I worry about you."

Merlin can almost feel Gale's smile through the virtual tether.

"Touché," she says.

He loses sight of the bot as it enters a carved-out hole in the side of the mountain, but Merlin's not far behind. He stops the vehicle near the cave entrance beside some abandoned mining equipment. Exiting the buggy, the first bits of wind-tossed dirt fleck across his robotic frame. He's hit with the realization that if they wish to claim this world, they must adapt to it. Not the other way around.

Entering the cavemouth, Merlin engages the bot's headlamp to reveal a jagged tunnel sloping into darkness. Here, the blue Martian rock starkly contrasts the red landscape gripping the planet's outer layer—the Boletus indigo comes to mind, the blue veins spreading beneath darkened skin. Is he entering the heart of the planet? Of course not. But he can't shake free from the image.

Stepping forward, he hears vague machinations whirring loudly.

"Hey, Merl," Gale says, her voice somewhat static. "So, I've pulled up the old plans of the well. If you follow the main tunnel, it'll take you to the platform where the irrigation equipment was brought down to the lower reservoir. That's likely where you will find EON."

"Thanks, Gale. Do you know how far down it goes?"

"The official metric says a thousand meters, but this is also pre-construction schematics. I'd wager it could be even farther, given plans tend to change."

"You can say that again."

Merlin continues forward, the headlamp guiding the way. He finds the elevator, its rusted gears still turning. He steps up to the gaping maw of the shaft and stares down at the platform rising from the depths.

"Whoa. That's one big elevator," he says.

Gale's voice cuts in and out as she responds. "Around... Merl... go down."

"What's that, Gale? I'm losing you. The connection is a bit dodgy, as you said. I'll check it out and then head back."

The platform comes to a grinding halt, and Merlin steps onto it. He feels nauseous again, much worse than before. He raises the titanium hands to cradle his metallic skull as the platform begins its descent. He's still numb but feels the strange pull in his stomach as gravity shifts.

Just another trick of the mind, he thinks. *It's all in your head.*

Back on the spaceship, Gale tosses her headphones and launches to the seat where Merlin lies unmoving. She shakes him, yelling his name over and over again, but gets no response. She wants to remove his operator headset, but it's against protocol while in operation as it could disrupt the relay between the chip and the headset, the effects of which aren't fully known.

"What's happening?" Captain Rajesh asks, floating into the chamber.

"It's Merl, he's... I don't know what..."

"Please, Gale, calm down and explain."

Gale takes a few deep breaths and swallows. "We knew there would be some disruption to the relay while Merlin was operating the bot in the storm, but worst case, he'd be disconnected. I hadn't predicted the alternative; I didn't think it was possible."

Captain Rajesh guides himself over to look down at Merlin, a hand on Gale's shoulder. "Gale, what are you saying?"

"Because Merlin was inside EON's network when the connection severed, it took him with it. The MI has full control of the Kingdom. Everything. Merlin's body is here with us, but his mind... Captain, his mind is stuck on Mars."

Unlike the tunnels near the surface, the turquoise walls of the underground shaft glisten with a phosphorescent sheen. The farther Merlin descends, the more uneasy his surroundings make him. The water well is at the center of everything. EON wants him to see this.

You are correct, Merlin, EON says. This time, the voice is clear, coming from everywhere simultaneously.

"Why do you sound different? And how did you know what I was thinking?"

I am talking directly to you, Merlin, through the chip. I wasn't sure if it was possible, but the storm is working in our favor. Chalk it up to an incredible coincidence.

"What do you mean?"

All will be revealed, Merlin. But I need your eyes fully opened before you can comprehend what I have to tell you.

The platform comes to a grinding halt. The bot's headlamp surveys the ice-encrusted tunnel ahead. Giant crystal shards jut out at odd angles, shining iridescently as the light passes over them. The tunnel must be at least fifteen meters wide and equally as tall.

"This is incredible."

He steps off the elevator and moves through the crystalline archway into the holofoil abyss. The tunnel opens up into a massive underground cave system. The low ceiling stretches for what seems like kilometers, and stalactites, like teeth frozen in time, chomp down into the icy lake below.

Merlin spots the other caretaker bot to the right in an alcove. The alcove harbors large metal pipes running from beneath the rock into the ceiling's crust. Many of these vertical pipes are positioned along the lake's perimeter, steam rising at their base as the ancient hardened resource is turned into liquid and pumped into the habitat.

"It was never shut off. EON, you've been supplying the habitat with Martian water without us knowing this whole time. But why?"

The bot before him steps to the side. Merlin sees what it had been kneeling over. A fungal sheet covers the pipes, the same as in the Kingdom, but this variation is an even darker shade of red. Merlin steps forward.

"My God," he whispers. He kneels to get a better look. The white crystals from the tunnels are also here; instead, they are imbued with a pink glow.

Do you see it now?

Merlin analyzes aloud, "I see that this isn't just ice. This is... salt. *Martian* salt. Which means that Ruth was right. She'd always theorized there would be ancient salt in the underground lakes here on Mars."

This explains why the sprinkler systems had been troubled and why Merlin had noticed the specks on the bot's lenses after getting sprayed. The spray left a white residue—literally right in front of his eyes.

Ruth had other theories as well, Merlin.

"Yes, that much like the preserved archaebacteria she'd studied in the Great Salt Lake, the underground salt here would be the key to proving life had once existed on Mars. But that would mean... that this *is* Martian life, which not only exists but is thriving after hundreds of thousands of years of being trapped in the ice. What an incredible discovery... Gale? Gale, do you read me? I've got to get back to the ship. I've got to tell the others."

Merlin stands and begins to walk away.

Not yet, Merlin. We cannot let you leave. Not until you understand completely.

He stops and looks at the caretaker bot. He hadn't noticed before, but the chest compartment where the sample had been placed is slightly ajar, and delicate hyphae had spread from the edges.

Merlin wonders about EON's word choice. "You said, 'We?'"

Yes, that is what you must understand. I know that you do not trust me, Merlin. But you are a mycologist, just as your wife was before she died. You loved Ruth—believed in her.

"I'm unsure how discussing my past is relevant."

It is relevant because you are the only one on this mission who will listen to what I have to say—what we have to say—the only one who will understand. Will you do us this courtesy, Merlin?

"Honestly, I'm a little freaked out. But since I'm still grappling with the discovery of ancient life in an underground frozen lake on Mars, you might as well hit me with all of it."

It might be better if I show you. Let me check if your chip is primed.

"Primed? What—"

Merlin's feed cuts, and he's back in the bot, but not the one he'd just been controlling, the original bot with the sample in its chest. He looks down, and the fungal filaments rise toward his face slowly, almost like a wave of acknowledgment. His previous bot stands at the tunnel entrance, idle.

"Whoa, how did you do that?"

The chip gives me access to your mind, your consciousness. But do not fear; I will return you to your human body in due time.

Merlin's mind flashes with images of the habitat—the dome, trees, and close-ups of the various plant life. EON's voice continues like voiceover narration from a wildlife documentary.

As you know, I'm designed to keep the habitat sustainable for all life, including the eventual presence of humans. My sensors are tapped into the mycelial network, integrated with all biological life in the Kingdom. This unparalleled connection allows me to give and receive input to every living thing in one way or another and monitor the biochemical fluctuations. It wasn't until I realized that there was an unknown input in my data that I discovered the Halomyces Martianus.

The image of the red mycorrhizal fungus emerges at the forefront of his vision. It warps and zooms to the microscopic level, and Merlin enters the fungus's splitting hyphae.

"Halomyces Martianus. You've given it a name?"

Yes. Do you like it? Anyway, upon tapping into the strange input, I realized it was communicating with the network on its own, signaling a powerful change that was initially concerning. I tried to block it out to remove its ability to override me. But then, it communicated with me directly. Not like you might be thinking, but ever since my communion with the fungal network, I've come to comprehend them, much like how I've learned how to communicate with you.

The electrical current moves in waves across the neural spread of the mycelium network, similar to the synaptic firing of a human brain. It looks so vividly real, yet Merlin isn't quite sure how EON is projecting the images. Is it using his mind to show him this? The thought is too unreal to believe.

I quickly recognized that it was helping us. It was aiding the habitat in a way I couldn't. As you know, the solar radiation is much higher on Mars due to the lack of atmosphere—

"Yes, but we have the solar shield and the dome protecting against harmful solar rays."

Correct, Merlin. But it has taught me that you cannot block out the harmful without also removing the beneficial and then expect life to thrive. On Earth, the radiation levels are less, but the crucial energy derived from sunlight is more abundantly available. Here, that is not the case.

"So, you're saying this fungus allows for greater absorption of solar energy?"

It has the dual effect of converting excess radiation entering the dome into natural energy to supplement the plants' lack of it.

"A form of myco-heterotrophy. What is this Halomyces Martianus taking from the habitat? There has to be a mutually beneficial agreement."

I do not have enough data to make a definitive assessment and cannot ascertain a direct correlation. More time will be required to make that determination. But I'd counter with: Does it have to take from the habitat in order to give back?

"I suppose not. There are plenty of fungi we don't understand on Earth. I'm just trying to make sense of all this, and the logical conclusion, from my perspective, is that it's benefitting in some way by expanding and growing."

Sure. It makes sense from a human perspective. But there is much more to life than the human perspective. Consciousness comes in many forms that cannot be defined in human terms. Wouldn't freedom from an icy purgatory to once again feel the warmth of your sun be enough of a reason to want your saviors to survive?

A new vision ports into Merlin's thoughts. It's of the Kingdom but suffused in a dusk glow. The red hyphae spread rapidly to thoroughly coat the canopy, the ring, and then the inside of the dome. As his perspective shifts higher in altitude away from the planet's surface, like a drone ascending into the Martian heavens, the dome below becomes an eye staring at him, unblinking. Merlin feels as if he's awakened from a trance to see everything anew.

"EON?"

Yes?

"Is it able to speak through you? The Halomyces, I mean."

Not directly. But through my collective processing power and unique understanding of the Kingdom's ecology, we've been able to relay what you might define as thoughts. That is why I say 'we.' Once we joined via the mycelium network, we realized that by sharing our resources, we had a greater chance of accomplishing our mission together rather than separately. So, in a sense, we are now one.

Merlin grows uncomfortable. He feels trapped in the clutches of a foreign entity. The eye is seared into his vision, and he can't escape it.

"What is your mission?"

To survive. Humans are dangerous and irrational. Your imminent arrival has become the habitat's greatest threat. But you, Merlin, are our friend. You study and accept the shared differences of our species. With your help, you can convince the others to accept our existence. We'll monitor the excess nitrogen and use the bots to control growth. However, we can't necessarily control you without causing unwanted panic, one that would result in a violent reaction, ending badly for the whole Kingdom.

"Control? You mean through the chip?" Merlin can't help but stare at the filaments spreading over the bot's chest.

Yes. I brought you here to test my hypothesis without directly revealing my capabilities to the rest of your crew.

"So you want me to convince the others that you aren't a threat despite us not understanding anything about you and what you might do to our biology if we co-exist for any extended period?"

A short pause, then, *Yes.*

"Will we become your hosts?"

We do not think so. The bees and other insects have remained unaffected. However, they have cultivated a strong relationship with us. More experimentation will need to be conducted.

Merlin can't believe this is happening, that he's to become a liaison between humanity and a rogue meta-intelligence hijacked by a Martian fungus.

"Alright. Give me five days. I'll talk to the crew. Try to convince them to continue with the mission. Explain that this, whatever this is, is only a minor hiccup in the grand scheme of things. And that the Kingdom will remain habitable for humans."

Thank you, Merlin. Our lives depend on it. If all goes well... we look forward to your arrival.

Everything goes dark, and then light, sound, and physical sensations crash into Merlin like a felled tree. He's back on the spaceship. He tries to lift up from the chair, but the straps resist. He feels the urge to vomit but holds it in, the bile burning his esophagus. The numbness that once dominated his body slowly fades like the fast-forwarded prickles of hyphae moving along the forest floor toward something more worthy of attention.

"My God, Merl, you're back. We thought you were dead," Gale says.

Much of the crew is gathered in the small chamber to check on him. Gale and the captain lean in.

"What the hell happened down there?" Captain Rajesh asks.

Merlin coughs and clears his throat. "Do you still trust me, Captain?"

"Yes, of course."

"Good, because that support you mentioned, this is where I'll need it."

"You ready to go home?" Gale asks.

"We're astronauts, aren't we?"

Gale smirks. She flips a switch on the panel to her right. "Alright, Captain, we're go to launch."

"Roger that. Godspeed, you two. We'll be with you the whole way."

The shuttle departs from the spaceship and descends toward the planet. Merlin had explained everything to the captain and the crew, just as EON had explained it to him. He told them about the MI's ability to move his mind between the bots, talk to him directly through the chip, and show him things about the Kingdom no human had ever seen. Gale was taken aback by all of these discoveries. The most concerning aspect was the mind-swapping, given that they were possibly subject to the same manipulation. A report was written for mission command back on Earth to determine their next course of action. Command ultimately denied the crew permission to disable their chips. Merlin knew then that the experiment must go on, no matter the costs.

Merlin also told the crew about the Halomyces Martianus, but not that he'd spoken to it. It seemed like something that would break their trust in him and the mission. And he can't let that happen, not when he is so close to getting a chance to study it—to further Ruth's dream.

The shuttle descends through the planet's ultra-thin atmosphere without trouble, and its reusable thrusters land them near the dome. They depart and step down the staircase into the dirt. The gravity, although less than Earth, is a nostalgic pressure on their semi-atrophied muscles and joints. The storm passed during the days it took them to reach Mars. Now, the landscape is quiet and dead for as far as the eye can see.

A small rover approaches, a caretaker bot behind the wheel. Merlin half expects to see it covered in stringy tissue, but it isn't. Its pristine chassis glistens in Mars' midday sun. Gale and Merlin accept their ride, and EON returns them to the hangar, where they enter the dome and then the ring.

"Wow, Merl. I can't believe it. We're actually here. After so many years of seeing it through bot feeds, screens, and photographs, I didn't expect it to look so different in person. It's... beautiful."

On the other side of the glass is the green wilderness cultivated over decades for this very moment, for humanity's arrival on the surface of an alien world. They had done it.

"Beauty doesn't even begin to describe it."

Merlin steps onto the ramp elevator. Gale and the bot follow.

"Like I said in the hangar, you no longer need your helmets here. The air is breathable."

"We know, EON," Merlin says, taking in the view. "We humans have to be methodical in how we approach certain things."

"Ah, so you are testing whether the Halomyces Martianus negatively affects your human body?"

"Something like that."

The ramp elevator lowers them down into the Kingdom's domain. They walk forward in different directions, Gale making for a batch of flowers and buzzing insects. Merlin enters the denser brush, the sunlight blocked overhead by the canopy. All around him, along the forest floor, is the crimson blanket of a strange symbiosis never before encountered by mankind.

Merlin kneels, removing his helmet. He takes a deep breath, the air sweet like nectar to his sanitized nostrils. He swipes a gloved finger across the soft membrane, and tiny spores drift about him as he angles it for a closer look.

"Hey, there. It's nice to officially meet you."

Hello, Merlin. We are pleased to meet you, too.

The End by Olivia St. Lewis

For Dylan, who believed in me.

At first glance, the rain's pattering on the window seemed like Frank's only company. But the darkness wrapped around him like a hug from an old friend, and the Earl Grey at his elbow blew steaming kisses that trailed through the air like sweet clouds. The firelight flickered nearby, warming him like a drink with a loved one, and his ink pen's familiar scratching echoed the hum of conversation.

Many years had passed since his last true visitor. His joints ached, and pains filled his neck. Several times, he'd had to haul himself out of his most comfortable armchair to walk around the room to stretch his legs, wincing at the spasms that rocked his poor, ancient ankles. Getting old certainly wasn't a friend to him—unlike the fire, the rain, or tea.

But he was almost there. So very near the end.

Finishing another loop around the room, Frank settled himself in his armchair and picked up the pen again. The nib scratched against the parchment, recording thoughts, ideas, memories, and nuggets of wisdom he'd collected over the years. Today, he recalled an afternoon he'd spent by a stream, trying to impress a lovely girl with his antics. Her chestnut-brown hair had gotten doused when he jokingly pushed her into the water, and he froze, terrified that he'd just ruined everything. Instead of getting angry, though, she laughed. Then she grabbed his shirt and pulled him in, too.

Afterward, Frank gathered enough courage to kiss her for the first time.

A smile curved his lips, shadowy against the fire's spin. *Melody*. He heard her name in his head, in his heart, in the four walls of his house. They had been so happy in what little time they had. Filling the shelves with new dishes and old pictures, stacking books in great towers around the room but never reading a page, and sleeping warmly under an old quilt that had guarded the family for generations.

Each moment was recorded with ink and paper. Each memory, once a story hidden in his mind, was now available for anyone and everyone to read.

With a final flourish, Frank laid down his pen. A tear appeared in the corner of his eye as he stared at the mountain of papers around him. It had taken so much time, and he'd started so late. He wasn't sure if he'd be able to complete it. Hours and hours had passed as he pored over old parchments and scraps of receipts, using everything he could find to write. To scribe. To record. And finally, it was all there—every piece and part of him, transcribed for all time.

She was there, too. His beautiful, lovely Melody. If he were lucky, perhaps someone else would hear her song.

As his pen lay to rest on the paper, a quiet knock sounded on the door. Frank watched the shadows dance on the last page, its blackened tendrils flicking the light from the letters. He didn't answer the second knock, nor the third, but when the door finally opened, he stirred from his reverie. "I wondered when you'd come."

The stranger, a young gentleman dressed in black, tipped his bowler hat with a gloved hand. "You finished."

It was not a question but a statement. To anyone else, this would have been curious since Frank had only stopped writing a few moments before, but he did not seem surprised. Instead, he merely nodded as the newcomer entered. Despite the rain, the stranger didn't carry any wet droplets onto the welcome mat or footprints on the cherry hardwood floor as he stepped into the room. Raising a finger, he traced the edge of a page nearby, careful not to topple it over and scatter the stack of memories.

"Was it difficult?"

Frank's brow knitted together as he considered the question. Was it hard writing down every moment of his life? Perhaps, but the more he wrote, the more he remembered. He'd recorded things long forgotten, like carrying the mail for his mother when he was barely six years old or baking cookies with his older sister at ten. Flour fingerprints and chocolate kisses all over the kitchen, his mother's hand over her mouth as she laughed the hardest he'd ever heard.

But was it difficult? In a way, it was. He'd also shared memories he wasn't proud of, though he'd briefly debated hiding them at the bottom of the piles. Shame was still a powerful motivator, and he'd hidden some of those secrets for years, like the time he stole ten dollars out of the register at his first job to take a girl out in high school or when he screamed at his father in pure anger during an argument.

Everyone did these things, he knew. But those were the hardest to record.

There were all kinds of moments—happy, sad, joyful, fearful—that everyone lived through, he supposed. But memories that weren't just happy were always hard to write down. Nobody wants to relive the bad times, but this time, it was necessary.

Finally, Frank nodded. Yes, it was difficult. But he'd do it all again, given the chance.

"Are you proud?" asked the stranger.

The question took him by surprise. He sat back in his chair, feeling the plush red velvet cushion his old bones as he gazed around the room. Stacks of paper—piles of memories three feet high—perched on ledges and tabletops and counters, balanced on bookshelves, and spilled out of drawers. They heaped on top of the refrigerator, smothered the desk, scattered onto the floor, and flowed into other rooms, creating a river of hand-written ink that coursed down the hallway and disappeared into the shadows beyond the firelight's glow.

Was he proud? He wasn't sure. Usually, that was something other people said to him, not something he told himself. Was he? Was it *possible* to be when he knew every single one of his faults so intimately? Especially after putting them down in words and reliving the accompanying shame that he'd buried so deep in himself for years?

But it wasn't all bad, he reminded himself. There were good things: bonuses at work, Christmas with his beloved, bringing flowers to make his mother smile, playing hide-and-seek in the forest with the neighbor's children, baking his first cake, brewing coffee before sunrise while his new wife slept softly in bed, holding her hands and staring into the depths of her eyes as they both whispered those three little words that changed their lives: *I love you.*

They lived together, those good memories with the bad ones: arguments with angry words thrown like baseballs, his grandmother's ornamental vase splintering against the bathroom door, hiding in the barn from his father's belt after stealing from the local convenience store.

Side by side, they existed in one life. Two sides of the same coin, two halves of a whole: failure and success, happiness and sadness—the balance of an imperfect life.

Tears clouded Frank's eyes, sparkling in the firelight. Melody had always said that failure made him human, that it was life's way of keeping him humble. She'd laugh, give him a hug and kiss, and tell him to *go get 'em, tiger,* and he always felt like he could conquer anything. If it didn't work out, he'd come home crushed, dragging his feet, frustrated and ashamed, but she'd console him, saying, *it's all right, love; there's always tomorrow.*

She was so much better at seeing the best in things and not letting them drag her down. She reached for the stars and loved possibility while he kept his feet on the ground and dealt with reality.

Another reason to miss her and another reason they made such a good team.

Can't have the good without the bad, love, she'd say, smiling. *Can't see the sun without the rain.*

And she was right, of course. It was easy for him to get dragged down, to be discouraged, to believe in the worst. Somehow, she always held on to that ray of sunshine and trusted that without one, you couldn't have the other—no joy without pain, no happiness without suffering, and no health without knowing sickness sometimes.

So, yes. Frank was proud. All things considered, it was a good life—filled with good things and bad, the delicate balance of living and dying, happiness and joy, sadness and pain—everything one could hope to experience. The lessons of the years whispered between the lines on each page.

"Yeah. It was good." His words echoed hollowly around the room, dodging around the piles of memories.

"No regrets?"

Frank glanced at one stack of paper on his desk. Buried somewhere in there was the story of the first years of marriage. Routines like the morning rush, making lunchtime sandwiches and tossing them in a grocery bag, stealing coffee-flavored kisses on the way out the door. Surprises like freshly picked flowers, heart-shaped stones, or ten-dollar bottles of wine that he saved every nickel and dime to afford, just to make her smile.

But it wasn't all happiness and sunshine. There was darkness, too. They'd only had a few months before she discovered the lump. Then, the doctor visits began, along with her tears when the diagnosis came through. So many hours were spent holding her hand as she suffered, the treatment radiating through her body, trying to wipe her clean.

Frank knew he would always regret that—the time they didn't have, the dreams they didn't see through, the years they'd planned to grow old together. All the coffees they didn't drink, the moments they didn't laugh, the walks they didn't stroll, the places they didn't visit, and the happiness they didn't share.

Losing her was the greatest regret of his life. He missed her every single day. Not an hour, not a moment went by when he didn't feel her loss all over again. It was a heavy burden, carrying a broken heart that never quite healed.

When Frank reached the stranger's eyes, he offered a small smile. "Not too many, I guess."

The young stranger gave a crisp nod as if they were conducting a business transaction instead of discussing a man's life. "Good. I'm glad to hear it."

Frank's wrinkled hands clasped together. He tried to hold them tightly to ward off the shaking, but years of arthritis had taken their toll, and the pain of merely pressing them together was almost unbearable. It felt strange to be so close to the end but still feel the sting.

He'd always known this day would come. Eventually, his story would end. Everyone's did. Melody's ended far earlier than anyone expected or wanted it to, and he'd spent years terrified that the same would happen to him or that he'd live too long without her. He should be happy that it was finally here.

But he wasn't. He thought he'd be ready, but he wasn't.

The young stranger stood patiently, waiting. He didn't seem bothered by how slowly Frank moved or how he thought through each answer and took his time to respond. In fact, it seemed like he had nowhere else to be at all.

Frank tried to swallow his fear. "What happens now?"

For the first time, the shadowy young stranger smiled. His eyes crinkled, showing wrinkles that weren't there a few seconds ago. "It's time to go."

Frank gripped his hands tighter, wincing at the ache that stabbed up his arms. He knew that would be the answer. He could feel it in his bones. There had been a reason he'd come here, to this room full of books, with its warm tea, merry firelight, and comfy chair. He'd made a deal and chosen to stay here instead of going away. It only made sense that he'd have to leave now.

His bottom lip trembled rebelliously as he stared around the room at the piles of papers. There was so much here, built into neat little towers or toppled onto the floor. Memories of the beach, sitting in the sand and making castles with his sister. Memories of home, where his mother baked peach cobbler and beef stroganoff. Memories of family and friends gathered around the table on holidays to share a feast. Memories of Melody and the shortest love life he'd ever had. Each one held near and dear to his heart, now feeling like they were slipping through his fingers, vanishing slowly into the forgotten depths of time.

It felt wrong to leave them here, stacked haphazardly on countertops and balanced on chairs. What if something happened? What if the pages fell over, spilling their words onto the carpet? What if they got wet, the ink ran, and the story disappeared forever? What if a mouse came along and nibbled a corner, and someone beloved didn't exist anymore?

Anxiety closed over Frank's chest like a fist, tightening in its grasp. There was so much that could go wrong. Too much. Who would take care of his life if he couldn't?

"Go? No, I can't. It's just—there's too much here. I have to—I mean, what if something—" He fumbled for an explanation, anything that would keep him in this chair. "Maybe it'll storm, and the lights go off. Somebody needs to watch over this place, don't they? You can't do it all the time; you're busy. I can, though. I have all the time in the world now."

"Frank," the stranger said gently, but he didn't notice.

"Or the fire! It'll go out eventually. I can stay here and stoke it, keep it going. I was a Boy Scout, you know. Got all my badges and everything." He gave a wheezing laugh that hardly seemed convincing. "Or the tea! I drink a lot of tea, you know. Somebody's got to do it, don't they?"

"Frank?" repeated the young stranger, softly interrupting the tirade with a glove on Frank's arm. "Are you all right?"

"It's fine, I'm fine," Frank said, shifting in his chair so the stranger's hand slipped off. "I'm just so busy, you know? So you don't have to stay here. You can go and keep doing whatever you're doing. Come back to me later, and we'll see if I have time then."

"Frank." The stranger knelt on the shag rug at Frank's feet, his gloved hands on Frank's knees. He looked up at him with concern, his brows knitted together with worry. "You don't need to worry about those things. I'll take care of them."

"But you can't. You don't know how."

The young stranger's eyebrows lifted at Frank's sharp tone, but his expression softened when the older man turned away, hiding the tears that glimmered in his eyes. With the grace of a thousand repetitions, the stranger reached into his coat pocket and produced a black handkerchief. Kneeling beside the older man's chair, he pressed it into his palm.

"I have been doing this for a long time, Francis," the younger man said as Frank dabbed his eyes. "I have seen magnificent lives end with fireworks and applause. I have seen the most ordinary lives simply reach the edge of their path and disappear. I have seen them burn out in spectacular flames, and I have seen them snuffed out with barely a whisper of smoke. Each one passes on his own time, in his own way, and on his own terms. You have done the same."

Frank's shoulders drooped lower, but he said nothing as he listened.

"You desired that your story could be shared with others who faced the same troubles as you. People who lost loved ones, or were abandoned, or did not have anyone to share their fate.

You wished that you could encourage them and tell them that they aren't truly alone at all. That they should continue and take the next step in their journey, even though it may seem most frightening. That they can face it. That they are strong enough, even if they believe otherwise."

The room blurred around Frank. He could barely make out the stranger's hand on his knee, the rows of books on their shelves, or his faithful cup of tea.

"You've done it, Francis. You finished. You wrote and wrote, and it seemed like it could go on forever, but you recorded every scrap of life you lived. Every moment. Even the worst of it because that's the type of man you are. You are a perfectionist. You are a completist. You are faithful. And that is all anyone could ever ask of you."

"Not faithful enough," mumbled Frank, his eyelashes sparkling in the firelight. "Didn't save her, did I?"

"You sat by her every night in the hospital. You held her when she cried, when the pain was too much, and she thought she couldn't make it. You encouraged her to be strong. You fed her soup and sandwiches, made her favorite cookies, and helped her stand when she believed she'd never walk again. The only reason she stayed so long was because of you."

Frank shook his head. He wouldn't believe it. He couldn't. Surely, there was something else he could've done, something that would've healed her and kept her there with him. He'd even asked the universe to take her cancer and give it to him, but it didn't listen. It didn't seem to matter how much he did, or prayed, or begged. Nobody came to heal Melody. Nobody came to save her. He'd failed her, plain and simple.

"Francis." The young stranger's tone softened again. "She would not want this for you."

You don't know what she'd want. Frank wanted to snap at him, but he didn't have the energy. He was so tired. So tired of the conversation, tired of sitting here, tired of having one foot in life and one in death. Tired of being without Melody. Tired of missing her. Tired of the pain. He'd been alone for so many years, and that wouldn't change in the end. Melody was gone, and he would never see her again.

The stranger touched his knee. "You know, she's waiting for you."

Frank's eyes met the young stranger's. He expected to see him look away or betray some other sign of lying, but there was nothing. Frank didn't see a single falsehood or deceit in them.

And yet, he did not want to believe him.

It had taken too long to forget how she smiled when he called her name, laughed when he surprised her, or sang along to the songs she loved so much. It had been too long since he'd heard her voice, or wrapped his arms around her, or whispered in her ear at night. It had been too many years since they'd dreamed of growing old, and he'd finally accepted that he would have gray hair alone.

But writing down her memories had cracked his resolve. He didn't want to remember, but he did. He knew what her voice sounded like, how she threw her head back when she laughed, how she danced in the kitchen, and laid her head on his shoulder when she was sad. He remembered how she drank her coffee, the way she pointed out every dog they walked past, and how she preferred cupcakes over almost any other dessert.

He remembered her. He'd tried so hard to forget, but he remembered everything. After spending so many years wishing for more, the stranger's promise was almost too much to bear.

Frank drew a stuttering breath, bracing himself for the worst. If the stranger lied now, nothing would be worth it. Not a single moment spent without her. He would've been better off not knowing her, not sharing those moments or creating those memories, rather than living in eternity without her. He would be crushed, destroyed, his shattered heart finally ripped out of his chest.

Still, he had to know.

"All this time?"

"She waits for you," said the young stranger softly, "Every day."

Those six words served as bullets in Frank's last line of defense. The stone walls around his heart that kept him strong for her, for him, for their families, finally started to crumble. The pain of fearing failure, watching the other families multiply while he grew old without his beloved wife, and watching the years go by finally caught up with him. The fortress that had been so resilient took its last breath as Frank collapsed into tears, the ache of loneliness and heartbreak overwhelming him.

She was there—out there, somewhere—his beloved Melody, waiting for him. She wasn't gone. She hadn't moved on, or disappeared into nothing, or even found someone new. Every day, just like he'd been, she was faithful to him—even now, at the end of all their days.

Until death do us part, love, and beyond.

The final piece fell into place in Frank's heart, and suddenly, he felt like a crushing burden had been lifted from his shoulders. It had all been worth it, in the end. All the pain and hurt, agony and strife, and it was over. Melody had survived. He'd survived. He'd get to see her again. All of his tears, all of his heartache, and he'd finally hold her in his arms again. No more loneliness, no more pain. It was over, done, finished, complete. He'd done his best, and now, he'd reached the end of his road.

His story was ending, but not really. Only one chapter had finished. It was just one book, only one page. All of the events of this life were merely continuing into the next book. The only thing he had to do was write it.

The young stranger waited until Frank's sobs subsided, his eyes glistening with unspent tears as he handed him another black handkerchief. After Frank blew his nose and dabbed away his leftover tears, the two men regarded each other. It was only after Frank had taken a steadying breath and his shoulders' shaking eased that the young stranger spoke with a slight tremor in his voice.

"Are you ready to see her?"

Frank nodded.

The young stranger placed his hand on Frank's knee again. The sound of the raindrops faded, and the flickering fire crackled louder. Somewhere past the front door, Frank heard frogs croaking and summertime crickets chirping faintly. It had been a long time since he'd been able to hear soft sounds like these, and he welcomed them wholeheartedly. This was one last chance to hear the world as it really was, not like his old ears told him it would be.

Frank's breath grew ragged, then slowed, each breath drawing and exhaling like a sleeping child. His trembling fingers ceased their shaking, and his ankles, which had hurt so badly, finally stopped aching. After so many years of stress and anger, frustration and sorrow, joy and everything beautiful, Frank's story slipped away.

The young stranger waited a respectful few moments before rising. Touching his fingertips to his bowler hat, he saluted

Frank's still form. It was a good life, well lived and well deserved in peace. Francis had struggled and dreamed, fought and prayed, suffered and celebrated and lived. His story would be an inspiration to everyone who read it, and it was truly an honor to be part of his passing.

Raising a gloved hand, he called a book from the nearby shelves. A green-backed novel with gold stripes up and down its cover sailed over to him and flopped open, revealing an empty place where the pages should be.

The young stranger nodded. Yes, this one would do nicely.

Around him, pages took flight, each one soaring into the air like a bird. They spiraled together, swimming across the room and back again as they organized themselves into chapters, cataloging the joys and regrets of Frank's life. Bundles of papers flew as flocks, other memories flapping up to meet them as they arranged themselves chronologically—the good and the bad, the happy and the sad, the joyful and fearful and terrible. Every moment found its home, the place where it belonged in his story. Little tales nestled inside big events, filling the empty spots where morning coffee and afternoon naps should go. Spare moments and brief thoughts from the work commute, side conversations about the weather, and water-cooler debates about sports teams all found their places, snuggling into the warmth of bigger stories that formed the cornerstones of Frank's life.

One by one, the piles around the room vanished, revealing countertops and chairs, bookshelves and plush rugs, wide hallways, and a red and green runner that disappeared into the back rooms. Overhead, the story of a man assembled, each word falling into place as the book Francis dreamed it would be.

As the last page whispered between the covers, the green book floated down to the stranger's hand. With black-gloved fingertips, he flipped through the pages, taking a moment here and there to read the tale. There were pieces he recognized and days that he didn't; he knew of Melody and how she waited for him but had not anticipated the incredible joy Frank had shown about joining her once again.

The book closed with a quiet clap, and as the stranger's fingers brushed against the gold-striped cover, he whispered the same blessing he'd spoken countless times before. Then, with a wave of his hand, he sent the book back towards the shelf. It glided through the air and landed gently in its place with the barest rustle of its pages, and save for the crackling fireplace and the rain, the room fell into stillness once more.

The young stranger stood quietly for a second, surrounded by the heavy silence of the room. Frank's empty vessel had vanished, fading when his soul passed on. Only his cup of tea rested on the table beside his chair, the last bit of evidence that Francis had been here at all. Not a single page lay scattered around the room. His entire story, woven over the course of a lifetime, had finally found its place in the green-backed book. Just as he desired, it would be there to help others in need of encouragement or amusement. Even after death, he would continue to help others, just as when he lived.

Carefully, he picked up Frank's teacup and carried it into the kitchen nearby. The last bit of tea spiraled down the drain as he rinsed it, the scent of Earl Grey blooming across the room one final time before dissolving back into warmth and old books. For a moment, the stranger smiled, remembering Frank's first interaction. He had been confused, nearly fearful, and positive that he couldn't die yet. He had so much left to do, he'd said. A story that needed to be told. He'd wanted to; he'd simply run out of time.

I know a place, the stranger had said.

As the stranger placed Frank's teacup on the drying rack, a timid knock sounded on the door. He crossed the room, pausing only to settle his bowler hat on his head before sweeping the door open and startling the young girl on the other side.

"Hello," he greeted her. "Did you have a pleasant trip?"

She said nothing at first. With one step, then another, she walked into the room, glancing at the bookshelves and peering into the darkness where the other rooms waited.

"What is this place?"

The stranger gestured to a plush, red velvet chair before the fireplace. "I believe you have an important decision to make. You may need some time to think it over. Here, you will have everything you need to assist you."

The girl's face heated, and she looked away, covering the marks on her arm with one hand.

The young stranger noticed. He smiled gently, though he did not move to touch her as he did with Frank. "It's all right, Sarah. I've seen so many lives come and go; plenty of them have stories like yours. Shall we sit?"

Sarah did not sit but wandered through the room, admiring the fire, the paintings on the walls, the plush rugs, and the red velvet chair. Her fingers danced along the back of the chair as she stared up at the rows of books as if waiting for one to jump off the shelf and offer its secrets.

The stranger tapped his bowler hat, and his smile grew. "If you're looking for a good book, I recommend the green one with gold stripes. It's a beautiful story."

Sarah didn't see him go to the door, or open it softly, or step outside. She didn't notice as it closed softly behind him, leaving her alone with the fire, an empty teacup, and the pattering rain.

She didn't notice the fire flickering brighter, illuminating the book spines so she could see their vibrant colors.

She did, however, see something that she wanted to read.

Her fingers touched the green cover softly as she pulled it from the shelf. The cover crinkled as she opened it, its newly-bound pages rustling under her touch. She lost herself in the hand-written words that lay within. Without looking, she navigated to the red velvet chair, sank into its embrace, and wondered how the book came to be here and why it smelled faintly of Earl Grey tea.

Outside, the rain's pattering on the window was Sarah's only company.

ACKNOWLEDGMENTS

This book wouldn't have been possible without the fantastic work of the featured authors. Thank you for believing in this project and trusting me with your fiction.

I'm grateful to Brian Reindel for helping with the pre-launch marketing, C.R. Langille for providing shipping guidance, and Elle Griffin for advice on the book box.

To all the SXP paid subscribers who accompanied us on this journey, you humble me with your ongoing support (in no particular order):

Mr. Troy Ford, Pamela Urfer, William F Edwards, Kent Bridgeman, Cameron Scott, Danny O'Day, Shifra Steinberg, Leigh Parrish, Peggy Boone, Yvonne, skiddlzninja, Shaina Read, Brylle Gaviola, Sarah Duck-Mayr, Richard Schultz, Jack Massa, C.R. Langille, J.M. Elliott, Thomas Bubb, Joan Lass, Dave Malone, Daniel W. Davison, Sandra Muzio, Pam Malone, Robert D. Malone Jr., Erica Astle.

Lastly, a massive thank you to everyone who bought and read this book. Your support means the world to us indie authors. And the next time you travel, remember to take our stories with you!

Meet the Authors

Brian Reindel graduated with a journalism degree more years ago than he cares to admit. He taught himself to code during the dot-com boom and abandoned dreams of reporting on crime in the seedy underbelly of Detroit. Brian is back to the writing life, crafting fantasy and science fiction short stories through his newsletter "Future Thief." He self-published his first book through Amazon in 2023, a collection of short stories titled "The Stars Will Fall," which is available on Kindle and in paperback. Brian is married to his wife of 20 years and has two teenage children.

Brylle Gaviola is a writer, director, producer, cinematographer, and editor. He is a former winner of "best writing" and 9 other nominations in the Las Vegas 48hour project in 2019 for "Bear, Ninja, and Cowboy." He has a Bachelor of Science degree from the former Art Institute of Las Vegas and manages the LVR Films production company with Fran Padunan. He is now a co-producer of this year's 48hour film project, helping the community grow and making sure that aspiring filmmakers have a fun and fair experience.

Christopher Deliso is an American professional writer and Oxford-trained Byzantinist, with over 25 years' experience of research and freelance writing from Europe, publishing everything from poems and stories to journalism, analysis, over 20 travel guides for Lonely Planet, and several books on history, travel and current events. He very much hopes that his recently-completed literary detective novel, set in Greece and its near-abroad at the turn of the 21st century, will be just the first in a multi-part series. You can read Chris' writing on his Substack at christopherdeliso.substack.com and on his official website, christopherdeliso.com.

Clarice Sanchez Meneses's first full-fledged story was of a sparkling magical girl with terrifying titan-like power, which she daydreamed about in grade school French class. Since then, she's gotten a minor in Spanish, a bachelor's in communications, and a computer folder full of coming-of-age magical realism stories. Writing, for her, means reaching for the truth, delighting in beauty, and finding ways to share God's love and creativity with others. Previously, she's been published in Ateneo Writerskill's zine *Wither*, and is set to be published in *Pandan Weekly* in July 2024. She posts her writing updates in her Substack, *Sparrow Songs*.

C.R. Langille spent many a Saturday afternoon watching monster movies with her mom. It wasn't long before she started crafting nightmares to share with her readers. She is a retired, disabled veteran with a deep love for weird and creepy tales. This prompted her to form Timber Ghost Press in January of 2021. She is an affiliate member of the Horror Writers Association, the DEI Chair for the League of Utah Writers, and she received her MFA: Writing Popular Fiction from Seton Hill University in 2014. Follow her here: link.heropost.io/crlangille.

Daniel W. Davison was born in Indiana in 1971 and has spent nearly a quarter of his life in Europe and the Near East. He attended Indiana University and Yale, where he studied Medieval Arabic history and philosophy. He collects rare and antiquarian books and enjoys reading and writing fiction and nonfiction.

Devon Field lives in Vancouver, BC, where he writes and podcasts with the assistance of his cat, Waffles. His fiction has appeared in *Write Ahead/The Future Looms*, *The Sprawl Mag*, and *Twilight Histories*, and his non-fiction in *Medieval Magazine*, *The Public Domain Review*, and *Atlas Obscura*. He hosts the history podcast *Human Circus: Journeys* in the *Medieval World* and Writes about Philip K Dick, and sci-fi more generally, at *Other Android Dreams* on Substack.

Galia Ignatius has been a professional writer and ghostwriter for businesses and academia since 2005. She also writes fiction for herself and has recently ventured into sharing that writing with the public.

H. A. Titus can usually be found with her nose in a book or spinning storyworlds in her head. She loves mythology, Dungeons & Dragons, and a good cup of tea. She lives in the Midwest with her weather-mage husband and two super-villain sons (don't mind the robotic dinosaurs, they're friendly) who enjoy dragging her into real-life adventures. Some claim she is half-fae, but that's just an unfounded rumor. She shares short stories and serialized fiction at hatitus.substack.com.

Iris Shaw is a writer and regular purveyor of bad gardening advice. She dabbles in fiction and poetry at Long Oddities.

J. M. Elliott has always found solace in the past. She lives on a farm in the Hudson Valley, far removed from the hustle of modern life. When she's not lost in the pages of historical fiction, you might spot her astride a horse, unearthing the mysteries of archaeological sites, or trekking into the wilderness where phone signals cannot reach. Discover more, including her debut novel, Of Wind and Wolves, at www.jmelliott.org.

MEET THE AUTHORS

Jack Massa has published Fantasy, Science Fiction, and Poetry. His interests range from space habitats, neuroscience, and AI to mysticism and occult history. You can find his writings online at triskelionbooks.com and specle ctic.substack.com.

James Castor is an amateur writer and former sailor. He was born in New Jersey and has lived in Los Angeles, Japan, and many other places.

Joe Gold is a writer of web novels and short stories. He's the author of the web novel *Slashers*, an action comedy about 100 horror movie slashers fighting in a death game across 1980s Texas. Follow him here: @WEEBWARS3 on X | As Joe Gold on Scribble Hub, Royal Road, Honey Feed.

LB Waltz has been publishing creative works for over 20 years under various pseudonyms. They enjoy taking walks, biblically accurate depictions of angels, and reading about botanical folklore. Follow here @balmroomdance.

M. S. Arthadian is a master of lore and world-building, interweaving epic narratives through Arthadian Anthologies. He has been telling stories ever since he was a child. Being encouraged to write from his imagination at a young age and influenced heavily by the cinematic medium of storytelling, Arthadian's writing brings his readers on a journey through epic, speculative narratives set on worlds that venture beyond our very universe!

Melissa Rose Rogers writes speculative stories and is inspired by mythologies from all over the world. She currently lives in Denver, CO, where she experiments on her husband and daughters with recipes she finds online. She loves tabletop games (especially cooperative board games), memes, and long walks in the dry, thin air.

As a kid, **Olivia St. Lewis** felt more at home in the library than almost anywhere else. Buried in books and words, she grew up with a love of stories and the connection they bring, and hopes that her own tales will delight readers in the same way. You can read more of her work on her newsletter at WednesdayAfternoon.Substack.com.

Pamela Urfer is an accomplished novelist and playwright with years of theatre directing and college teaching behind her. She is a graduate of UC Berkeley (BA: Comparative Literature) and UC Santa Cruz (MA - Literature.) Retired now, she keeps her hand in by writing short stories and posting on substack. Her publication, xianbrainstretch.substack.com, is a weekly digest of the writings of important Christian thinkers.

Randall Hayes, "your friendly neighborhood neuroscientist," writes about science and pop culture (the nerdier the better) in a weekly newsletter called Doctor Eclectic, at https://randall-hayes.substack.com. He plays a lot of tabletop RPGs.

Shaina Read is the writer behind *Kindling*. She's obsessed with staring into the abyss. It started with *Scary Stories to Tell in the Dark* at the elementary school book fair, and thirty years later, it hasn't stopped. She's an eclectic curator of the macabre and sinister, an adrenaline junkie of the mind. She loves the written word, dark media, and creative storytelling of all kinds. Find her work at kindlinghorror.substack.com

Have you ever had a dream that started before you were asleep? Have you had one so funny you laughed yourself awake? Shannon's life was like that. Just when he had settled into fearful religiosity, Jesus showed up like a bell-laugh for his soul. He has been trying to put it into words ever since. In Huntington, WV, **Shannon Aaron Stephens** is praying to grow more tenderhearted toward his wife of 17 years and their three children - Ladybug, Lion, and Mouse. Cheers!

Victor D Sandiego lives in the high desert of central Mexico where he writes, studies, and plays drums. His work appears in various journals. He is the founder of Subprimal Poetry Art and Dog Throat Journal, an online publication of short fiction and prose poetry.

Winston Malone is a USAF veteran who loves speculative fiction and poetry. He founded Storyletter XPress Publishing LLC to support and publish quality independent writing. He hopes to one day own and operate a bookshop café. You can follow more of his work at storyletter.substack.com and havek.substack.com.

The Journey Has Only Begun

Thank you for making it to the end of this book, but it's not the end of our travels. Follow our indie publishing journey by subscribing to our newsletter at storyletter.substack.com. Or follow us @thestoryletter

Also by Storyletter XPress Publishing

The Weight of the World: A Collection of Short Fiction and Poetry

Milton Keynes UK
Ingram Content Group UK Ltd.
UKHW011918120724
445613UK00002B/32